About the Author

Kiltie Jackson grew up in Scotland, moved to London and then finally settled down somewhere in the middle.

She now lives in Staffordshire with six cats and one grumpy husband.

Her debut novel 'A Rock 'n' Roll Lovestyle' was released in September 2017 and 'An Artisan Lovestyle' followed a year later.

'An Incidental Lovestyle' is the third book in 'The Lovestyle Series'.

If you would like to read more about Kiltie, you can find her on the following:

Website: www.kiltiejackson.com

Facebook: www.facebook.com/kiltiejackson

Twitter: www.twitter.com/KiltieJackson

And So It Begins...

Amber Fisher walked over to the fridge in the corner of the large, family kitchen. She paused, with her fingers on the handle, to look at the photograph stuck to the front of the pale blue door.

One small piece of paper...

So many memories...

There had been an argument between her mum and dad when her dad had put it there, held in place by two fridge magnets – one in the shape of a bottle of champagne, the other a party hat. Both were mementoes from the evening the photograph had been taken – her parents' joint fiftieth birthday party. With barely a week between them, it had been an obvious decision for any celebration to be a joint one.

The brand-new, pale blue, fridge-freezer had been her mother's pride and joy and she'd still been in the honeymoon period when her dad had placed the photograph on it. She didn't want anything to mar its pristine exterior but her dad had simply smiled, turned up the song on the radio and had whisked her away from the cooker and into his arms, crooning the love song in her ear as they'd danced around the room.

Amber smiled now, as she had smiled then. Her parents had been childhood sweethearts who'd met on their first day of school and had gotten married as soon as they'd turned sixteen. Their elopement to Scotland, in the school holidays, had become a family legend. Everyone thought her mother was pregnant but they couldn't have been further from the truth. They didn't have Amber until they were twenty-five and her sister, Saffy, hadn't appeared for another ten years after that. No, it was a very simple case of being in love and it was a love that had grown deeper every year since.

The thought of the thirty-fifth wedding anniversary they would no longer see, made Amber's fingers tighten on the fridge handle. She took a deep breath to steady the emotions rocking through her and the photograph blurred as her eyes welled up again. She wiped them angrily and wondered how it was possible to still have tears left. The days and nights she'd spent crying should surely have emptied the well inside her, but it seemed to be bottomless for still they came.

She pulled the door open and grabbed the bottle of chardonnay from the shelf. The initial plan had been to have just one glass but, upon reflection, she figured even the whole bottle wasn't going to be enough. Not for what she had to do.

She picked up the glass from the work top and carried both it and the bottle up the stairs. The house was quiet. Saffy had had a New Year sleepover with her best friend, Brioney, and wasn't due home until later that night.

Amber walked along the corridor until she came to her parents' bedroom. She'd only been in there once in the last nine months and that had been the day she'd chosen their outfits for the undertakers.

She let out a sigh and pulled on her gloves. It wouldn't have made any difference what she was wearing – gorgeous Jeff wouldn't have been interested in a dumpy, boring, old ginger-nut like her. Someone as gorgeous as him could have his pick of any beautiful woman who crossed his path, she wouldn't stand a chance. Not that it mattered much anyway – when it came to relationships, she wasn't interested. They were more trouble than they were worth. That didn't mean she couldn't look though. There was no harm in perusing the menu, even if you had no intention of eating.

She pushed him from her mind and made her way down the path towards the village. She'd told Sukie a very small lie, having said her bus was due half-an-hour earlier than it was but, when she'd stepped off the bus that morning, she'd realised she'd never had a good look around the village and she wanted to do so before she left. She was sure Sukie wouldn't have minded but she didn't want to risk giving offence so it was easier to change the time the bus was due.

She stepped into the little high street and found herself standing by a small row of shops on her left. Across the road from where she stood was the village green. A rather quaint pub – which looked genuinely old – sat at the top end of the green and she was sure, in the dusky gloom, she could make out a village pond too. Talk about idyllic!

She strolled along the pavement, taking time to pause at each shop window to look in. The haberdashery had a pretty display of knitting needles, brightly coloured balls of wool, a matching Arran knit jumper and the paper pattern detailing how to create the eye-catching garment. Next to that was a ladies dress shop and their window was decked out in cool wintery shades of pale blue and white. A beauty and hair salon rubbed shoulders with the dress shop and Jenny could see that this was great placement for both shops. Ladies, who've just had their hair done, often fancy a new outfit to complete their look or, the other way round, a new dress looks so much better with a smart, fresh hair-do.

She walked past the closed French restaurant which brought her to the bottom end of the green and alongside an old-fashioned, red telephone box. She couldn't help but smile as memories of her childhood came back. Her aunt hadn't been one for "new-fangled gubbins" and so it had often been a quick trot to the phone-box in all weathers whenever there had been a need for a phone call. Thankfully, her aunt had eventually relented and one had been installed just before she began university.

She crossed the road to walk along the opposite side of the green and up towards the bus stop. A glance at her watch told her she still had fifteen minutes to spare so she wandered slowly past the shops on this side. The butchers had now closed and the bakery looked as though it was about to do the same. There were a handful of cakes – looking utterly delicious and mouth-watering – left in the window and the assistant behind the counter was serving a young girl. As she watched, the assistant came and removed the last custard slice which she placed in a bag and handed to the teenager. Jenny quickly moved on before she gave in to temptation herself. Eating cake when you're fourteen is a lot different to eating cake in your forties – it doesn't shift quite so quickly, as all those mince pies from Christmas were keen to remind her.

The next shop after the bakery was empty. She looked up and saw the "For Sale" sign above her head. Jenny stepped back and looked the building up and down. It was white with blackened timbers and had large bay windows. She stepped closer to the windows and it appeared, to her inexperienced eye, that both the muntins and the individual panes of glass were nearly all original. She would hazard a guess that it was probably built in the late 1500's or early 1600's. She crossed the road to the bus stop which was directly opposite and turned around to see the building in its entirety. It was really beautiful. There were three floors that she could see – the ground floor with the bay windows, the first floor and then a second floor with three dormer windows. She surmised that was probably the attic. It put her in mind of the shops one would find in a Dickensian novel and it was a shame to see it standing empty. It had so much potential and she wondered why it was for sale.

She looked around to see she was alone at the bus stop and, when she took her phone out of her bag, Jenny noted it was still five minutes until the bus was due. She fiddled with the useless piece of technology – her more polite name for this particular piece of kit – and was quietly delighted when she managed to get into the camera function. She took a few photographs of the old shop and also of the seller's board – it would be something to look at when she indulged in her little pipe dream of one day owning her own book shop. She could put it on her Pinterest boards alongside all the other quaint little buildings that tickled her imagination. She was putting the phone back in her bag as other people arrived to stand beside her, also waiting for the bus. She suspected that, as it was the last one of the day, it might be busier than usual.

A few minutes later the bus came around the corner and trundled to a halt. Being at the head of the queue, Jenny was the first to get on. She flashed her return ticket to the driver and took a seat about two-thirds of the way up. She sat on the opposite side to the driver with the intention of seeing a different view on the way home, although, it was now almost dark and the only thing she was likely to see was her own reflection in the window.

Thankfully, she always carried her e-reader with her, so she had another option. She looked towards the doors to see if there were many more passengers to get on and saw the young girl who'd been in the baker's shop slip past the driver while he was busy sorting out change for the passenger in front of him. She hurried up the gangway and sat in the seat directly in front of Jenny. She opened her bag, took out a book and immediately immersed herself in it, now oblivious to all around her.

Jenny looked back out of the window and said nothing. She'd snuck a free bus ride more than once when she was in her teens – it was almost a rite of passage for any teenager – and she wasn't going to upset anyone by telling tales. She sneaked a peek over the girl's shoulder to see what she was reading and was thrilled to find the text of "Anne of Green Gables" looking back at her. This had been one of her favourite books when she'd been growing up and she was delighted to see that, in this age of computers and CGI technology, the simple story of a red-headed orphan still had the power of enchantment. With a small nod of approval, she settled back in her seat and, following the young girl's example, took her e-reader out of her bag and was soon lost in the dirty, criminal underworld within her crime thriller.

A noisy commotion dragged Jenny away from the gang-riddled council estate in East London and back to her seat on the bus home to Oxford. A ticket inspector had gotten on and was asking the teenager in front of her for her ticket. A ticket Jenny knew she didn't have.

'I did have one, I must have dropped it when I got on,' the girl said, in a sulky, mutinous voice.

'Well, that's not good enough, young lady. If you can't show me a ticket, you will have to buy another one or get off the bus.'

'I don't have any money to buy another one…'

'Then you need to get off. We can't allow free journeys.'

'But this is the last bus. I need to get home.'

'Not my problem.'

Jenny leaned forward. 'How much is the fare, I'll pay for it?'

The inspector turned to her and asked in an officious voice that immediately set Jenny's teeth on edge, 'Is this minor with you, madam?'

'What difference does that make? I'm offering to pay her fare, surely that's all that matters?'

'I'm sorry, but, if this girl is not with you, then I cannot accept you paying her fare.'

'WHAT? Where is the logic in that? Are you seriously going to dump a vulnerable child in the middle of nowhere, in the middle of the night, on her own? Are you out of your tiny mind?' Jenny's dander was up now. What a complete moron this man was.

'Driver, pull over at the next bus stop. This bus is going nowhere until this girl alights.'

Jenny pulled her mobile phone out of her bag, thankful now that she'd had a play about on it earlier because, without any ado, she took a photograph of the inspector's ID.

'I'll be making sure your superiors hear about this. You should be ashamed of yourself. Do you practise at being a nasty little man or does it come naturally?'

As she spoke, the bus slowed and pulled over into a bus stop. The inspector turned back to the young girl, 'Right then, missy, this bus doesn't move another inch while you're still on it. So the choice is yours – you can upset all these *paying* passengers who just want to get home or you can get off! What's it going to be?'

Chapter Four

Jenny watched the tail-lights of the bus disappear into the darkness before looking at the young girl standing beside her. 'Well, I suppose we should be grateful the driver at least had the decency to drop us at a stop with a proper shelter.' She nodded her head towards the little wooden hut behind them which also sported, miraculously, a light that worked. 'Shall we sit down and decide what to do next?'

The teenager slouched her way over to the shelter and sat down heavily upon the wooden bench inside. She looked up at Jenny. 'I'm sorry to have been so much trouble. I did have the money but then I saw the lovely cakes in the bakery, and my tummy was rumbling big style... I just couldn't resist, I had to have one. I used my bus fare to pay for it.' She hung her head, clearly upset at the trouble she had caused.

Jenny sat down beside her. 'Hey, don't worry about it, we can fix this. And, if I'm being honest, they *were* very delicious looking cakes. Was it tasty?'

The girl looked up and treated her to a wide, brace-

Chapter Five

Saffy looked at the woman sitting beside her. She had gorgeous rich, red hair – just like her heroine, Anne Shirley, in her favourite book, "Anne of Green Gables". Saffy was a bit jealous because she'd wanted red hair ever since she'd first read about Anne Shirley but was stuck with a mousey-brown colour instead. The woman had a lovely, generous smile and looked what her dad would have called "cuddly". Mind you, that might just have been the coat she was wearing which, in Saffy's opinion, was really quite gross. Bright orange was bad enough but quilted too…? The bad coat aside, however, she reckoned the best thing about Jenny was that she hadn't spoken to her as if she was a stupid child although she did have an air of authority about her. Saffy wondered if she was a teacher. That was the kind of vibe she was giving off. Saffy thought for a moment then decided it would be safe to tell her things.

'My name is Saffy Fisher, I'm fourteen, I'll be fifteen next month and I live with my big sister, Amber. She'll be twenty-five in March. Our parents died in a helicopter crash in Vietnam last year.'

'I see. That must be quite difficult for you both.'

'It's been hard but Amber has tried her best to keep things going. She says it's important for me to have stability. Sometimes though, I think she's too strong. She only cries at night when she thinks I can't hear her. She never cries in front of me.'

'Perhaps that's why she's been getting into trouble at work? Maybe her grief is coming out in other ways.'

'No, it's something else. She's got a secret. She hasn't told me it but I know what it is.'

Jenny looked at Saffy. 'How do you know it, if she hasn't told you?'

Saffy grinned at her. 'Because I sneaked into her bedroom when she was in the shower and found an envelope lying on her bed. I looked inside and found out she was adopted when she was a baby.'

'She was *what*?' Jenny's handbag fell onto the floor of the hut with a loud thunk.

Saffy leant down, picked it up and handed it back with a smile on her face. 'Yeah, I know! How cool is that?'

'And she didn't know she was adopted?' The disbelief was clear in Jenny's voice.

'Nope! Well, I don't think so. She was all normal-like up until New Year and then, on New Year's Day, she began to clear our parents' bedroom and she's been weird ever since. So, I'm guessing she found the envelope then.'

'So, when you say weird – in what way?'

'Well… kinda spaced out. She's always lost in her thoughts and hardly speaks. It's like she's thinking *all* the time. She's also drinking more wine than she used to and I think that's why she's getting into trouble at work – she's been going in late and hungover. She doesn't normally work on Saturdays but she had to go in today to make up for the time she's lost from being late.'

'Well, it's good of her employers to allow her to do that. Not all bosses are so kind.'

Saffy shrugged. She wouldn't know about that. All she knew was that, right now, Amber had to be careful because she couldn't afford to lose her job. 'Can I let you in on a secret, Jenny?'

'Of course you can. I won't tell anyone.'

'Amber really likes Pete Wallace and I went to Lower Ditchley today to try and get his autograph. I thought it might cheer Amber up.'

'I see. And did you have any luck?'

Saffy hung her head. 'No. I waited by the gates to his house all day, but he didn't come out. I missed my lunch – that's why I was so hungry and bought the cake. It was all a waste of time and look at the trouble I've caused,' and she began to cry.

She felt Jenny's arm around her shoulders and she was pulled into a warm hug. Saffy let herself be comforted by the soothing words Jenny was crooning above her head and the hand gently rubbing her back helped to ease her upset.

Jenny and Saffy were still sitting cuddled up together when they heard a car approaching. With Sukie's words playing on their minds, they shuffled down the bench until they were sitting tightly in the shadows in the corner of the hut. Upon hearing two small toots of a horn, they let out a sigh of relief and made their way to the side of the road where Jeff had pulled up in his car. Jenny opened the back door for Saffy to get in before sliding awkwardly into the front seat next to Jeff.

'Oof!' She suddenly found herself engulfed inside her big padded coat. Sitting down hadn't been an issue on the bus with its rigid, upright seats but the bucket seats in the Jaguar had her sliding down inside the coat and it had flown up around her ears. She tried to push the coat down while sitting herself up but each time she just about managed it, she slid right down again. To add insult to injury, her arms were flapping about somewhere above her shoulders. Jeff's muffled voice floated down to her, 'Jenny, may I suggest taking your coat off. The car is rather warm and I'd hate for you to be hot and uncomfortable.'

She hoped her reply, 'Good idea, I'll do that,' was coherent as she wriggled around, trying to find the door handle. The only way this thing was going to come off in a way that might be considered elegant, was by getting out of the car and removing it outside. She felt one of the car doors being opened and closed before the one by her side was opened and a warm hand took a hold of one of hers.

'This way, Jenny.'

She allowed Jeff to guide her out of the vehicle and, once she'd undone the buttons, he helped her to take the erstwhile piece of clothing off whereupon he carefully folded it and placed it in the boot while she sat back down inside the car. She was about to close her door when Jeff took hold of the handle.

'Please, allow me,' he said, as he gently closed it before moving around the front of the car and getting back in, grinning at her as he put on his seatbelt.

His face was lit up from the dashboard lights and she smiled at him in deep embarrassment. She forced herself to look away and turned to make sure Saffy had done up her belt. Satisfied that she was secure, she turned back and thanked Jeff for going to all this trouble.

'Jenny, it isn't a bother. I had to drive back to London anyway – I'm merely taking a different route home.'

'A less direct, more out of the way, route!'

'I prefer "scenic"...'

'It's pitch black out there..., how can that be scenic?' The young voice from the back seat broke into the conversation.

'Oops, I'm being rude. I didn't introduce you. Saffy, this is Jeff and Jeff, this is Saffy.'

'Pleased to meet you,' they both replied in unison, which resulted in laughter from Jeff and giggles from Saffy.

Jeff looked at Saffy in the rear-view mirror. 'Saffy, if you could give me your address and post code, I'll pop it into the sat-nav and get you home.'

Jenny pulled her mobile phone from her handbag, while Jeff set the route and began driving. A few moments had passed in silence when Jenny let out a frustrated squeak. Jeff glanced across to see her swiping furiously on the phone.

'What are you doing?'

'I'm trying to find the maps on this thing. I've only had it a couple of weeks and I just cannot find my way around it at all!'

'What brand is it?'

Jenny held the device across for Jeff to look at.

'Ah yes, that one is a bit of a bugger. I had that model before I upgraded. If you swipe to the left, and again...'

Within a few seconds, the app Jenny wanted was sitting proudly on her screen. She opened it up and typed in Saffy's postcode. 'Well, that's handy!'

'What is?' Jeff looked over as she peered at the map on her screen.

'Saffy lives not too far from me. It's maybe about ten minutes away in the car. I can probably get a bus from there, once you drop her off.'

'You'll do no such thing! For the sake of ten minutes,

I think I can drop you home too.'

'But Jeff…, you've already put yourself out so much by picking us up and taking us into Oxford. I don't want to impose upon you any further.'

'Jenny, it's not an imposition, I am more than happy to help. Honestly! So, let's not say anything more on the matter.'

'Okay, if you insist.' She smiled her thanks, put the phone in her bag and sat back to listen to the DJ's talking on the radio.

It didn't take long for them to drive into the Oxford suburbs and the streets became wider and better lit. After some light-hearted chat, Saffy had fallen quiet and then asleep and the remainder of the journey had passed in silence. They soon pulled onto the brightly lit gravel driveway of an imposing Victorian house and Jenny turned round to waken her up.

She got out of the car and was helping Saffy when the front door was flung wide open and a young woman came haring across the gravel. Her strawberry blonde hair was in disarray and she was clearly upset. As soon as Saffy stepped out onto the driveway, the woman grabbed her and pulled her into a hug, all the while berating her for causing so much trouble.

'Where on earth have you been? What have you been up to? I've been worried sick about you! Your text, "Hit a small bit of bother, will be home soon, don't worry", told me absolutely nothing! And of *course* I was going to worry, you stupid girl!'

Saffy wriggled out of the embrace. 'As you can see, Amber, I'm fine. Jenny looked after me. It's not my fault the bus inspector was an asshole.'

'Bus inspector? What? Exactly where *have* you been today?'

Jenny stepped forward at this point. 'Hi, I'm Jenny. Saffy's telling the truth – the bus inspector *was* an asshole. As for the rest, however, I'll let her fill you in on that.'

'Thank you so much, Jenny, for looking after her and bringing her home safely. I'm really sorry for any trouble caused. Would you like to come in for a cup of tea or coffee?'

'Thank you for the offer but I'd better get on. It's Jeff who's the real hero of the hour; he came to the rescue of us both.' She indicated towards the car where Jeff leant forward and waved through the windscreen. 'He went out of his way to bring us home and I have no desire to inconvenience him any further.' She turned to Saffy who came forward to give her a hug.

'Thank you, Jenny, for being so cool. You're awesome!'

Jenny grinned at her words. 'So are you, young lady, but next time... Take enough money for the bus AND a cake!' She gave her a wink and got back into the car, waving goodbye as Jeff reversed back onto the road to take her home.

Chapter Six

Jeff drove back towards the main road, following Jenny's directions, and onwards to her home. As she had stated, it was a mere ten minutes later when they were pulling onto her driveway.

He'd barely stopped the car when she jumped out, leant down and said, 'Thank you so very much for all your help today. You were extremely kind. And thank you for bringing me home too. I won't keep you any longer as you've still got to get home yourself.' She'd closed the door and was halfway up the steps at the front of the house by the time he'd extricated himself from his seatbelt and gotten out of the car.

'Jenny! Wait! You've forgotten your coat.' He retrieved it from the boot and walked over to where she'd stopped at the front door. As he walked up the steps towards her, he said, 'Would you like to have dinner with me? We passed some little restaurants on the way here. I'm sure one of them must serve something nice. What about the Italian? Fancy some pasta?'

She looked down at him. 'Don't you need to get

home? It's getting late.'

'It's not even seven o'clock yet. I'm in no rush to get back to London. And, by the time I do get there, it'll be too late to eat a decent meal. If you won't join me for dinner, then it'll be cheese on toast for one when I get home.' He gave her what he hoped was a charming grin.

After what felt like forever, she smiled back. 'Oh, go on then! Although the Chinese restaurant is much better than the Italian and we stand a better chance of getting a table. Come on up, I need to feed my cats. I'll call the restaurant and book us in before we go.'

Jeff went back to lock up the car, all the while wondering where the sudden urge to act on his feelings had come from. The outcome had fallen in his favour, however, and he wasn't going to question it too closely. He'd learned from his assistant, Elsa, that sometimes you just need to live in the moment and not question everything – some things are just meant to be.

He followed Jenny inside. The small hallway ran from his left to his right with a white painted door at each end and another just in front of him. A thick, deep-pile, oatmeal-coloured, carpet embraced his feet. To his right was an open, polished wood, staircase. As Jenny hung up her coat, she pointed to the door opposite him. 'The bathroom is in there, if you should need to use it.'

Jeff smiled. 'Thank you. I'm okay for now though.'

She nodded then pointed towards the stairs. 'Please go up, I'm going to quickly change. I'll be with you in a few minutes.'

Jeff made his way up the stairs and stepped into a large, open-plan room that took his breath away. The first thing he'd become aware of, as he'd walked up, was the high apex in the roof above him. This must have been the attic area before the house had been converted into flats. Directly in front of him was a huge French window which filled almost the entire wall. Where the slope of the roof met the white painted surround, another smaller window had been installed, thus ensuring the maximum amount of light filled the room. He slowly turned around, taking in the pale cream, corner sofa which was set out to face the window. It had bright red throws upon it and a bright red rug was sprawled across the floor at its feet, pinned down by a large, old sea chest, complete with all the iron locks and fixings. At the far end was an open-plan kitchen with a breakfast bar facing into the room. Between it and the sofa, a small oval dining table was placed with four chairs around it. The dark oak laminate flooring ran the length of the room. It was a warm and inviting space and it suited Jenny down to the ground. There were a few ornaments dotted about and some paintings on the wall. His artistic eye told him the pieces were originals and unique. The lady has a good eye, he thought to himself.

He was walking over to take a closer look at one of the paintings when he heard a snuffling noise coming from underneath the sofa. He was about to bend down for a closer look when two furry faces peeped out. One was a tabby, the other ginger and white. He put his hand down for them to sniff but they backed up and disappeared from view.

'They're not used to visitors and tend to be rather shy, aren't you boys?'

Jenny had come up the stairs but her shoeless feet were the reason he hadn't heard her approach. 'Do you like cats?' she asked, as he straightened up.

'I don't mind them, although I confess I don't know much about them. I grew up with dogs,' he answered.

'Well, I suggest you stand back because you're about to witness the phenomena that is the speed at which cats can travel upon hearing a tin of food being opened.'

Sure enough, Jenny had barely popped the lid on the

can she'd taken out of a kitchen cupboard when two streaks flew past him and skidded to a halt at her feet.

'Now then, Winston, Churchill, are you going to be good boys and say hello to our guest? It's very rude to ignore people.'

It seemed that neither of the cats were bothered about their lack of good manners as both of their attentions stayed firmly on Jenny, watching her spooning the food into their bowls.

'Winston? Churchill?' he asked.

Jenny smiled at him. 'I grew up close to Blenheim Palace and spent a lot of time there. I always had a bit of a fascination of the man, so, when it came to naming the kittens…' She gave a small shrug.

'I like it. It's clever and unusual. Much better than Tom and Jerry or Tony and Adam!'

'I won't tell Sukie you said that!'

Jeff grinned. 'She already knows! My football affiliations lie with Tottenham – any Arsenal reference was never going to go down well.'

'It's because of Tony and Adam that I ended up with these guys. I always got my feline fix with them but, when Sukie moved, I had to make alternative arrangements. Elsa moved in with Puddle, but it wasn't the same.'

'Oh, you know Elsa? I knew she lived in Oxford before moving to London…'

'Yes. Sukie owns the flat below. That's how we know each other. When she married Pete and moved over to Austria, Elsa moved in for a few years. It's now rented out to a young, married couple but I don't see them very often.'

'Honeymoon period?' Jeff asked.

Jenny smiled as she replied, 'I think so.'

Jeff looked at the two cats whose faces were now

buried up to their eyes in the bowls and felt a growling in his stomach. 'Are you ready to go? Ever since you mentioned Chinese food, my mouth hasn't stopped watering.'

'Ready when you are!' came the prompt reply.

The waiter smiled, took their menus and walked off after taking their order. An awkward silence fell over the table as Jeff realised he knew absolutely nothing about Jenny and wasn't sure where to start without sounding either intense or creepy. This wasn't a planned date where the exchange of life stories was generally a given. The spontaneity of the situation had put him on the back foot. He decided to simply jump in and prayed he came over as sincere.

'So, Jenny, what do you for a living?' Oh dear lord, he thought, could I have made that sound any more like a school headmaster?

'My job is one of those which people always consider to be rather dull and boring but which I find very fulfilling.'

'You're an accountant?'

'Noooooo, but I am a librarian, which many think is about as much fun!'

'I suppose someone has to be!' Did the wide grin on his face convey that he was joking with her? Her laughter told him he was in the clear.

'I'm a very lucky librarian, though, as I work at the Bodleian Library.'

'Wow! That is definitely not your bog-standard library.'

'That's for sure.'

'So, I suppose this leads me to what may, or may not be, an obvious question but, do you like reading?'

Jeff was intrigued to see Jenny's face light up as she answered his question. 'I love reading and I love books. I love the feel of a book and I adore old books. The smell from the paper, the beautiful covers... And some of the illustrations are simply stunning.'

They sat back as their food arrived and was placed in front of them. While they ate, Jeff listened as Jenny spoke more about her work and he was in no doubt that she enjoyed it greatly.

'What kind of books do you like to read?' he asked, as she deftly skewered a piece of sweet and sour chicken with her chopstick.

'Thrillers and romances – if the two genres cross, even better. I don't mind if they're historical or current, I'll read them.' She went on to name a number of her favourite authors and Jeff was surprised to hear her name a few that he himself enjoyed.

'That's not the answer I was expecting from an academical librarian. I thought you'd be saying William Shakespeare or Lord Byron with some Charles Dickens thrown in for light reading.'

Jenny smiled at him again. 'Been there and done those. My Masters in English Literature saw to that!'

'Wow! Again! Although I shouldn't really be surprised since you work in one of the top libraries in the country. I guess one of those would be part of the remit. Did you not fancy being a professor?'

'No, that wasn't for me. I kind of fell into being a librarian, it wasn't planned. I started off as a student cataloguer, which went rather well, so I was asked to assist with some other projects – being a university library, there are always projects going on. Anyway, my diligence was noticed and I was asked if I would consider a full-time position. I was working on my Masters at the time and they promised flexibility with my hours to allow for study and research. Well, as you can imagine, I was perfectly placed for the latter. That was almost twenty years ago and I've never worked anywhere else.'

'Would you like to? Is there something else you want to do?' He watched as she hesitated. He could see she wanted to say something but was nervous about doing so. 'I can see from your face there is… Let me guess, you want to be a Hollywood actor?'

'No!'

'Hmmm… An intrepid explorer in the deep, dark, jungle?'

'Urgh! No!' This was accompanied by a distinct shudder.

'Ah! I've got it! You want to run away and become a clown in the circus!'

At this, Jenny threw her head back in laughter. Jeff felt a thrill go through him at the sight and sound of it.

'There is a certain appeal to that last option but no! The truth is, I would love to run my own bookshop. I've got all these ideas in my head of how it would be.'

'So why don't you?'

'Oh, I couldn't. It's just a pipe dream.' Jenny shook her head.

'Of course you could. With your librarian experience, I'm sure you'd be a natural at it. Tell me more, please.'

He watched her hesitate again before taking the plunge and telling him what she'd always hoped for.

'It would be a specialist bookshop – I'd stock only thrillers and romance. Those are the two biggest selling genres so I figure I'd save a lot of money by stocking only those. Surely it's better to have a large choice of what people want than a little bit of everything of which sixty percent would never move?'

'That makes sense to me.' He nodded his agreement.

Just then, Jenny leant across the table and stage

Chapter Seven

Jenny smiled as her colleague, Hilary, moaned upon hearing a group of squealing children gathering in the vestibule. 'Oh no, not another school trip…! I could really do without one of those today.'

The children were completely ignoring the teacher who kept telling them to shush, and, when she looked a bit closer, Jenny noted the "children" were actually teenagers. Now she understood Hilary's dismay. All too often, they were the ones who caused more grief as they often played up while trying to show off to the members of the opposite sex in the group.

'Do you want me to take it?' she asked.

'No, you're fine, Jenny. I'll do it. It's my turn.' Hilary stood up wearily and gathered up her clipboard.

'Well, feel free to give me a shout if they get too boisterous, okay?'

'Thanks, I will.' Hilary gave her a tired smile before walking off.

She was just turning back to the computer when she heard a voice calling her name. She looked around and was pleasantly surprised to see Saffy waving wildly at her from the middle of the group. Jenny waved back and mouthed over to her, 'Come and see me when you are finished.'

Saffy gave her a thumbs-up to let her know she'd understood.

An hour later, Saffy arrived at Jenny's desk with a face that was flushed and eyes that were sparkling. 'We saw where they filmed Harry Potter! It was AMAZING!'

'Are you a Harry Potter fan then?'

'Oh yes! Mum and Dad took me to the film studio place in London a few years ago and I loved it. I didn't know they had filmed here, so close to home.'

'They filmed in several spots around Oxford AND also got inspiration for several props and costumes you see in the films. You should take a visit to the Natural History museum – I'll bet it won't seem so boring now.' Jenny winked at her.

'I'll be making a point of it. Anywhere else?'

'Christ Church College – the Great Hall there is where they got the inspiration for the Great Hall in Hogwarts. Furthermore, the staircase up to the Great Hall was used in the film.'

'I could walk up the same staircase as Harry Potter…? Awesome!' Saffy went all dreamy-eyed at the thought.

'Yes, you could, but there have been a great many footsteps up and down them since – sorry to burst your bubble!'

'Ah, but he was there. That'll do for me!' Saffy's grin was infectious and Jenny couldn't help but grin back.

'So, what are you plans now? Have you finished school for the day?'

'Yeah, we're done. I'll probably have a wander around the shops and then get the bus back home.'

'Well, if you don't mind waiting an hour, I can give

you coping?'

Amber looked at her suspiciously. 'Why are you asking that? What is it to you?' Her tone was defensive and Jenny quickly tried to reassure her.

'Saffy told me what happened with your parents and that you're now her legal guardian. That must be so hard, especially with everything else you've had to deal with. Saffy seems really clued up and mature so I'm sure caring for her isn't difficult but that doesn't mean the responsibility is any easier to bear. So, I'm asking again, how are you coping?'

Amber stared down at the table and Jenny watched the turmoil on her face – the desire to spill the truth fighting with the need to appear strong and in control. Finally she spoke.

'It's been hard. Very hard. Some days, just getting out of bed feels like a mammoth task. If it wasn't for Saffy...'

'But if it wasn't for Saffy, you wouldn't have suddenly become a parent. You wouldn't have to feel that you need to be strong all the time because someone else is relying on you for their welfare.'

'I was doing okay. Sorting out getting them home, and then the funeral, helped to take my mind off it all but now... Now I have too much time to think and my head feels like it's about to burst.'

Jenny nodded. 'And I suppose the other thing was a shock you really didn't need.'

Amber's eyes narrowed as they turned towards Jenny. 'Other thing?'

'Being adopted.' Jenny was taking a punt on the fact that Amber hadn't spoken of this to anyone.

Amber's mouth opened and closed but no sound came out.

'Saffy knows. She told me.'

'How on earth does *she* know?'

'Teenage girls snoop. Apparently she noticed a big change in you after New Year but didn't know why so she sneaked into your bedroom one day and found the paperwork.'

'Oh, for goodness' sake! I've been trying to hide this from her because I didn't want her to deal with any more upset.'

'She's anything but upset – in fact she thinks it's a bit of an adventure – but I do think she might be a bit upset that you haven't shared this with her.'

'I just don't know how to. I feel my whole life has been a lie. How can I explain things to Saff, if I can't explain them to myself? I'm so... unsettled. I'm questioning everything in my life now and I no longer feel like me. I've suddenly become a person with an unknown past and it's twisting me up. It's so hard to describe.'

'Don't you have anyone you can talk to? Aunts? Uncles?'

'No. Or not any that I feel close enough to. Our family only ever get together for special events – christenings, weddings, big birthdays and...' She fell silent.

'Funerals.' Jenny sighed as she filled in the gap. 'Look, I know you really don't know me from Adam but I don't mind being an ear for you. Maybe the fact you don't know me might make it easier to talk freely.'

Amber hesitated again. Jenny looked her over as she waited. She suspected that, when her dark, strawberry-blonde hair was freshly washed, her bluey-green eyes had some sparkle and her bony, skinny body regained the weight she'd clearly lost, Amber was a gorgeous looking girl. She discreetly looked around the kitchen and her eyes were drawn to a pin board on the wall where she saw that she was right. A picture of a slightly younger Amber was on there and she could see just how much weight she'd lost. The girl needed support, someone to help and be there for them both, but there didn't appear to be anyone to help her. She was all alone and being crushed under the weight of the troubles life had heaped upon her.

'Amber, please..., let me help you.' She gently placed her hand on top of Amber's.

Without any warning, the girl let out a howl of intense pain and tears began to pour down her face. Jenny moved her chair and pulled her into her arms as the soul-destroying sobs racked through Amber's body.

Chapter Eight

Jeff pulled onto Jenny's driveway just after eleven o'clock on Saturday morning. He quickly glanced around to ensure there was no one to see him licking the back of his hand and sniffing it. His breath smelt fine but he popped a Polo mint into his mouth just to be on the safe side. He'd had chicken kiev for his dinner last night and hadn't given any consideration to the possibility of garlic breath until he'd gone to bed where, once the thought was in his head, it had been impossible to shift. As the thought was settling in and making itself comfortable, it hooked up with the nerves he was feeling at finally having a "sort-of" date with Jenny. The two evil little miscreants had combined forces which meant he'd had a restless night and had finally fallen asleep a couple of hours before his alarm went off. He tried to stifle a yawn as he got out of the car and went to ring the bell for Jenny's flat. However, before his finger even touched the pad, the door opened and she was standing in front of him.

'Hi Jeff, I saw you from the bedroom window and didn't want to keep you waiting.'

Oh, crap, he thought, did she see me checking my breath and trying not to yawn? I really hope not...

'I'm sorry?' Jenny had been talking and he'd missed what she'd said.

'I was saying thank you for coming with me today. I'm not really sure *why* we're going but I'm looking forward to having a nosy around the shop.'

'It's my pleasure. I seem to have some kind of perverse liking for looking around properties – be they up for sale or just generally. I love those TV shows where they do the houses up, or build fabulous grand things in the middle of nowhere. This is the perfect day out for me.'

He held the car door open for Jenny as she slid in. Part of her coat was hanging out so he carefully tucked it in before closing the door gently.

Once he'd negotiated his way out of the gates and had pulled into the traffic, Jenny turned to him and, with a little conspiratorial smile, said, 'I'll let you in on a secret, Jeff... I love those TV shows too. That one where the builders all go and do up the homes for the people who have been struck by some kind of tragedy... Makes me cry every time! No matter how often I say it won't get me this time, it always does.'

Jeff smiled back. 'I'll let you in on my secret... It does for me every time too!'

Jenny gave a small laugh and, as they indulged themselves by sharing their favourite home make-over moments, Jeff felt himself beginning to relax. He felt sure that today was going to be a good day.

It didn't take too long for them to get out of the suburbs and onto the country roads. The journey flew by and, in no time at all, they were parking up in a small car park near the village green in Lower Ditchley. They walked slowly towards the shop and gave it a good look over in the pleasant wintery sunshine. Against her better judgement, Jenny was already envisioning beautiful, colourful, book displays in the big bay windows on the front.

'What do you think, now you're seeing it in the flesh, so to speak?' she asked Jeff.

Jeff looked the building up and down with a critical eye. 'I'm guessing it dates from the 1500s, maybe a tad later, with its traditional white plaster and black wood construction. Three stories high, from what I can see… I only glanced at the specifications last week, when I looked it up in the restaurant. I was more interested in the open day, if I'm being honest. Have you read them?' He glanced down at her.

'No, I wanted it to be a surprise. I didn't want to risk seeing something different in my imagination and then be disappointed if the building didn't match up.'

'Well, shall we go in and see what's what?'

Jenny smiled at him, the excitement beginning to really churn up in her tummy. 'Lead on, MacDuff!'

They were crossing the road when a woman with long, dark blonde hair, stepped out of the bakers next to the old shop. She locked the door and turned to walk towards Jenny and Jeff as they stepped onto the pavement. They all met at the door where Jeff stepped back and indicated for the women to go in ahead of him.

Jenny went in first and had to blink a few times before her eyes adjusted to the gloomy interior after the brightness outside.

'Good morning, welcome. I'm Fiona Parkridge, the estate agent in charge of the property. Please may I take your names?'

Jenny gave both her and Jeff's name which the agent

marked off on the paperwork in front of her.

The blonde woman stepped forward and spoke in a soft, quiet, voice. 'Hi, my name's Samantha Curtis and I own the bakery next door. I'm not on the list as I didn't realise I had to register. One of your earlier visitors mentioned it was an open day today so I thought it would be okay to just pop in. Is it a problem?'

The agent looked Samantha up and down then gave a small sigh. 'No, it's fine. Please have a look around and don't hesitate to call me if I can be of assistance.' She handed brochures over to the three of them while explaining they contained the details of the property along with the measurements for each room.

'Has it been busy?' asked Jenny. 'Have you had much interest?'

The agent gave a small grimace. 'There was plenty of interest until I informed them the property cannot be converted into flats, or developed in any way to provide residential dwellings. There's a covenant on the land with rather strict caveats. This was stated on the website but it's surprising how many people don't read all the information.'

'What about the retail side? Has there been much interest there?' Jeff looked up from the brochure as he asked his question.

'Not really. It's a small village with not much going on. I think any business would struggle unless they were able to provide an essential requirement, such as your bakery for example.' The agent nodded towards Samantha.

'I see, thank you.' Jeff turned towards her. 'Well, Jenny, shall we have a wander around?'

Jenny looked at Samantha. 'Would you like to "wander" with us, Samantha?' she asked with a smile.

'Oh, thank you, I would, if you don't mind. It would

be nice to have someone to bounce ideas off, if required. And please, call me Sam.'

'Jenny.'

'Jeff.'

They all shook hands before turning as one to begin looking around.

'Did you know the owner, Sam?' Jenny asked as she walked over to take a closer look at the small panes of glass in the window, checking they weren't cracked and that the wooden muntins hadn't begun to rot.

'Yes, I did – Frank Wilson. He was a lovely man. The ironmonger's was in his family for over a hundred years but neither of his daughters wanted to take it on when he retired.'

'That's a pity,' Jenny sighed, 'although I don't suppose there's much call for that kind of business anymore. People don't seem to repair the way they used to. It's a throw-away society we live in these days.'

She looked around the front room of the shop with a keen eye. Behind the counter, where the agent was standing, was a bank of small wooden drawers. They all had little brass handles on them and spaces for labels to advise what was inside. Jenny's first thought was that removing the wooden counter would open up that area and, if she took out some of the drawers, the spaces could be used to put books in or even little knick-knacks to make the room seem more homely. She'd always envisioned her book shop to be cosy and welcoming. A nice coffee machine in a corner so customers felt no need to rush and some chairs and small tables scattered around to relax in. She could even try to put together a book club so that people could meet up and chat about what they were reading.

She closed her eyes and let the vibe of the room flow around her. Yes, it felt right. There was warmth in the hospitality.'

Jenny smiled at Sam's question. Even though she knew her dream stopped here, she hadn't been able to resist asking.

'From what we know of the building's history, it began life as a coaching inn and maintained this status for several centuries until, in the mid 1800's, there was a serious fire which resulted in the building being quite badly damaged. It was closed up and left in that state until around the 1880's. It was purchased, repaired and became the ironmongers for the next 120-odd years. I would, therefore, suspect that due to having been a catering establishment back in its early history, you would be able to make such a change if desired.'

'I'm guessing that would need to be done via the local council or parish?' Jenny was flicking through her brochure, trying to find the answer to her question.

Fiona looked at her. 'Actually no, it would be agreed with the landowner. All the properties in the area are leasehold, although I can assure you that the value of the lease is minimal. The landlord has to give permission for a change of use to the property. Fortunately there is now one in situ again and this will make gaining permission slightly easier. I don't know if you've heard of Pete Wallace, the musician, but he's the owner of the land upon which this village, and Upper Ditchley three miles away, sits on. You would need to arrange an appointment with him to discuss that option further.'

'Thank you, Fiona, for the information and for being so helpful. We need to think over what we've seen and learnt and give everything some consideration.' Jenny caught Jeff's eye as he replied and worked on smothering a giggle as they made their way out of the door.

Chapter Nine

Once outside, Sam said goodbye and began walking off.

'One minute, Sam.' Jeff looked at Jenny. 'Why don't we all go for something to eat and drink? That pub over there looks very nice. Sam, would you care to join us?'

Jenny looked at her watch. 'My goodness, its one thirty, I didn't realise we'd been in there so long!'

'I... err... don't you have things you wish to discuss?' Sam looked at Jeff and Jenny.

'Yes, we do, but I think you could add some valuable input. You're local to the area, you might be able to help with any questions we may have.'

'Please join us, Sam.' Jenny had warmed to the quiet, unassuming woman as they'd walked around the shop. She was attractive with her long, dark blonde hair and brown eyes. She had curves in all the right places and appeared to be totally unaware of her beauty. She was naturally friendly to Jenny and hadn't flirted at any time with Jeff, which said a lot. She was a woman's woman and this made Jenny feel very comfortable in her presence.

feel of the building but, the truth is, it's far too big for me. I can't afford to take it on so you don't need to worry about me competing with you for it.' She gave a small rueful smile.

He looked at Jenny who gave a small shrug. 'I'm the same as Sam. I loved it. I loved the feel of the history which is steeped into its bones, the overall air of cosiness and I *know* I could do so much with it but the building is just too big. I only want to sell romance and thrillers. I don't need that much space.'

'I thought the same. I agree with you both but I don't need that much space either.'

'Excuse me?' Jenny looked at him, wide-eyed. 'When did you decide you had an interest? I thought you came along just to humour me.'

'I did. Initially... But, as we were looking around, a nugget of an idea began to grow and both of your comments have made me realise it might be worth discussing further.'

'Oh! Well, spit it out!' Sam leant forward as she spoke. 'Don't keep us waiting.'

'How would you feel about us going into business together? The three of us! Sam, you could have the area out by the conservatory. It's right through the wall from your shop so you could knock through a doorway which would give access directly from the bakery into a café area. Jenny,' Jeff turned to look at her, 'you could have the front of the shop plus a portion of the back area next to the café. I'm sure that dividing wall could come down which would open it all up to give a nice airy space. You could choose to either put up decorative screens between your area and the café or keep it all open-plan. You could also have some of the cellar for your crime section.'

'Okay. So what would you be doing?' Sam nodded at Jenny's question.

'I would take the upstairs room with a view to selling antiques, curios and, of course, paintings although not to the same standard as those I sell in London. I'm thinking more along the lines of supporting local creatives – you know, artists, sculptors, hand-crafts, etc. What do you think?'

The expression on Jenny's face told him what she thought. She was battling between shock and surprise. Eventually, she was able to speak.

'But… What about your place in London? Don't you have to be there?'

'Not anymore. Elsa has the place running like clockwork, she's completely on top of everything and she has an incredible gift for selling and for spotting talent. I'm pretty much surplus to requirements these days.'

'But, Jeff, that's your whole career, why would you give that up?'

'If I'm being honest, Jenny, it's lost its thrill lately. I've become bored with it. There's no longer a challenge. I didn't realise this until we were throwing out the ideas on what we would do to the shop and I felt a frisson of excitement that I've not felt for quite some time. Besides, I'm only a ninety-minute drive away from London if Elsa did need me for anything. Maybe I could go down one day a week or something…' He smiled around the table. 'So, what do you both think? Is it floating your respective boats?'

Sam gave a big sigh. 'It sounds wonderful and it's a perfect solution but I simply can't afford to buy in. Almost all of my capital went into the bakery. I created it from scratch and industrial ovens don't come cheap. Nor do French, antique, display cabinets!'

Jeff nodded as she spoke then looked at Jenny. 'Jenny?'

A few seconds passed before she answered him. 'I

love it! It's a great idea. I didn't fancy taking on such a large establishment on my own but sharing it would be perfect. And what you've suggested, Jeff, sounds like a great plan. We'd all complement each other and could offer a more enjoyable shopping experience.'

'Ahem! Are you two listening to me? I can't afford to be a part of your plans.'

Jeff thought for a moment before leaning forward. 'I have a suggestion to put on the table. Jenny, if you are not happy with it, promise me you'll say so.'

'I promise!'

'Right, Sam, there are two possible options we can consider. Number one – Jenny and I buy the property fifty-fifty between us, pay for all the alterations and then you rent the space. Or, number two – Jenny and I buy the property between us BUT we hold your third for you. You can then pay a portion off either every month or every three months, whatever suits you best, over a set period of time. Hopefully, the café would give you an income boost which would help you to do that.'

He looked at them both – would they feel as excited about this venture as he did? He wasn't usually an impulsive man but everything about this whole idea felt so right. He'd watched Jenny as she'd walked around the shop; her eyes had been shining and her face had glowed as they bounced ideas around on how to do it up. He'd been truthful when he'd said he hadn't felt like that for a long time and he wanted to feel that thrill again. He loved his art but, after all these years, maybe a little change wouldn't be a bad thing.

'Jenny, how do you feel about that? If it's all too sudden, or you want more time to think about it, please say so. This is only a suggestion.'

He felt his insides gently squeeze when she smiled at him and replied, 'If I'm being honest, Jeff, I was thinking something similar myself. I think having the café as part of the set-up would really enhance the chances of the whole enterprise being successful. I'm completely flexible on either option. Whatever works best for you, Sam.'

'But, neither of you know me? Why would you do that?'

'Sam, Jenny and I barely know each other either but sometimes fate works in funny ways and puts people together who can help each other out.'

'Jeff, are you *sure* you want to join in this venture? It's a big step down from a posh gallery in Mayfair, you know.' Jenny gave him a pointed look.

He gave a small sigh. 'Honestly Jenny, I really do. I need a new challenge and I want to do something different. I also want a more relaxed pace of life. I wouldn't be able to do this in London because I need to provide a certain standard there so I'd have to do high-end antiques. Well, I no longer find much fun in that – people buying pieces because they'll gain interest over time, not because they've actually fallen in love with the picture or the item. I want to see people look overjoyed because they've found a vase that'll be perfect in the alcove in the hall and who don't care that it's not Ming Dynasty or the like. I've lost the enjoyment in my work – it's time to move onto something new.'

'I can understand that. I love working in the library but I need something else now. I feel more fired up right now than I have done for a very long time. I think we can do this and do it well. I really do.'

They looked at Sam expectantly. She hadn't yet given them an answer. 'Are you both absolutely sure about this?' she asked. When they both nodded enthusiastically, she threw her hands up in surrender. 'I'm in! I'll do it! I like the payment plan option if you are both happy to in touch in the next few days to confirm our intentions.'

They all stepped out of the shop, waited for Fiona to lock up before shaking her hand and saying their goodbyes. When she'd driven away, the four of them turned to look at the shop front again.

'So far, so good,' said Jenny. Jeff and Sam nodded their agreement.

Sukie and Pete welcomed their guests and, once drinks had been sorted out, they sat down and listened to their plans.

'We wanted to do this informally first, Pete,' said Jeff, 'before we got too hooked on the idea and had to deal with the disappointment if you refused our requests or were advised they were not in your best interests.'

'Well, first off, I'd say it's too late to worry about getting "hooked" on the idea because I can see that all of you are like kids at Christmas! The excitement could be cut with a knife.' Pete smiled as he looked at the expectant faces in front of him. 'Secondly, you have no reason to worry. I think your plans sound excellent although knocking through from the bakery into the shop...?' He looked at Charlie. 'Charlie, do you think it's feasible?'

Charlie nodded. 'I can't see any reason why not. I know enough about structural issues to believe it will be a goer, but it needs a qualified surveyor to sign it off for insurance purposes.'

'Thanks.' Pete looked back at Jeff. 'If the surveyor is happy that knocking part of the wall out between the bakery and the shop won't cause any problems, then you have my full permission to go ahead. I'll tell Kara to put it in writing for you.'

'I don't want to put a spanner in the works here, but do you honestly think your venture will be successful?' Sukie looked around the table. 'The village isn't that big, and while I will never knock the option of there being a bookshop close by, I am concerned that the overall footfall may not be enough to keep you going. Don't forget, I used to do the risk calculations for a large business and it was my job to look for the weak spots. I just want to be sure you know the risk you're taking.'

Sam leaned forward and cleared her throat before speaking. 'When I moved here five years ago, the village had a little tearoom and it did very well for visitors because we used to get tourist coaches stopping off for mid-morning or mid-afternoon tea breaks. When Rose and Doris – the two ladies who owned it – retired and sold up, the tearoom was turned into a restaurant. With its demise, the tour companies changed their routes. Although we had the pubs, they're not for everyone and it was the "quaint little English tearoom" that was the main attraction. I believe, if we informed the tour companies of our intentions, they could be persuaded to put us on their maps again. Depending how quickly we can get everything sorted, we could be up and running for the beginning of the summer, which would be perfect timing.'

Sukie smiled. 'Now that I did not know, but it's very interesting... Very interesting indeed! Please, give me a few moments, I've got some ideas brewing...'

She sat back, pulled a pad towards her and began to scribble down her thoughts. After about fifteen minutes, she sat forward. Everyone else around the table looked at her expectantly.

'I have a few suggestions to make but, before I do, may I ask the three of you a question – how would you

'By other commitments do you mean Sadie?'

Jenny nodded. 'She's in her eighties now and, although still sprightly and with every marble she was born with still intact, she's also all alone. We're her only family, there's no one else to keep an eye on her.'

'Continuing with the assumption the shop purchase goes through, what are your plans? Have you given any thought to where you'll live? Or if you'd prefer to commute?'

'Sukie, it's all happened so quickly, I'm still trying to come to terms with the fact that my long-held dream could be about to become a reality. Barely eight days ago, I was sitting at the bus stop admiring the old building across the road and now I'm sitting here, about to put in an offer to buy it! I've not had a chance to think about anything else.'

'Okay, let's talk this out and see if it helps. Firstly, where do you want to live – do you want to commute?'

Jenny thought before she answered. 'I love my flat, as you well know, and I don't think I want to sell it. The drive out here isn't too bad – depending on the traffic it's approximately thirty to forty-five minutes, door-to-door. I'd be going against the traffic – out of Oxford when everyone else is coming in – so that helps.'

'Do any living premises come with the shop?'

'There are rooms on the top floor which we all agree could be converted into a small flat but Jeff will be living in it as he's the one moving the furthest distance.'

'What's he doing about the shops in London?'

'I think he's planning to give Elsa a promotion to manager – he says she's pretty much doing the job already so she may as well have it on an official basis. He does seem really keen to try something new. To be honest, this is all rather scary but, at the same time, really thrilling.'

'Okay, so Jeff's going to live above the shop.' Sukie was quiet for a moment. 'Now, as you've already pointed out, it's a forty-five-minute drive at the worst which is potentially an extra hour and a half being added onto your day. That's okay until you consider all the other aspects of being your own boss – stocktaking, shop and window displays, special events and bookkeeping, to name just a few. If business is good, you'll only have time to do those things after closing. Do you really want to add ninety minutes onto a twelve or thirteen hour day?'

'When you put it like that, no, not really.' Jenny grimaced at the thought.

'And then, of course, you've got Winston and Churchill to think about. It's not fair to leave them alone for such long hours. If you were local, you'd be able to pop home to see them for ten minutes.'

She let out another sigh. 'I know. They're my other worry.'

'Hang on a minute, let me get Pete.'

Sukie left the room and returned a few minutes later with Pete following behind. The twins ran in, both dressed in their pyjamas. Their little curls were still damp which suggested they'd just had their bedtime bath.

'Right you two. On the sofa and behave. Read your books.' He handed over some picture books for them to look through.

Jenny was impressed when they both did as they were told. 'My! You've got them well trained!'

Pete smiled. 'They know the drill – if they mess about, then they go to bed early. If they behave, they can stay up a bit longer. It took a while and a few tantrums for the message to sink in, but perseverance won the day. They're really good now and we get to spend a few extra precious minutes with them as a result.'

Sukie sat back in her chair and Pete perched on the

Chapter Twelve

'You're doing WHAT?"

Jeff looked at Elsa and tried not to laugh at her open-mouthed, shocked expression.

'You heard me,' he replied. 'I've bought a new shop in Lower Ditchley with Jenny Marshall and Samantha Curtis and the three of us will be running it together—'

'But... But... But what about this shop and Knightsbridge? Are you selling them?'

'Elsa, stop interrupting. Let me speak! I'm not selling the London shops and you are being promoted to Area Manager. I am putting you in charge of running them both. You're practically doing all the work these days, I'm just giving you the title to go with it.'

'Are you accusing me of pushing you out? I can't help that I get so enthusiastic over what we do here...'

'Elsa, Elsa, Elsa...' Jeff smiled at her. 'You're not pushing me out – you're making it easier for me to move onto a new challenge. I really want to take this step, and knowing I'm leaving all this in your very capable hands, means I can go for it without worrying over the galleries here.'

'Jeff, I don't want to be looking a gift horse in the mouth here but I can't do everything – what about the insurance valuations?'

Jeff took a hold of Elsa's hands. They were sitting in the office of the Mayfair shop and he'd just received the news that their offer on the shop had been accepted. It was now full steam ahead to get all the paperwork done and the sale completed as soon as possible in order to give them time to do the alterations needed before the planned opening at the end of May. It was going to be tight but they reckoned it could be done if everyone pulled together. Charlie had offered to project manage the renovations for them and he was pulling in a few favours with friends in the building trade to ensure everything went to plan.

'Elsa, you are more than capable of doing the valuations – you know you are – but, if you would prefer, I will be back here a couple of days a week and you can schedule appointments for me then.'

The uncertainty on her face told him she wasn't convinced.

'Look, why don't we shut up shop – it's only an hour early – come downstairs to the flat and I'll tell you everything over a bottle of wine? Do you and Danny have plans tonight or can you stay a bit late?'

'No, we don't. Danny's working on the new pieces for his next exhibition in the summer so I was planning a quiet night in with Puddle and a chick-flick. I can stay a bit later.' Elsa walked over to lock the door and close the window blinds while he switched on the answer machine.

Ten minutes later, they were sitting on the twin sofas in Jeff's basement flat under the gallery and he was filling her in on all that had happened in the last two weeks. When he'd finished, Elsa just sat staring at him. 'Well,

Chapter Thirteen

'You're doing *what*?' whispered Amber, her dismay clearly written all over her face. In the short time she'd known Jenny, she'd become extremely fond of her and appreciated the advice and help she imparted so kindly. It had been such a relief to finally have someone she could talk to about everything and she'd really unburdened herself to Jenny, letting out all the pain and heartache she'd had to shoulder alone since the death of her parents last year. Jenny had also taken Saffy under her wing and had let her sleepover at her place a couple of times in order for Amber to have some time off from being a "parent" and go out with her friends.

Jenny leant across the table and took Amber's hand. 'It's okay, I'm not deserting you. We can still have our weekly dinners although I may need to rearrange the day, but that won't be for a little while yet. I was also thinking that, as Saffy will soon be fifteen, maybe she could come and work in the shop on a Saturday? It would give her some working experience, teach her responsibility for earning her own cash and gives you back a bit more "me" time, which you desperately need. What do you think?'

Amber looked at Jenny's hand in hers. The nails, on the unadorned, long fingers, were short and unpainted. The skin was soft and unblemished. She'd commented before that Jenny had such lovely hands and had been advised that the constant wearing of gloves among all the old books she often handled, had protected her hands considerably.

'Tell me what you're thinking, Amber.' Jenny squeezed her hand and she realised she hadn't answered Jenny's question.

'I think... I think that sounds good. I'm sure Saffy will love working with you in the shop but you'll need to run it by her yourself.'

'Naturally, but I had to see how you felt first before putting it to her. Now, why don't you tell me what you are feeling?'

Amber gave a small smile at Jenny's question. Somehow, she always managed to put her finger right on the sore spot and push at it until the truth came out. 'I'm not sure... Upset maybe because it's been such a comfort knowing you were close by – your friendship and support has been a blessing. I'm also scared that you'll move on with this new chapter of your life and forget us and... Well... I guess I'm annoyed that I've become so dependent on you in such a short space of time and while I *should* be sitting here wishing you well and good luck, I'm actually thinking "What about me? What happens to us now?"' As she spoke, her eyes filled with tears and one slipped down her cheek when she raised her head to look at Jenny.

Jenny slipped her free hand into her cardigan pocket and pulled out a fresh tissue which she used to wipe the tear away before handing it to Amber.

'Amber, I promise you that I will not forget you and

Chapter Fourteen

'You're *WHAAAAT*?'

Jenny tried not to cringe as Sadie's indignant screech ripped through the air. She was tired, it had been a traumatic day and it wasn't over yet. She'd gotten to bed late last night after staying longer at Amber's than she normally would but it had been clear that Amber was putting on a brave face and it had been necessary to give her further reassurance that their new friendship was not going to cease.

Then, when she'd finally gotten to bed, she'd tossed and turned for most of the night as she'd worried over how it was going to go down when she handed in her notice for that was the next task on her "To Do" list. Now that their offer on the shop had been accepted, it was full steam ahead on making this massive change in her life and that included saying goodbye to the place where she'd worked for almost half of her life. In the end, however, she'd worried unnecessarily for her boss and colleagues had been delighted to hear she was taking this adventurous step into an unknown future and had wished her well. Although she was only required to give one month's notice, Jenny had offered them six weeks to give them plenty of time to find a replacement. However, with all the cuts going on through the university, there was no guarantee she would be replaced.

All of that had been easy, in the face of informing Sadie of her new plans. She had yet to broach the suggestion of her moving to live in the newly-built retirement village although she'd brought the brochure Pete had passed on and had the company website already loaded on the tablet currently hidden in her handbag. She was under no illusion that Sadie was going to put up one hell of a fight over this and she was going to have to be very canny and savvy if there was to be any chance of getting the feisty old bird on board.

'You heard me, Sadie,' she replied, swallowing down the sigh that had threatened to slip from her lips. 'I'm moving out to live beside Sukie. I've bought a shop with Elsa's boss, Jeff, and we're going to run it together.'

'Good on ya, gal! Nice to see you've finally got some gumption in you and the balls to take such a brave step, especially at your age! You're not exactly a young thing, are you?'

Jenny practically choked on the drink of wine she'd just taken. 'I'm not *that* old, Sadie! I'm only in my mid-forties!'

'Well, it's old enough when you've been standing still for as long as you have. Pulling up those roots won't be easy, I can tell you.'

'Sadie, I've wanted my own bookshop for longer than I dare think. Yes, it's scary – very bloody scary, if I'm being honest – but it's also hugely exciting.'

'I'd be lying if I said I wasn't going to miss you, lass, but I'm sure you'll sell or rent your flat out to someone nice so I'll simply work my charm offensive on them.'

Okay, thought Jenny, that's the first bombshell dropped, time for the considerably larger, second one to go.

'Actually, Sadie, if I'm being honest, I don't want to leave you here on your own. I've grown so fond of you and it would be horrible not seeing you every other day. I enjoy your company very much.'

'Well, I confess I'm rather partial to seeing you every day, love, but life moves on. We'll just need to adapt.'

'What if we didn't have to adapt? What if we could still hang out a few times a week – like we do now? Would you like that?'

Sadie looked at her through her spectacles, her eyes scrunched up as though trying to read her mind. 'What exactly are you saying, girl? C'mon, spit it out!'

'I want you to move out to Lower Ditchley with me.'

'Do you mean... share a home?' Sadie's voice had dropped down an octave and was ominously quiet.

Jenny took a deep breath. Here goes... 'Not quite. There's a new retirement village opening up close by—'

'RETIREMENT VILLAGE? DID YOU JUST SAY 'RETIREMENT VILLAGE'...?'

'Hear me out, Sadie, please—'

'Hear you out? You want to stick me in some geriatric hellhole, full of doddery old cronies, and LEAVE ME TO ROT?'

'No, it's not like that—'

'I'd say it's exactly like that! Do you honestly think I would choose to hang out with decrepit, broken-up, coffin dodgers? I'd rather live in Outer Mongolia before I'll do that!'

'Sadie! Will you be quiet and let me explain!' Jenny hadn't meant to use her "librarian" tone on her friend, her words had just come out that way – although, it had shut Sadie up, so maybe not such a mistake after all. 'Sadie, I actually require your help. My mum, Bernie, has been struggling to maintain the house since The Judge died. She's been talking about selling it and downsizing but, so far, she's only giving the suggestion lip service. I need to find a way of convincing her that moving is the right thing to do.'

'And how can I help with that? Dumping me in amongst a bunch of piss-smelling, saggy bone-bags is hardly going to bring her round is it?'

Jen couldn't help smiling at her choice of words. 'Okay, before I go any further, let's get one thing cleared up here – you are not being *dumped* in some old-folks home! A retirement village is merely an establishment which has strict controls over who can live on the grounds and there is usually a minimum age requirement – fifty-five tends to be the norm. You have your own home – this particular one,' she gestured at the brochure which she'd pulled out of her bag, 'has an assortment of houses or apartments, all of which are newly built. There are communal facilities such as a gym, a swimming pool, a spa, a restaurant, a bar and some small shops. You can have your own mode of transport but they'll also be running a mini-bus into Oxford five times a week. It is NOT an old folks home in the way that you think, and as you'll have your own, private, accommodation, you'll be able to get away from any that do happen to smell of piss!'

Jenny thrust the brochure at Sadie and it took all of her willpower to maintain a poker face when curiosity got the better of her and she took it from her hands.

As Sadie began to flick through it, Jenny continued, 'Now then, back to what I was saying about Bernie. I think this place would really suit her. The only friends she had were the wives of The Judge's cohorts. Now that he's gone, she's no longer invited out to dinner parties or social events and, though she won't admit it, she's lonely. She needs to move, make a new life and find some real friends. That's where you come in – on the couple of occasions when you've met, you've both gotten on rather well and I think, given the chance, you could be good friends. With your feisty spirit, you would soon knock any melancholy out of her and get her smiling again. I reckon you could persuade her that this,' she nodded at the brochure in Sadies's hand, 'would be a good way to move forward. So, what do you say, are you up to the challenge?'

Sadie didn't answer immediately. Instead, she pointed to some photographs in the brochure. 'Are these the houses you mentioned?'

Jenny looked across. 'Yes, they are. They're kinda smart, wouldn't you say?'

She received a grunted response and held her tongue while Sadie looked through the brochure a second time. Eventually she said, 'I've brought my tablet with me, if you wanted to look at their website. They have additional photographs on there and more information…'

'Oh, go on then, let me see! I'm not saying yes, mind, but I suppose there's no harm in looking. You can take me out for a look around on Saturday – just to get a feel of the place.'

'Sure, I can do that. I'll phone tomorrow and make an appointment. How about I ask Bernie to join us? We can pretend that you would like her there for a second opinion because you trust her more than you trust me – does that sound like a plan? I'm sure that, once she sees what's on offer, she'll be more amenable to the idea of finally making the steps to letting go and moving on.'

'Yes, alright then. I'll play along if it helps your mum. It would be nice to see her again, it's been a while.'

'I'll text you tomorrow with the details. Now, I'd

better get to bed. I'm shattered and the next few weeks are going to be manic so I need all the sleep I can get now.' .

She bent down to pick up the brochure but Sadie quickly put her hand upon it. 'I'll keep a hold of this for now. I want to have a proper read of it so I can prepare questions for Saturday.'

Jenny sucked in her cheeks to prevent the smile that threatened from breaking loose. It would never do for Sadie to know she'd walked right into her carefully laid plan.

'Okay, no problem. Here, I'll leave my tablet too, should you want to look up anything else. Goodnight.' She kissed Sadie on the cheek and left.

As she made her way up the stairs, the grin she'd been holding back escaped and spread across her face. She knew that, once Sadie and Bernie were together, they'd talk each other into moving. She just had to remember to phone her mum tomorrow and fill her in on the plan. She was sure Bernie would play along for she hadn't been lying when she'd told Sadie about the lack of social life her mum now had – she'd just omitted to mention that Bernie was actually very keen to sell the old marital home and get her life back on track.

'Oops, my bad,' she chuckled aloud, as she let herself into her flat and closed the door behind her.

'Sukie, you told me this was a cottage! This is NOT a cottage!'

Jenny, Sadie, Bernice and Sukie were standing outside

the Little Gatehouse. Jenny had taken Sadie and Bernice to look around the retirement village and it was looking like it had been a successful trip. They'd totally clicked upon meeting again and it appeared as though both were interested in making the move to live there. They had some more comprehensive paperwork to look through and think about before going back for a second visit later in the week. Bernie had offered to collect Sadie as Jenny would be at work.

They'd stopped for lunch at The Inn on the Green and Jenny had given them a small tour of the village although Sadie already knew it rather well from her regular bus visits to Sukie.

Now it was Jenny's turn to view her potential new abode. Sukie had met them at the gate by the church and had led them along the short path to where the house stood. And it was most definitely a house.

'Well... I suppose it's not a cottage in that it doesn't have a thatched roof and roses around the door but it's not exactly huge.' Sukie tilted her head to one side as she spoke.

'Sukie, we don't all live in Austrian castles or stately homes – compared to my little two-bedroomed flat, this is huge!'

The building in front of them was built from the same Cotswold stone as the manor and sported two large bay windows on the ground floor with a big solid, black painted, front door in between them. The first floor had three wide, tall, evenly spaced, windows and, above them, a sharp pitched roof rose up into the tall trees which surrounded the house.

'Come on, let's go inside and see what you think.' Sukie led the way through the front door, Sadie and Bernie hot on her heels. Jenny lagged behind, however, a little bemused by this turn of events. The size of the

101

property didn't actually bother her – she'd lived in large houses for a good part of her life – it was the surprise of expecting something small and quaint and being presented with the equivalent of a miniature stately home.

'Sukie, how on earth can you call this "The Little Gatehouse"? It is anything but little.'

Sukie was standing in the large, airy, hallway as Jenny walked in the door. 'Err... because it's next to the little gate that leads to the village...' she replied. 'The Big Gatehouse is the one down on the main road next to the big main gates.'

Jenny had no answer to that. 'Fair enough! I suppose it makes sense when you look at it like that,' she grinned.

She looked around the hallway where they all stood. The flooring was simple chess board, black and white tiles laid in a diamond formation. The walls were a gentle cream with white dado rails halfway up from the floor and deep, grooved, white skirting. It was a nice size – not so big as to feel cavernous but not so small that the four of them standing there felt crowded. Towards the back of the hall, the staircase, with its sweeping bottom step, made its way up along one wall to a small landing which ran from one side of the hallway to the other.

Sukie led them into the two rooms at the front of the house, one on either side of the main door. They were almost identical in both size and layout with the large bay windows on the front and a smaller window giving a side-view into the trees. The ceilings were lower than that of the hallway and this gave them a cosy feel. Both had lovely open fireplaces with, as Sukie explained, gas-effect fires for ease and comfort.

'One room is the dining room and the other the lounge. You can decide which is which although I do believe that room,' she pointed across the hall to the room on the left of the front door as they faced it, 'gets more sunlight in the summer months.'

She turned on her heel and led them through a door into the large, bright, kitchen-diner which ran the full width of the house.

'Wow!' was the collective response from Sadie and Bernie. Jenny was too gobsmacked to say anything for the room was amazing. The walls were a soft, gentle, buttercup colour and the flooring was pale oak, varnished floorboards. The kitchen area was to one side with rich cream units and an Aga-effect cooker. A breakfast bar split the room and on the other side opposite, was a large empty space which would be perfect for either a table or a large, comfy sofa. The floor to ceiling windows looked out onto a decking area which led down into the walled garden. It was currently still barren looking but Jenny could see some small green shoots beginning to peep out of the tubs on the deck.

'Those are bi-fold windows, Jenny, which open all the way back. Perfect for warm, balmy, summer nights.'

'It's utterly gorgeous, Sukie, it really is.'

'You've yet to see the upstairs, come on.'

On the journey home, Jenny and Sadie agreed that the two vast bedrooms on the first floor had been quite something with their en-suite bathrooms and walk-in dressing rooms although Jenny's personal favourite had been the third bedroom up in the attic. It had two dormer windows looking down into the walled garden, and also came with en-suite facilities. Sukie's suggestion of making it into a little studio flat for Saffy, when she came to visit, had been perfect and Jenny knew her young teenage friend would love it. All in all, the house – albeit larger than she'd anticipated – had been stunning and she'd already been positioning her furniture when Sukie had told her what the monthly rent would be. Jenny had been appalled at how ridiculously low it was and had made every effort to make Sukie see sense and charge her the going rate but Sukie had refused to budge, saying she held rather a big soft-spot for this particular house and she couldn't be happier that one of her best friends was going to be living in it. She'd also said that if Jenny felt that strongly about the price, she could make up the difference in bottles of wine when they, once again, met up in the evenings to chew the fat and put the world to rights. Jenny had finally given in and agreed that *that* was the best kind of rent she could think of.

control. 'I'm so sorry,' he choked out, 'that was extremely rude of me but your forthright delivery is truly refreshing, I love it.'

'She's always been like that,' Rose whispered, 'just opens her mouth and spews forth. No filter is what I think they call it these days.'

'You think correctly, Rose, but I prefer straight-talkers, you always know where you stand with them.'

He turned back to looking at the now, fully exposed, glasswork. 'So, ladies, what can you tell me about this. Why was something so stunning hidden away from view?'

'It was the war.' Doris spoke while Rose nodded by her side. 'When the moon was shining, it reflected off the glass. This broke blackout rules and the owner was told to take it down. There was also a rumour that the iron would be taken away and used for weapons. Well, old Mr Wilson was having none of that, he loved this conservatory – he used to grow tropical plants in it, just like that place near London – so he had it all encased in wood, which he painted black, and hoped those in authority would forget about it. The villagers all swore to keep his secret and, over time, people did forget. Even I'd forgotten about it until I saw the wood panels come away. I was only about eleven but seeing it again now, it feels just like yesterday when he would let me visit and teach me all about the gorgeous plants he was growing – *pyrethrum roseum* was my favourite, I've never forgotten that one. I clearly had a thing for roses even then.' She smiled gently at Rose who smiled brightly back.

Charlie felt a small lump rise in his throat as he witnessed the obviously deep love between the two women. 'But…' he croaked. He took a small cough to clear his throat and tried again. 'There's no evidence of this inside. It's a solid ceiling in the glass-panelled room.'

Doris gave him a mischievous smile. 'Come with me and bring a ladder and a crowbar!'

When they were inside, she pointed up at the ceiling. 'Break through the plaster and look for a join. Although, before you do, you might want to cover the floor in dust sheets, it could get messy.'

Charlie went back outside and called Robbie and his men in. They laid down dust sheets as instructed, divided themselves across the room and began carefully pulling away the plaster on the ceiling. After fifteen minutes, Robbie let out a yell. He'd located a join.

Charlie rushed over and they each carefully slipped a crowbar into the weak spot and began to slowly prise away a large wooden panel. As they worked the bar along the join, pulling out the old nails, Charlie could see daylight – albeit rather dull – through the increasing gap. When the entire panel had been removed, he grabbed a torch and rushed back up the ladder. He stuck his head through the large, gaping hole in the ceiling, switched the torch on and let out the biggest of gasps when he saw what was around him.

He heard Jeff call up to him, 'Well, what can you see?' but he was spellbound and unable to talk. After a few minutes of silent looking, he came down the ladder, turned to Robbie and said, 'Robbie, could you and the boys continue working on removing this ceiling, please. Jeff, you need to come with me.'

He went over to the tool deposit in the far corner, picked out a second crowbar, a claw hammer, and practically ran towards the stairs. Jeff, Doris and Rose followed eagerly behind. When they'd all arrived on the first floor, and stepped carefully around the dresser Jeff had been sanding, Charlie walked over to the wall directly opposite the windows which looked out onto the village.

'Jeff,' he looked at his brother, 'you mentioned you wanted a window in this wall to let in more light.'

'Err... yes, that's correct.'

'Good! Because I think you're about to get a lot more light than you bargained for!' As he spoke, he ran his fingertips over the wall, occasionally stopping for a few seconds before moving along again. 'Ah, here we go.'

Just as they had downstairs, Charlie began removing the plaster on the wall. This was thinner than the stuff on the ceiling and came off quickly. When another wooden panel had been fully exposed, he used the claw hammer to ease out the nails and slowly removed it, telling Jeff to close his eyes before he did so. He put the panel to one side, took Jeff's arm and guided him across the floor.

'Okay, stop here. Now open your eyes...'

Jeff hesitated for a moment. What on earth was he about to see? He savoured the anticipation for a few more seconds and then...

'Oh! My! Goodness!' He felt his mouth drop open with wondrous surprise for, in front of him, was an exquisite wrought iron balcony. Beyond it he could see Robbie and his men as they removed more of the ceiling panels downstairs. He turned to Charlie. 'I don't believe it, how come no one knew of this?'

'I did!' Doris piped up.

Jeff and Charlie gave her an exasperated look before setting to work on removing the remaining wall panels. It didn't take long until they were all down and the full scale of what they'd uncovered could be seen. Nearly half of the downstairs ceiling was gone and there was enough light to see the beautiful, intricate iron work across the roof and the beams extending from the balcony across the empty space to the glass wall on the opposite side.

Finally, Jeff found his voice. 'Charlie, I don't know what to say. It's just… amazing! This is going to change the whole ambience and feel of the shop. Jenny and Sam are going to love this. Well, I hope they will.'

'Of course they will, what's not to love about it? It's just given you a whole new marketing vein. A newly discovered, one hundred year old, Victorian conservatory will have them all queueing up for a look-see. Now, let's go back downstairs and help with removing those final panels and we can see how awesome it looks from down there.

When they all arrived back down the stairs, Doris and Rose made their way to the front door. Doris looked back at Charlie and Jeff. 'Thank you for letting us look around today, it's been fun, hasn't it, Rose?'

Rose smiled her agreement as Charlie thanked Doris for the information she'd given them. 'It would have taken us longer to make this discovery, had it not been for you. Thank you again. And, if you know of any other secrets this building might be keeping, you're more than welcome to share them.'

'Well, young man, when you have a few minutes to spare, may I suggest you remove all that hideous plaster and wood around the staircase…'

And, with those words still hanging in the air, she gave him a wink and breezed out through the door, closing it firmly behind her.

Chapter Sixteen

Jenny stood looking around the shop and marvelled at how bigger, brighter and airier it felt since Robbie and Charlie had removed all the wooden panelling in the conservatory and, on Doris's hint, around the staircase. The latter had revealed another wrought iron treasure – a gorgeous, intricate stair bannister which matched the rest of the ironwork they'd discovered; the small sweeping stairs at the bottom gave the shop a more luxurious feel.

The downside of these discoveries, unfortunately, was that they had increased the painting time considerably. Previously, all the wooden panels would have been done in a couple of days with the aid of paint rollers. The ironwork required a more delicate approach. It needed a good wash down as, despite being protected within its wooden enclosure for almost eighty years, it hadn't been protected from dust and dirt. The original paint had flaked off in several places which meant some careful sanding was needed before it could be repainted by hand and using small paint brushes. It had easily added several extra days of labour onto their already tight schedule.

'I think it's safe to say we've just lost any free time we may have hoped for in the next eight weeks,' Jenny said.

Jeff, who was standing next to her, agreed. 'It's a good thing I'd decided to move into the flat this weekend – it means I can work later without having to bother Sukie.'

'She'll miss you being around. With Pete away on tour, she's enjoyed having you stay. She was telling me the twins don't quite have the same level of conversation as yourself.' Jenny smiled as she relayed the information.

'Well,' Jeff said, 'she's still got Charlie as a house guest so I'm sure he'll be able to prevent her sinking into full-blown mummy-brain.'

'I've got a suggestion!' Jenny turned to Saffy who was standing on her other side, between her and Amber. They'd come along to help bring over the boxes she'd packed up, ready for moving into the Gatehouse. Amber had offered to help with the transport as her parents' large SUV was still in the garage and it needed a good run out to keep it ticking over. This had been a blessing as Brian the Beetle was certainly not the man for the job.

'And what is that?' Saffy's face was glowing with her idea and Jenny couldn't wait to hear it. She had grown incredibly fond of both girls and Saffy was so lovable and sweet, it was impossible not to adore her. Jenny had to make an extra effort to be firm with her, when it was required, because it would be so easy to capitulate every time Saffy turned her beautiful smile on her.

'I can come and help. School finishes next week for the Easter holidays and I've got nothing to do because Amber's at work. I can do washing and painting.' Saffy grinned as though this was the obvious answer to the problem.

'Actually, young lady, you'll have year-end exams to study for. Just because I'm at work, and not able to watch over you, doesn't mean I expect you to sit around doing nothing.' Amber gave her sister a gentle nudge with her elbow.

'Oh, Amber, you can't seriously expect me to study all day, every day! That's not fair!'

'Wouldn't you rather be hanging out with your friends?' Jenny couldn't figure out why a fifteen-year-old girl would rather be washing and painting in an old shop than dreaming over pop stars, or gaming, with her friends.

'I can't. They're both going away on holiday. I'll be pretty much on my own.'

'Well, I have an alternative suggestion.' The idea had just come to Jenny and she spoke before she had the time to change her mind. 'I'm moving into the Gatehouse on Saturday and it has a couple of spare bedrooms. Why don't you come and stay with me for a bit. You can do studying in the morning and then come to the shop to help in the afternoon.'

'Oh WOW!' Saffy's face lit up with joy. 'That would be awesome! Thank you, I'd love to do that!' She threw her arms around Jenny's waist and gave her a big hug.

'Excuse me, I think I should have a say in this decision, Saffy.' Amber's tone was slightly cool and Jenny suddenly felt awkward. She hadn't meant to tread on any toes. Damn! She should have discussed it with Amber first. She said as much, while apologising for speaking out of turn.

'Jenny,' Amber smiled, 'I've got no problem with your suggestion, and I'm really grateful for it, I just don't think you should be burdening yourself with a teenager when you've got so much to do.'

'Amber, I would never consider either of you a burden. If I'm being honest, having Saffy to stay would be a benefit. You see, the house is a little isolated, given its location, and as much as I can't wait to move in, it'll feel strange not to have any neighbours close by. I've never lived *that* alone before and it's going to take a few weeks to adapt. Having Saffy to stay the first week or two will make it easier for me. And, if you like, you could come and stay over the following weekend. We could have an early celebration for your birthday on the Saturday night, since it falls on a weekday this year.'

'Oh yes, that's a WONDERFUL idea. Go on, Amber, let's do that. It'll be fun.' Saffy nudged her sister back.

'Well... When you put it like that...'

'YES!' Saffy fist-punched the air, knowing that Amber had given in. 'I'm off to find Charlie, he'll need to make sure he has a hat and hi-vis to fit me!' She scurried off, leaving three bemused adults behind her.

'I think she's developing a little crush on Charlie, I'd better go and make sure she doesn't chew his ear off too much.' With a parting grin, Amber followed in Saffy's wake.

'That was a very kind thing to do.' Jeff smiled at Jenny.

'Oh, it's nothing. Saffy's a great kid, she'll be fun to have around and we'd be daft to say no to the extra help. It's not like we don't need it!' She felt her face warming up and made a point of looking down inside her rucksack to prevent Jeff from noticing. They'd spent a lot of time together, since the night he'd come to her rescue, and nearly double that time talking on the phone as they discussed shop business. When the shop business was concluded, they'd occasionally carried on talking, getting to know each other, and she was growing quite fond of him. Along with Saffy and Amber, it felt as though she now had a little family... Well, almost. They weren't "hers" as such but a bond had grown between them all. It was nice.

'Ah, here we go.' She pulled a tape measure out of her bag with a flourish. 'Jeff, do you mind helping me to take times bigger than the first, slowly peeled itself away from the ceiling and dropped onto the third glass cabinet with a deafening crash. This time, the noise was so loud that Matt must have heard it for he stopped drilling. A second later, Robbie's phone rang and Matt was on the other end asking if he was okay. 'I am right now,' he replied with a sigh, 'but I don't think I will be for much longer.'

Matt appeared in the bakery within a few seconds, breathless from running, and took in the carnage in front of him. 'Oh, fuck!'

'Yup! Oh, fuck indeed, Matt.'

'Shall I get some dust sheets to cover them?'

'I think they call that "closing the stable door after the horse has bolted"! No, just leave them for now. Let's get this wall sorted out first and then we'll deal with the ceiling.'

They spent the rest of the day, and half of Tuesday, finishing the doorway. When it was done, it looked quite good. The stone had been left exposed and the finish was rough and uneven but it would be a sacrilege to hide the beautiful stonework edging behind plaster.

When he was satisfied the structure of the wall hadn't been compromised from their efforts, Robbie removed some of the supports and turned his attention to the ceiling. The plaster which had fallen was dry and brittle and, when he climbed up to inspect what was still on the ceiling, he found it to be the same. It crumbled at the smallest touch. He breathed a small sigh of relief that the fault hadn't been entirely his but it was a small victory in the face of what lay below him. Had he known the ceiling was in such poor condition, he'd have had the cabinets removed from the room. As it was, he'd just moved them away from the area he'd been working in, thinking they would be perfectly safe.

He came back down to floor level. 'Matt, go and get

sheets to put over the floor and these cabinets. The whole of this ceiling needs to come down so let's make it easy and put most of it onto sheets that we can lift up afterwards.'

'Shall I clear this debris off the units first?'

'No point right now as more is going to come down and you'll need to clean them a second time. We can sort them tomorrow. We'll bring down the rest of the plasterwork this afternoon, I'll check the joists and laths above are dry and secure – we may as well take advantage of this disaster to ensure there's nothing else wrong up there – and then tomorrow, we can begin to re-plaster. It'll need two coats of lime plaster but we should have enough time for it to dry before we have to decorate in here. We can amend our schedule to make this and the kitchen the last to be painted. That should give us some breathing space.'

The following day, satisfied the ceiling laths were in good condition, Robbie put on the first layer of plaster. He hadn't done a lime plaster for a number of years and he enjoyed working with it again. He'd started early and had finished by lunchtime. He stood below and looked up at his morning's work. It looked not too bad at all. He had to leave it now for a few days to dry and then he'd come back on Saturday to check it over for any holes that may need filling before he put the second layer up on Monday.

He smiled as he picked up his jacket. He needed a shower to wash the plaster off himself and a couple of pints to clear the dust from his throat. He'd come back this afternoon and begin clearing up the mess the old ceiling had created.

RUINED ME!' she screeched.

'Sam, I'm sorry. Please, let me explain...'

'There's nothing to explain... You've destroyed my dream. My beautiful work counters...' She began sobbing again.

'Here, Sam. Come with me. Come on, let's go to your cottage and make you a cup of tea.' Jenny put her arm around Sam again and began to walk her towards the back door. She looked over her shoulder at Robbie, 'You'd better come too and explain exactly what happened in here.'

'No! I don't want him anywhere near me!' Sam screamed as Robbie followed them out.

'Sam, we need to know what happened and how it's going to be put right.'

When they were settled around the table in Sam's cottage, Robbie explained what had happened.

'I'm so sorry, Sam, I really am. The ceiling plaster looked fine and I had no idea it was in such poor condition. When was it last painted?'

Sam hiccupped as she answered, 'November last year. There were a few cracks and it didn't look good so I gave it a couple of coats.'

Robbie sighed at her reply. 'If only I'd known that... I could have removed your counters from the room and taken the ceiling down in a controlled manner. As it was, it looked fine so I simply moved them away from where we were working. I thought they were safe.'

'So, what next, Robbie? Are you planning on clearing up the mess or were you leaving it for Sam to do herself?' Jenny gave him the look which had left many back-chatting students quaking in their trendy Doc Martens.

'I'm clearing it all up, that was my plan for this afternoon. I've also been in touch with a couple of restoration people I know who may be able to mend the cabinets. I'll be sending pictures to them this afternoon, once I've cleaned them up. Sam,' he looked towards her, 'do you have photographs of how they looked beforehand so they know what to work to?'

When Sam nodded that she did, Jenny replied, 'Okay, now we know what's what, Robbie, I suggest you crack on with getting that mess cleared up. Sam, find those photographs and email them to Robbie. When you've done that, you can come and give me a hand in the shop and, in return, I'll help you to wash down the bakery when Robbie has finished doing all he needs to do.'

'Thank you, Jenny but that doesn't solve the problem of the shop being out of commission. Robbie's just said it'll be at least another week before I can get back in there. It might be only three days but I can't afford another three days.'

'Can I make a suggestion?' Robbie looked at Sam.

'Are you still here?' She glared back at him. 'I don't want to hear any suggestions from you. In fact, I don't want you anywhere near me or my property. Fuck off, you little Irish oik!'

'Sam!' There was no hiding the shock in Jenny's voice.

'No, it's okay, Jenny. Sam's upset and I've been called a lot worse over the years.' He stood up and made his way to the door. 'All I was going to say is, is there any way you could offer a short-term delivery service to cover the few extra days the bakery is closed? I'll pay the expense of the fuel, it's the least I can do.' He gave them both a sharp nod and walked out.

Jenny turned to Sam. 'That's actually not a bad idea... Could it be done?'

'I suppose...' Sam chewed on her thumbnail for a moment before continuing. 'I could print off some flyers, pop them through letterboxes and put some up in the shop

I'm only seventy-eight, you know, not eighty-seven! I'm not in my dotage just yet!'

'Sadie, this time last month, you WERE in your "dotage" so don't start that one with me! I'm just checking you've got everything before I go.'

'I'm fine, Jenny. I promise to keep my phone by my side at all times. I'm going to be busy packing up my things so there's no chance of anything untoward happening.'

'No climbing up any ladders, do you hear me? I'll be over on Thursday to take down curtains, pictures etc., and to clear any top shelves I haven't yet done.'

'Okay, okay. Now, will you get going before someone in the street calls the RSPCA to deal with those damn cats!'

Jenny gave her a hug and set off, turning up the classical music radio station she'd put on in the hope it would lull her caterwauling felines to sleep.

Jeff met Jenny when she drove into Lower Ditchley. He'd helped the removal men to back up the narrow pathway along the side of the church and had given them access to the house. Under Jenny's instructions, the furniture from the old spare room was the first of the items to go in. This cleared the way for the cats to be released upon her arrival. Jeff carried Churchill and Jenny took Winston. They ceased their non-stop howling the minute she opened the carriers.

'Oh boy, silence has never sounded so good!' she said, as she slipped out the bedroom door and checked it was firmly closed behind her.

'Were they like that for the whole journey?'

'Yup! I've never been so tempted to open a window and let them loose as I was today. Has the fridge-freezer been installed yet? I need to make sure there are some bottles of wine in cooling. I reckon I'm going to need them tonight!'

'I don't think your fridge will be cool enough by then but, as Sukie has invited us both for dinner tonight, you don't need to worry. I'm sure she'll have a couple of bottles all nicely chilled.'

Jeff knew for a fact she would as he'd put two bottles of Champagne in the fridge earlier, especially for celebrating Jenny's move. He should have moved into the flat over the shop last week but, upon moving an old, decrepit wardrobe, they'd found an external door they hadn't known about. It had taken a bit of effort to get it open, despite the key hanging conveniently by the side, but the lock had pretty much seized up and several squirts of WD40 were required to get the mechanism moving. When they had finally gotten it shifted, the old, iron, spiral staircase on the other side didn't look safe enough to take anyone's weight. No one had been aware of its existence because it was covered in ivy and came down on the other-side of the courtyard wall. This was when they realised that the overgrown area at the side of the shop was actually a small lane which appeared to lead to the old, bricked-up stables. They'd all been so busy working on getting the inside ready, that the outside hadn't yet been fully explored.

Robbie had promised to put a new door in next week so Jeff could move in without any further disruption and the outside stairs would be the first priority once the shop had opened. Sukie had expressed her delight at Jeff's extended stay because Pete was still touring and not due home for another ten days. She'd mentioned to Jeff how much she'd enjoyed having him and Charlie around the

Jeff looked on bemused. 'Something you ladies want to share here?'

To his eyes, Jenny appeared to be glowing as she replied, 'When Sukie and I were neighbours, we spent many nights talking politics and discussing "society today" over bottles of wine. In the summer, it was up on my roof-terrace, in the winter, it was down in Sukie's cosy lounge. I have to confess I've missed them but don't tell Sadie, she likes to think she's still one of the girls. Unfortunately, as much as I adore her, it wasn't really the same.'

'Actually, it's one of the things I've missed since moving away from London, having girlie nights in. They're something quite special,' Sam said quietly.

Sukie turned to her and, leaving one arm over Jenny's shoulders, put her other around Sam's. 'Then you must join us. The more the merrier.'

'Ahem! Excuse me! What about me? I don't know anyone here. Can't I be an honorary girl – at least until I can wrangle my way onto the local darts team or whatever they do for sport around here?' Jeff made a point of assuming an affronted look which caused the ladies in front of him to giggle before turning to laughter when he walked in an exaggerated cat-walk swagger towards the dining room.

'Carry on like that, my son, and you'll be more of a girlie than we are,' mocked Sukie. Amidst giggles and laughter, the three women made their way into the dining room behind him.

'Sukie, that was delicious. Thank you, I really enjoyed it.' Jenny leant back, rubbing her stomach. 'I really shouldn't have had that second portion of sherry trifle but it was utterly scrumptious, I couldn't resist.'

'Oh, don't worry about that, Jen, life's too short to fret about every morsel that crosses our lips. There's nothing wrong in having indulgent moments, they make up for all the crappy ones we have to endure.'

'Sam, you own a bakery and sell sumptuous cakes and pastries – of course you're going to say that,' Jenny giggled.

'Good point but I do also believe it. Life is for living, so live it!'

'I'll drink to that,' Jeff raised his glass in yet another toast. They'd already had several when the champagne had been cracked open but no one was complaining at another one.

'Life is for living, so live it!' they all chorused together.

Jeff put his glass back on the table. 'Women look better when they've got curves and stuff anyway. Most men don't actually like the washboard look all those magazines try to sell. As an honorary girlie, I say "Jenny – eat what you damn well please!", and, as a normal bloke, I say "Jenny – your figure is absolutely perfect and don't you ever worry that it isn't".

Sam and Sukie laughed as Jenny blushed deep scarlet. 'Thanks, Jeff. I'll err… keep that in mind,' she mumbled.

Sukie took the bottle of wine out of the cooler and refilled their glasses. 'So, have you come up with a name for the shop yet?' she asked, 'I need to let the travel companies know so they can include it in their blurb.'

Jenny, Sam and Jeff all looked at each other. 'Ahh… Urm… No, not really. Nothing is coming to mind.' Jenny answered Sukie's question.

'What? Nothing at all?'

'Well… There was "Jeff 'n' Jen's Pokey Bookshop"…'

'Pokey Bookshop? Seriously? Why?'

'Because Jeff's merchandise is going to be so eclectic! He's planning to stock the place with small prints and paintings, sculptures, pottery, patchwork quilts and hand-made jewellery, but he's also giving free rein to his love for antiques. He plans to have these peppered around the room on his renovated display shelves and cabinets – expensive carriage clocks will sit on shelves next to low-priced glassware and oddities such as a pair of Victorian opera glasses. He's refused to streamline his purchases and is simply buying what he likes in the hope others will like them too. It's going to be one of those rooms where you "poke" about in the hope of finding a hidden gem, hence the "pokey" bit.'

'I see. But "Pokey Bookshop" is not going to work because it sounds like a shop which is a bit of a dump. Sorry but I have to be honest.'

'I think that's a clear enough way of telling us to dump that idea,' Jeff looked around the table.

After a few minutes, where they all stared at each other and into their wine glasses, Sam eventually broke the silence. 'There was something I thought of but... Well... You'll probably think it's silly...'

'Sam, in the absence of *anything* else, please just spit it out.' Sukie gave her a smile of encouragement.

'How about "Jeff 'n' Jen's Cabookeria"?'

'Huh?' Jeff's face expressed his puzzlement quite clearly.

'I'll explain,' Sam cleared her throat and took a drink of wine before continuing. '*Ca* from café, *book* from... well, book, and *eria* from galleria. A galleria is a collection of small shops underneath one roof. Also, a gallery is where works of art are displayed. So it's kind of a play on words. Ca-book-eria. Cabookeria!'

She grabbed her glass and took another big sip when she'd finished. 'See, I said it was silly...'

'No, that's not silly at all.' Sukie shook her head slowly.

'It's really clever.' Jenny smiled.

'I think it sounds fabulous, I like it.' Jeff smiled too.

'Only one thing, let's lose the "Jeff 'n' Jen" bit. I think it's too long-winded and we are hoping that, one day, you'll be an equal partner, Sam.' Jenny spoke gently to Sam who was now blushing from the praise being given to her.

'I agree,' Jeff said. 'We should keep it simple. How about "The Cabookeria"? And perhaps the signage, and our logo, could be "The" in simple, cursive font and "Cabookeria" in bold capitals. Just my suggestion, of course…'

'It's perfect!' Sukie nodded along with Jenny. Sam gave a squeak of delight which caused everyone to laugh again.

It was decided.

Their venture would be called *The Cabookeria*.

Chapter Nineteen

Jenny, Jeff and Sam walked slowly around their shop and wondered how they'd managed to get everything ready for the grand opening the following day. The books were all laid out smartly on their shelves and on the small tables dotted about. A couple of high-backed chairs were positioned "just so" in front of the bank of drawers which had so attracted Jenny that first day. As she'd envisioned back then, some had been removed to allow books to stand in their place, others stored extra copies of the books lined up above them. A small, hand-woven rug had been purchased from one of Jeff's handiwork suppliers and it lay upon the shining, wooden floor between the chairs. Brass standing lamps with delicate Tiffany shades, stood behind each chair to provide the readers with additional lighting in the darker months of the year.

The large double fronted windows contained displays which showed off all aspects of what was available inside – Jeff's shabby chic bookcases held some of Jenny's books while some of his delicate pottery was set out on a table alongside cake stands which Sam would replenish each day with fresh wares. Small pastel-edged chalkboards advertised their opening times, special offers and invitations to the passers-by to step inside for a leisurely browse.

Jenny's old-style cash register stood proudly on the massive writing desk she'd spent hours sanding down and re-staining. The carpenters had fallen under her spell and, when she'd asked them to make a few adjustments to it – such as making pedestals to raise its height, and putting a false front with shelves into the footwell – they had been only too happy to oblige. These shelves now held little pocket-sized books of humour, poetry, Shakespeare sonnets and even baking recipes. The book shelves, some tall and some small, were arranged in such a way that a natural corridor had been created to lead the browsing shopper towards the back of the shop and the area which had once been dull and dingy was now light and vibrant thanks to their beautiful conservatory.

They stood admiring Sam's café area which filled the glass and iron structure. Sam had fallen in love with the Victorian ironwork and had declared she would be running a Victorian tearoom. Giant ferns were strategically placed to provide privacy and to minimise the echo, all the tables were covered in dark green damask table cloths with pale cream lace covers over the top and the chairs had all been re-upholstered in dark green velvet. Sam had accompanied Jeff on his forays to antique auctions and clearance sales to find beautiful Victorian crockery. It didn't all match but it did look fabulous. She, and her waiting staff, would be smartly dressed in ankle-length, dark green skirts, pastel green blouses and full-length, cream, bibbed aprons. When they'd dressed up for the promotional photographs, they'd looked amazing and it had been agreed that this would most likely be the best selling point for the whole shop. Jeff and Jenny felt it would look even better if the Victorian theme was maintained throughout and agreed they would also wear the same attire although Jeff did declare that he didn't have good hips for a skirt and would be better in dark green trousers, a pale green shirt with a dark green tie and a waistcoat. The ladies had teased him that he'd grab any excuse to don an item from his vast waistcoat collection and he hadn't disagreed.

Sam walked through the tearoom and straightened a table cloth here and there before they turned and made their way upstairs to Jeff's floor of goodies.

The name 'The Pokey Bit' had stuck and Jenny had arranged to have a little sign made up which matched their logo and shop signage – pale cream background with dark, racing green font – and it was placed at the top of the stairs. Jeff had been delighted with it.

The room was laid out exactly as they'd described it to Sukie the night they'd all had dinner. Jeff's shabby-chic dressers and cabinets were the perfect foil for some of the darker antique pieces he'd found. The bright daylight that came in through the conservatory had allowed him to paint one of the walls a dark racing green and it created the perfect enhancement for his prints and paintings. Wicker baskets, under the units, contained jewellery, throws, quilts and all sorts of small hand-made knick-knacks. It was a veritable Aladdin's cave and a place where "poking about" was encouraged. Jeff nodded his approval that his room was also ready for the following day.

They walked down to the cellars, the next stop on their pre-opening day walk-through. Jenny had put fresh whitewash on the walls and a thick, dark green, deep-pile carpet had been laid to add warmth. The rooms were cool at the moment but the newly added radiators would make them cosy in the winter. The bookcases down here held all the latest thrillers and a second reading place had been added but this time the lampshades were less frivolous – simple green glass shades – and brown leather, wing-back armchairs added to the ambience of crime and mystery.

The last port of call was Sam's bakery. Robbie had worked wonders and Sam was as pleased as Punch with it. By way of an apology, Robbie had laid down the black and white tiled floor Sam had really wanted but, due to cost, had had to remove from her renovation requirements.

He'd done this at his own expense. He'd also had her antique cabinets repaired, re-glazed and re-painted. They looked stunning and, when paired up with the new, freshly painted plasterwork and shining tiled floor, the bakery looked classy and sophisticated. Satisfied that everything was as ready as it could possibly be, the three of them stepped out the shop-door and stood on the pavement, looking about them. The exterior of the shop had been given a fresh coat of paint and it rose up brightly as the beacon of a new start for the village. The other shop owners in the village had been happy to come on board with this injection of life and they'd also made efforts to improve and freshen-up their frontages. Sukie had gotten everyone together in the village hall to announce the travel companies would once again be including Lower Ditchley in their schedules and she'd appealed to everyone to get behind the project. She was a natural orator with a very persuasive manner and, by the end of the evening, everyone had been fired up with enthusiasm and ideas had flown back and forth.

She'd teamed up with one of the ladies from the WI – Estelle Walton – and, together, they had been quite formidable. Essie, who'd grown up not too far from the village, had recalled being taken to a fun day out as a young child. A quick chat with Doris and Rose soon had them looking into the history of the Old May Fete. It dated back to the times of Henry II when men fit for fighting had to register with the local magistrate in the event of being required to go to war as there was no such thing as a standing army back then. Those who registered then marched through the streets of the village and the remaining villagers would stand and applaud them while the young ladies would throw flower petals in their path. In the evening, the lord of the manor would supply ale and sweetmeats on the village green, local bands would play and the villagers danced in celebration. As the centuries passed, the original origins were forgotten and it simply became a day of celebration. It had petered out around the 1970s but Sukie and Essie decided now was a good time to resurrect it. As a nod to the discovery of the conservatory, they'd gone for a Victorian theme and had managed to drum up a traditional Victorian funfair complete with a carousel, swing boats, helter-skelter and a variety of side stalls including a coconut shy, ball in the bucket, hoopla and hook the duck. The WI were running various competition stalls and Jeremy, the vicar, had agreed to do a stint in the old stocks. The large bucket of sponges was already waiting for his arrival the following day. Everyone participating would be in Victorian dress.

The last finishing touches were being put in place as Jenny, Jeff and Sam looked around in awe. They'd all been so busy inside, they hadn't noticed the goings-on outside.

'Wow!' Sam looked on in amazement. 'I know Sukie told us what was planned but this is much more than I imagined.'

'Yes, she's done a fabulous job. I'm gobsmacked.' Jenny was smiling with delight as she looked about her. This was fabulous.

'You do realise this is all your doing, Jenny

Marshall?'

'Eh? How do you figure that one out, Jeff Rowland?'

'You fell in love with the shop that day back in January.'

'Yes, I did, but you were the one who all but dragged me out to view it the following week. Something I would *never* have done on my own.'

'I wouldn't have known about it, had you not told me.'

'Will you two stop bickering! It doesn't matter how we got to this point, the fact is that we did. And I, for one, am as excited as hell for tomorrow.' Sam smiled at her brothers-in-arms. 'Now, I must say adieu, for I need to be up rather early to begin baking. I'll see you both here in the morning.' She gave Jenny and Jeff a tight hug then made her way home.

'Do you think it'll be okay, Jeff? Will we be a success?' Jenny's voice was quiet as she asked the question which had begun to niggle at her as the opening drew closer.

Jeff put a comforting arm around her shoulders. 'Of course we will, Jen. How can we fail? You must think positive. This shop is about to become the hub of the village and surrounding areas. Think of all the events we've got planned along with the various meet-ups you've organised – The Knitting and Crochet Club, The Art & Antiques Appreciation Group, The Book Club... I already know your live event with the best-selling author, Michaela Balfour, is almost a sell-out. And other authors will be hot on her heels when they hear about us. The vision we had for this shop is about to come to fruition and you should be very proud of what we've achieved.'

'Hmmm... Well, we'll see, but – right now – I'm taking a leaf out of Sam's book and going home to bed. Tomorrow is going to be a long, long day.' She gave Jeff a peck on the cheek. 'Thank you,' she whispered, 'for making my dream come true.' Not giving Jeff a chance to answer, she scurried off around the green and disappeared along the alleyway towards the gatehouse.

Chapter Twenty

'Oh! My! Goodness! What a day! I'm shattered!' Jenny was flopped out on a chair in the conservatory, Sam and Jeff and Robbie on either side.

'I've sold every cake, teacake and loaf of bread. I don't think there's a single crumb to be found anywhere!' Sam had slipped off her shoes and was rubbing her toes. 'I haven't stopped all day.'

'Are you glad now that you got off your high horse and let me help you?' Robbie gave her a sneaky look before explaining to Jenny and Jeff, 'You should have seen the kitchen – well, you couldn't see it, the dishes were piled so high.'

'Someone put the dishwasher on the wrong speed so, what should have been a quick wash in forty minutes was actually a two-hour intense job! It backed everything right up!' Sam butted in before Robbie succeeded in making her look completely incompetent.

'I offered to do some washing up, to help out, y'know... Well, you should have heard her go off on one. Such foul language from such a pretty mouth! For sure,

'I'll have to say ten Hail Mary's to keep her eternal soul away from the gates of hell!' Robbie grinned as Sam swatted him playfully with her hand.

'What did you expect? The last time I let you loose around my bakery, you broke it!'

'But I fixed it all! Surely the nice tiled floor has earned your forgiveness.'

'Hmmm... I suppose.'

'And did I break anything today?' Robbie raised his eyebrows questioningly.

'No, you didn't. And yes, as loath as I am to say it, your help was much needed and greatly appreciated. Thank you for stepping in.'

'I'm always happy to lend a hand. And now that it looks like I'm going to be staying in the village for some time—'

'What do you mean "some time"? I thought you'd finished up here?' Sam's tone was sharp and caused both Jenny and Jeff to raise their eyebrows.

'If you'd let me finish... Sukie and Pete have asked me to take a look at their old windmill with a view to rebuilding and renovating it. They've had an idea of turning it into either a holiday let or a writers retreat. The latter, apparently, are becoming quite popular. Charlie and I will be assessing it next week. I've also had some of the villagers ask me to look at repairs they need doing on their period cottages. There's enough work here to merit staying around for quite a few months to come.'

'I see,' was Sam's rather cool reply.

'Look, Sam, let's bury the hatchet and move on. If you're all done here, can I take you for a drink over at The Inn? I think we've earned one.'

'Oh, if you must! Although, I owe you one for your help today,' she replied, standing up and slipping her shoes back on. 'Jenny, Jeff, I'll see you both tomorrow.

With luck, it might be fractionally less frantic.'

They left the room, arguing over who was buying the drinks.

'I give it a month,' Jeff said into the silence.

'Sorry?' Jenny looked at him in confusion.

'I reckon they'll be an item within a month.'

Jenny snorted. 'A month? Two weeks more like. The chemistry sizzles whenever they're in the same room.'

'That is very true. So, now we have to find someone for Amber. She's far too lovely to be on her own.'

'I don't think Amber's really in the market for a relationship right now. She's got a lot going on in other areas.' Jeff didn't know of the turmoil Amber was going through and Jenny wasn't about to tell him. It wasn't her secret to tell.

Amber and Saffy had stayed with her last night and, once Saffy had gone to bed, Amber revealed that she had finally sent off for her original birth certificate.

'I know it's taken me ages to decide, Jenny, but I was so confused. I took your advice in the end and waited until I felt calmer and could consider the issue rationally. I came to the conclusion that I'll never rest until I know the truth. The mystery will eat me up so better to face up to it, come what may.'

Jenny had taken a hold of her hand. 'Amber, whatever comes of this, you know I'll always be here for you to talk to and reply upon. You and Saffy feel almost like family to me now so please, never hesitate to come to me, if there's anything I can do.'

Amber had smiled at her words and leant against her, allowing Jenny to gently rub her back and give her comfort.

'Perhaps she could do with a distraction from her troubles…' Jeff continued to muse.

'Oh, give over, you old romantic, you! Fancy yourself

as a bit of a matchmaker do you? Well, all I will say is, don't give up the day job! Now, how about we make our way over to the pub for a quick drink too? I think we've more than earned it.'

'If you're insisting... I think I could do with a nice cold beer.' Jeff stood up and turned towards Jenny. 'Come on, give me your hand.'
Jenny placed her hand in his and Jeff pulled her to her feet then stepped back for her to lead the way.

Jenny stretched as she tried to suppress a yawn. She was shattered. It was the Sunday after the grand opening and the shop had been open every day. Going forward, they would be closed on Mondays and every second Tuesday but, as the opening had been on the Bank Holiday Monday, they'd had to do a seven-day stretch. She looked at her watch – only half an hour to go. The shop was quiet now, as most of the day-trippers were making their way back home. This gave her the chance to update her stock list. It was going to be a large order going through tomorrow and she'd be making it from the luxury of her bed with a large cup of tea by her side. She had planned a full-on pyjama day and she couldn't wait. The mobile phone would be switched off, she had stocked up on her favourite chocolate biscuits and, once the stock order had gone in, she would be curled up with her book and the cats. Oh, the bliss...

Just then, her mobile phone rang and, when she saw who was calling, she answered with a smile.

'Hey, Bernie, how are you? I hope you and Sadie are keeping out of mischief,' she said.

'Hi, sweetie, we're both well and I think we're

151

behaving – although, it really depends on what you consider to be mischief, I suppose.'

'The list is a long one…'

'Well, in that case dear, I'm going to take the fifth on this.' Jenny could hear the humour in Bernie's voice.

'Jenny,' her mum's voice grew serious. 'I'm actually calling to warn you that Oliver visited today. He was looking over the house when he saw the local newspaper lying on the table and read the story on the front page.'

Jenny let out a groan. The opening had been front page news for the local rag and it had generated a wonderful amount of publicity. She knew at least fifty percent of their footfall this weekend could be attributed to the article. The downside was it had brought her business to Oliver's attention and she could have done without that.

'What was his reaction?' she asked.

'It's Oliver, dear, he only has one reaction. He left here in a fury and I believe he's on his way over.'

A sudden screech of tyres and the slam of a car door told Jenny he'd arrived.

'He's here, Bernie. I need to go. Thanks for the heads-up.'

She bent down to place the phone in her handbag under the desk, taking the few extra seconds to collect her thoughts and prepare herself for the forthcoming battle as she heard Oliver's footsteps stomping through the door.

She forced a neutral smile on her face and stood back up. 'Good afternoon, may I help you— Oh, hello, Oliver, this is a pleasant surprise. How are you?'

'Don't act all surprised with me, I know Mother's been on the phone to you already, telling you I was coming over.'

'Fair enough, I'll dispense with the pleasantries too, since you've clearly left your manners in the car. Why are

Chapter Twenty-One

Going back in time…

'Jenny Marshall.'

Jenny, standing outside the governor's office, heard her name being called. She rubbed her hands on her maroon tracksuit – her palms were sticky with nerves – before opening the door and walking in.

'Good afternoon, Marshall. Are you okay today?'

'Yes, thank you, sir.'

'That's what I like to hear. Now, Marshall, I'll get straight to the point. You're due for release in six months but there are concerns over the lack of support you'll have when you leave. You have no family and, given the rarity of visits during your time here, I suspect few friends. The concerns lie in the fact that you may offend again.'

'I won't, sir. That's a promise. I don't want to come back here.'

'Marshall, of all the prisoners in here, you are probably the only one who I actually believe when I hear that statement. And I've heard it a lot.'

Jenny said nothing and waited for him to continue.

'I've requested your attendance here today to inform you of a new arrangement being considered to assist female prisoners who have either a minimal, or non-existent, support network when they are released. It is being trialled over the next year and I have chosen you as a candidate.'

'Oh!' Jenny looked at the governor in surprise. This was not what she'd been expecting. Her lack of an outside support network had been the reason her last two parole requests had been denied.

'Yes. The arrangement is for six trusted prisoners, who are due to be released within the next nine months, to be placed within the homes of people who are members of the Prisoners' Advice Service. These volunteers will help to guide you into work and back into society. It's a big adjustment to make, especially when your sentence has exceeded three years.'

'I see.' Jenny didn't really know what else to say in the face of this unexpected information.

'In the four and a half years you've been here, Marshall, you have been an exemplary prisoner. You've not only managed to keep out of trouble – an achievement in its own right – but it has been noted that, on a few occasions, you even managed to avert trouble occurring. Furthermore, your work in sorting out and maintaining the library has made you the perfect candidate for one of the available positions. The wife of an eminent judge, Judge Browning, is one of the volunteers in the trial. They live in Oxford and Judge Browning already has a job on offer for they have an extensive personal library which requires proper organisation and cataloguing. You would also serve as his secretary when required. It would seem that, for once, the workshops we offer here are actually going to have been worthwhile as I understand you took the secretarial course a few years ago.'

'Yes, sir, that is correct,' she nodded.

'Right then, I'll set the wheels in motion—'

'Sir?' Jenny interrupted him. 'May I ask a question?'

'Of course, go ahead.'

'Please, could you give me more information about the position?'

The governor looked at the paperwork in front of him. 'Judge Browning lives in Oxford with his wife Bernice and their son Oliver. Oliver is a year older than you. He is a student at the University studying neuroscience.'

'I see.' Jenny paused for a moment before speaking again. 'Sir, I don't wish to appear ungrateful but, is there another position available? You said there were six openings...'

'None that I feel would be suitable for you. Why do you ask? What is the problem? This is an excellent opportunity for you and one which most prisoners would give their right arm to be chosen for.'

The governor's tone was sharp and Jenny realised her next answer had to be carefully given or this chance could be snatched away from her. It may not be an ideal option but, when faced with another six months in this hell-hole...

'I'm sorry, sir, I didn't intend to sound ungrateful for this chance. It's just that, given what happened, I wasn't planning on returning to Oxford. My hope had been to make a fresh start elsewhere.'

'I understand that, Marshall,' his tone softened and Jenny quietly let out the breath she'd been holding. 'However, it is believed the familiarity of a location is less stressful for new-releases, while they are in the process of adapting to being outside again. It really is in your best interests to accept this offer. If you feel the need, you can move once the year is over.'

'I have to stay for a year? But my release date is only six months away, sir.'

'I know, but the terms of the arrangement are one year. There are two ways of looking at it – you either consider your sentence extended by six months or shortened by six months.'

'What happens if the arrangement doesn't work out, sir?'

'Are you planning on causing problems, Marshall?'

'No, sir, not at all. But what if the family don't like me, or I make a mistake in my work and they decide they no longer want me there?'

'I see. Then you would return to the prison for what would be the remainder of your sentence. So, even if you came back in seven months' time, you'd have to do a further six months.'

'Oh!' Jenny gulped. It had been bad enough coming to terms with five years of incarceration at the start of her term, coming back inside a second time, to finish it off, would be absolutely more than she could bear. No matter what, she'd find a way of getting through this. She had no choice.

'Then, sir, I can only thank you for your trust in me and I would be very grateful to join the trial. When does it commence?'

'In the next week or two, once all the paperwork has been completed.'

'Thank you, sir. Will there be anything else?'

'No, Marshall. You may leave. You'll be advised on your exit date over the next few days.

'Thank you, sir.'

Jenny turned and walked towards the door. Her hand was on the handle when the governor spoke again.

'Oh, Marshall...'

She turned around. 'Sir?'

'DON'T let me down on this, I'm trusting you. You are the only candidate I am putting forward so, if you show me up... Well, let's just say your return will not be a walk in the park. Am I making myself clear?'

Jenny swallowed. 'Err, yes, sir. You are.'

'Good.'

She quickly made her escape and scurried back to her cell, her mind whirling with the news.

Ten days later, Jenny got out of the car and looked at the house in front of her. It was an old, Victorian, detached property and was a reasonable distance from the road to the front door. It had huge bay windows on either side of the double-sized front door. The roof had several steep aspects, facing in a number of directions, and the garden to the front was landscaped with mature trees which proved to be a natural divider from the garden to the driveway. The afternoon sun shone upon the pale brickwork, making it look warm and welcoming.

'Come on then, Marshall, I haven't got all day. Get your stuff out of the boot.'

The prison officer, who'd escorted her on her journey, prodded her into action with her words. She opened the boot and pulled out the battered old suitcase she'd been given. There wasn't much in it – some books, a few journals, a motley collection of clothes which no longer fitted and a handful of photographs. The items rattled around inside the case when she lifted it out.

The large front door opened as they walked towards it and an elegantly dressed woman, followed by an austere looking man, came out to greet them.

Introductions were quickly made – 'Do you prefer Jenny or Jennifer?' the woman asked.

'I don't mind, although I'm usually called Jenny.'

'Well, Jenny, I'm Bernice, often also called Bernie, and this is Martin, although we always call him "Judge" or "The Judge". It began as a nickname and sort of stuck.'

Jenny smiled. The warmth being shown to her by Bernice was helping to soothe her nerves, although The Judge had yet to say anything other than, 'Hello'.

'Bernie, why don't you take Jennifer to her room while I sign the paperwork?' The Judge spoke over his shoulder to his wife as he led the escorting prison officer indoors and into a room. Although his tone had been neutral, Jenny began to suspect her place here was probably more at his wife's insistence than his choice.

Bernice smiled at her. 'Come with me, I'll show you to your room and then give you a tour of the house. We don't want you getting lost now, do we?'

She led Jenny up the beautiful open oak staircase which had a number of old oil paintings hanging over it. Jenny made a note to take a closer look at a later date; she was partial to a nice bit of art.

She followed Bernice along the corridor at the top. 'These rooms here are our rooms. The Judge doesn't like to share his breakfast time with anyone so we eat in our smaller lounge up here. You can have your breakfast in your room or downstairs in the dining room if you prefer. Just let Mrs Parker know and she'll make the arrangements.'

'Oh, I don't want to be any trouble – I'll do whatever is easiest for everyone.'

'You are not any trouble, I assure you.' Bernice smiled at her again. 'Now this here is Oliver's suite of rooms. He's just been offered a research position in neuroscience at the university so his hours at home can be sporadic. Sometimes we don't see him for weeks, and other times, we trip over him every day.'

Jenny said nothing and simply smiled at the information.

Bernice walked to the end of the corridor and turned a corner. There was only one door, at the end. She walked in and Jenny followed.

'Oh my goodness, it's beautiful,' she said. And it certainly was. The high ceiling, with gilt cornicing, along with the pale cream walls and double-aspect windows made the room feel bright, airy and fresh. A long way from the small, nine-foot by six-foot, cell she'd woken up in that morning.

There was a sofa and chair suite in front of an open fireplace. A television stood in one corner and a writing desk was placed in front of the windows which overlooked the garden at the front of the house.

'Through here is your bedroom and an adjacent bathroom.' Bernice opened a door in the far corner and led Jenny through.

The bedroom was pale lilac in colour and a huge carved bed with a canopy over the top, stood in the middle of the room. She could see, through the open door on the other side, an old-fashioned roll-top bath in the bathroom. 'Are these the original fittings?' she asked.

'Yes. They're quite beautiful but also hard work to look after. That's why we have staff, dear, I couldn't manage all this myself.'

'Do you have live-in staff?' Jenny began to think she'd landed in the middle of that television show from the seventies – Upstairs, Downstairs.

'We have two live-in and a woman who comes in every day. Mrs Parker is the housekeeper and cook. Bessie is the live-in maid and Mrs Forbes comes in to help her.'

'Where do they sleep?'

'Oh, they're in the servants quarters upstairs, dear.'

'But… why am I down here? I thought I would be working for Judge Browning?' Jenny looked at Bernice, her confusion clear to see.

'You will be, Jenny, but given where you've come from, I thought it would be nicer for you to have a fresh start with a pretty room and some space for you to call your own. I'm guessing it wasn't very nice where you were.'

'No, it was…' The words stuck in her throat. How could she explain the dismal, soul-destroying place she'd come from to someone who had clearly lived a privileged life? The way Bernice casually discussed her "staff" spoke volumes about her upbringing. 'It wasn't a nice place,' she finished simply.

'Well, you're here now and I hope you begin to feel at home soon. Now, why don't we hang up your clothes, have a little tour and then go down for afternoon tea. You can speak with The Judge and get to know him better. Don't be fooled by his austere appearance – he's really a pussy cat behind all his bluster.'

'That sounds nice. I don't have many clothes so hanging them up won't take long.' She opened the suitcase and took out the few items within it and placed them in the old mahogany wardrobe. The little underwear she had was quickly put in the chest of drawers but she wasn't quick enough. Bernice had seen it, hidden underneath her two jumpers.

'Oh, Jenny, this stuff is no good. I'm sorry, I don't mean to be rude but, honestly, I wouldn't even give that away to charity. Tomorrow, we'll go shopping and sort you out with a few outfits.'

'Thank you, I would really appreciate that. I have some money from my work in the prison and—'

'Oh, don't you worry about that. We're going to have a nice girlie day out and it'll be my treat. Now,' Bernice looked at her watch, 'we'd better get downstairs. The Judge is a bit of a stickler when it comes to eating times. I'll show you around afterwards instead.'

She walked back out to Jenny's lounge area, Jenny following behind.

'Oh, by the way, Jenny, while I remember, only the immediate family know of your circumstances. We haven't informed the staff for we feel it's none of their business so you have no need to worry about anyone looking down on you. This is your new start, my dear.'

She patted Jenny's arm before leading the way back down the stairs.

Jenny followed behind and felt the tension in her stomach begin to subside. Maybe her year here would be more bearable than she'd previously thought.

The first six months flew by. Jenny and The Judge came to an understanding and she found working for him interesting. She did any required secretarial work for him in the mornings and sorted out cataloguing the library in the afternoon. She found out the house had been built in the early 1800s by the Judge's, several times, great grandfather. The men in the family had all been lawyers and all had sat on the bench in the later part of their careers. The first one to break the mould was Oliver.

Oliver! The fly in her otherwise very soothing ointment! The apple of his parents' eyes, he was the worm in her new life. He'd arrived home the day after Bernice had taken her shopping, pulling up in front of the house in a sporty two-seater TVR, sliding to a halt and sending gravel flying everywhere. She had seen him through the window of the library and knew, straight away, that trouble was about to walk through the door.

The Judge was in Oxford working and Bernice had gone out to lunch with some friends, leaving Jenny in the house alone with only Mrs Parker and Bessie for company if she desired some.

Ten minutes after he'd slammed the front door behind him, Oliver walked into the library where she was writing the details of the books in front of her onto index cards.

'So, you've arrived then!' It was a statement, not a question, and made in an imperious voice as he walked towards her.

'Clearly,' was her short reply. She had no interest in engaging with him in conversation if he was going to be hostile towards her.

He stopped at the desk and picked up the cards she'd written out. 'Please be careful, they're still wet...' she said. The Judge had asked her to write the cards in fountain pen as he believed it gave a more professional look. Unfortunately, she'd run out of blotting paper and the cards were taking longer to dry off.

'Oh yes, so it is,' said Oliver, as he slid his thumb across three of the cards, smudging the words together. 'Oops, look what I've done. Sorry about that.' He threw the cards back on the table, his tone anything but sorry.

'So, why are you here?'

'I'm sorry?' Jenny looked at him in confusion. 'You know why I'm here. To help your father...'

'I know about that,' he answered, 'I want to know why YOU are here. What are you hoping to gain? Do you intend to fleece them? Are you trying to worm your way in with the hope of getting money from them?'

'NO! I am not!' she replied indignantly. 'I'm here as part of my rehabilitation, as well you know.'

'Hmmm… So you say…'

Jenny didn't reply to that, there was nothing to say.

'You know Father and I didn't want you here. You're Mother's little pet project. We tried to talk her out of it but she can be surprisingly stubborn – kept banging on about giving back to society. Father gave in eventually, but I've told her, in no uncertain terms, that I'm not happy with this and, if I have my way, you'll soon be back behind bars, jailbird, where you belong.'

He turned on his heel and walked out, leaving her feeling quite shaken up. She had no doubt he would stick to his word.

And he had. Whenever it was possible for him to cause trouble, he did so. He messed up her cataloguing on more than one occasion, meaning she lost several hours putting it all right again. He removed work files from his father's study, which resulted in The Judge blaming her when he couldn't find them. A valuable antique box had been taken out of the sitting room and placed in her bedroom, making it appear as though she'd taken it.

She couldn't say anything to Bernice or The Judge because Oliver could do no wrong where they were concerned. He'd had an older brother, named Martin after The Judge, but he'd been a sickly child and had died of meningitis when he was twelve. Oliver, on the other hand, had been quite robust all through his childhood and even into adulthood. Apart from the usual childhood diseases of measles and chickenpox he'd been as fit as a fiddle. Bernice had proudly told her that the only illness he'd managed to avoid was mumps, although it had caught up with him two years ago. However, Oliver being Oliver, he'd quickly gotten over it and hadn't even had a cold since then. The loss of their first child meant Oliver had been effectively wrapped in cotton-wool and thoroughly spoiled. Whatever he wanted, he got. Jenny could no more take her troubles to his parents than she could try to fly for she knew her words would fall on deaf ears.

That was until the day came when he pushed her just a step too far...

She was walking slowly down the stairs, her nose buried in a book. She'd found a first edition of Tess of the D'Urbervilles and was enjoying the smell of history which emanated from the dusty old pages as she read them. The story had really been gripping her attention and she was finding it impossible to put the book down. She stepped down from the bottom step and, without any warning, lost her balance and fell over, banging her forehead hard against the bannister as she went down.

The sound of laughter, as she lay there dazed, floated over to her. 'You should watch where you're going, jailbird, you don't want to have an accident now, do you?'

She slowly sat up, rubbing her throbbing head, and noticed some glass marbles on the floor around her. She watched as Oliver began to pick them up and put them back in the ornate vase outside the sitting room door. It was then that she realised he'd purposely set up the trap to make her fall. The pain in her head, along with the knowledge that he could have caused a more serious injury, was too much for her. All the injustices he'd piled upon her over the months welled up inside her and with the scream of a banshee howling from her lips, she rushed across the hallway and punched him square on the face. She felt his nose crunch beneath her knuckles before he fell over. The Judge and Bernice, upon hearing the commotion, arrived at the door of the sitting room in time to see the blood begin to pour down his face.

'WHAT IS GOING ON HERE?' yelled The Judge.

'Oh my God, Oliver...' screeched Bernice as she ran

to his side, already pulling her linen handkerchief from her trouser pocket. She tilted his head back and placed the insipid piece of material under his nose.

'It's her fault... She attacked me for no reason...' Oliver's voice was muffled under the handkerchief but they were all able to hear what he said.

'That's not true. He deliberately placed marbles on the floor so I would fall when I came down the stairs. Look at my head...' She pushed back her fringe to show them the vivid lump and bruise which was already forming.

'Well, a small bit of tomfoolery is not a good enough reason to react so violently,' The Judge admonished. 'A broken nose is far more serious than a bruise to the head. I simply cannot condone this. You've gone too far. I've overlooked the matter of your poor secretarial skills – losing those important files caused me great embarrassment – and, quite frankly, an illiterate could catalogue the library quicker than you have done, but I cannot turn a blind eye to this kind of behaviour.' He turned towards his wife. 'Bernice, I know you wanted to help people less fortunate but, in this case, I think the experiment has failed. I'll be phoning the authorities tomorrow to have Jennifer returned to where she came from.'

'NOOOO! Please, don't send me back. I can't go back.' Jenny began crying as the thought of returning to Holloway sent waves of panic through her.

'I'm sorry, young lady, but today you have crossed the line.'

Even though she knew she was wasting her breath, Jenny spoke up against the injustice. 'I didn't lose those files, Judge, Oliver took them so I would get the blame. He also keeps messing up the index cards in the library and moving things around to make my job more difficult. I am good at what I do, but I can't do it properly when someone is deliberately trying to sabotage it.'

'Oh, seriously, Jenny, do you expect us to believe that?' Bernice spoke up as she cradled her son, who was still lying on the floor, in her arms. 'Why would Oliver behave in such a manner?'

'Because he doesn't want me here! He calls me jailbird every time he sees me and won't let me forget where I came from.'

'Jennifer, like it or not, you are a criminal and you have been in jail. You can't expect to forget that.'

Jenny rounded on The Judge. 'You are wrong, sir. I am NOT a criminal but I have been in jail...' she spun on her heel, pointed at Oliver and screamed, 'BECAUSE HE PUT ME THERE!'

Chapter Twenty-Three

Going back even further...

'Mummy, _pleeeeeease_ can I go to the shop to buy some sweeties? I've still got money left over from my birthday. See!' Jenny held up her hand to show her mum the fifty pence piece that had been burning a hole in her pocket.

'Oh, I suppose so!' her mum replied, with a smile. 'Let me put Mandy back in her pushchair and we'll go to the little newsagent next to the crossing.'

'I'll help you.' Seven-year-old Jenny adored her younger sister and always enjoyed being able to help her mum look after her. It was the school half-term and, as a special treat, Mummy had brought them both to the park for a picnic. The park, however, was a bit of a distance from their house, so her mum had put three year old Mandy in her pushchair because it was too far for her to walk. She had even let Jenny push it once they'd gone through the park gates. Jenny would play with Mandy by pushing the pram really fast. She loved to hear her sister squeal with joy and giggle with laughter.

They'd had a lovely picnic and, afterwards, they played a sort of football. It was only gentle though because Mandy couldn't kick too far. Jenny didn't mind – she got to play proper football when she was at school.

'Right, have we got everything?' Both Jenny and her mum looked around to check they hadn't left anything behind. 'Looks like it. Come on then, let's go and get you some sweets. Hold onto the pram while I push it.'

Jenny held onto the pram and tried to pluck up the courage to ask the question which had come to her when Mum had said they were going to the newsagent. After a few minutes, she took a deep breath. 'Mum... When we get to the traffic lights, can I cross the road by myself please? We've been learning about the Green Cross Code at school and I know what to do. You can watch me to make sure I do it right.'

She looked up and gave her mum the wide-eyed look which she knew helped her to get what she wanted. It *always* worked on Daddy but sometimes her mum wasn't fooled by it. Her mum saw what she was doing and laughed again. 'Don't you be pulling the Little Miss Innocent look with me, young lady! I'm not your daddy, I'm not a soft touch.'

Jenny knew however, from her mum's tone of voice, that she'd gotten what she wanted. Her mum's laughter had given her away. Although, her mum laughed a lot so maybe she wouldn't be allowed. Sometimes, it was difficult to tell.

When they walked out of the park, and reached the traffic lights, Jenny looked up at her mum hopefully.

'Oh, go on then! Show me what you've learnt. Mandy and I will wait here by the wall for you. Now remember, straight into the shop – I'll be able to see you from here – and don't talk to any strangers. Okay?'

Jenny skipped on the spot. How grown up was she?

'I'll show you up to your room, Jenny. Take a few minutes to change and then come down to the kitchen. We need to have a talk.'

Aunt Clementine walked up the stairs in front of her and led her along a dark corridor. She opened a door and stepped back to let Jenny walk in ahead of her.

'Oh!' Jenny couldn't help but exclaim. All the furniture from her old bedroom had been moved here and it was laid out almost exactly the same. The door and window were in a different place but everything else was nearly identical.

'Uncle Peter and I brought it over during the week, when you were staying with him and Auntie Mary. We thought it might help you settle in. Now, that door there,' she pointed across the hallway, 'is the bathroom. It will be your own bathroom because my room is on the other side of the house and there is another one there which I use. I'll leave you to change into your jeans while I go and make us something to eat. Please don't take too long.'

Aunt Clementine walked out and left her standing alone. She went over to the wardrobe and opened the doors. Inside were all her clothes, even the ones she was too big for now. The pine toy box under the window had all her dolls and teddies on the top. They were even lined up in the correct order. The rug under her feet was the same fluffy one she'd had since she was little. Aunt Clementine was right – the familiar items did help her to feel a bit better.

She got changed and made her way to the kitchen. A plate of cheese sandwiches and a bowl of crisps sat on the table along with a jug of blackcurrant squash. Aunt Clementine was pouring hot water into a teapot.

'Hey,' she said, 'sit down and help yourself, I'll be there in a second.'

She placed the teapot on the cork mat, put a cosy over the top and sat down across from Jenny.

'Okay, first things first. I don't know how you feel but I think Aunt Clementine sounds very old-fashioned, scary, and it's a bit of a mouthful. How would you feel about calling me Auntie Clem? Would that be better?'

Jenny nodded.

'Here, have some squash.' She watched Aunt Clementine, or rather, Auntie Clem, pour out a glass for her.

'Now then, Jenny, we have some grown up things to talk about. I'm afraid I'm not very good with children and I often speak quite sharply. I apologise now for the many times I know I will do this to you. I also speak my mind but I won't apologise for that. Truth is the foundation of all good relationships so I ask that you are always truthful with me and I will always be truthful with you. Think we can manage that?'

Jenny nodded a second time.

'Jenny, I want you to feel at home here and I will do everything I can to help you with that. You'll need to move schools because it's too far to travel to your old one, and I know that will be horrible at first, but I hope you'll make new friends and you can bring them to the house any time you want. All I ask is that you must let me know beforehand. You may go into any room except my study. That is firmly out of bounds. I do important work in there and I can't risk anything being touched, moved or broken. Is that understood?'

Jenny nodded again. She was beginning to feel less scared now that she realised Aunt Clementine… Auntie Clem, was trying to help. Maybe she wasn't the nasty ogre Daddy had always said she was.

'Do you have any questions, Jenny?'

'Why did my daddy not like you?'

a bill to settle.'

She spun round and there he was, standing so close she could feel the heat of his breath on her neck.

'Err, yes, you do. Just let me, erm, get that for you.'

'Did you think we had done a runner?'

Jenny looked up from the calculator she was using to add up the total. 'The thought briefly crossed my mind,' she smiled.

'Now, why would we do that? This is the best Italian restaurant in Oxford, I'm not going to risk being barred over a few pound notes.'

A few pound notes? The bill was over fifty quid!

He handed over his credit card and, as she placed the carbonised receipt in the swipe machine, she noted his name – Oliver Browning. It had a lovely ring to it. He signed the receipt with a flourish and handed it back to her.

'I was wondering… If you're not too busy next week, would you like to go out with me?'

Jenny, busy with ripping off his receipt, raised her head so quickly she felt a crunching sensation in the back of her neck. 'I'm sorry… did you just ask me out?'

'Yes, I did. What are you doing on Tuesday night?'

Studying for an exam on Thursday, she thought, but her mouth took over and she heard the words, 'Not much,' slip from her tongue.

'Then, would you like to go to the cinema? I'll meet you outside the Odeon at seven thirty. See you then.' Not giving her any opportunity to speak, he smiled and walked out, leaving her quite flabbergasted behind him.

The next three weeks passed by in a hazy blur. Jenny was

rushing from exams, to study periods, to work and to Oliver. She was thankful she'd put in so much effort with her studies earlier in the year because she had very little time to cram anything in now. Oliver was around her all the time. They went for drinks, picnics, meals and, once, a long walk along the side of the River Cherwell. He'd barged his way into her life and she was loving every moment of it. She didn't know how or what she had done to attract his attention but she wasn't about to complain.

The day after her last exam, he asked her to dinner at his flat. 'Call it a celebration because I just know my little doctor-in-the-making is going to pass in style.' He leant down and gently rubbed his nose against hers.

When she arrived, the flat was in semi-darkness and candles provided the only light. He greeted her at the door with a glass of Asti Spumante in his hand. 'In memory of the night I asked you out,' he whispered in her ear. His breath tickled against her earlobe and sent frissons of excitement down her back. She suspected that tonight would be the night they first slept together. She hoped he didn't mind that she was a virgin and wasn't experienced. She was sure he wouldn't, he was always so sweet and kind.

The steak dinner was perfection and the wine was plentiful. After dinner, Oliver put on an album of Elton John love songs and they kissed on the sofa. Eventually the kissing led to more and Jenny found herself arching up beneath him. Oh God, how she wanted him. His hands were caressing every part of her and she wanted more.

'Come with me...' Oliver stood up, held out his hand and led her into his bedroom. He closed the door behind him and slowly began to undress her. Jenny shivered with anticipation. She couldn't believe this god-like human was about to make love to her.

All through the night, Oliver held her, stroked her and

'Maybe one day, sweet girl, but not yet. The upside of working in a university is that you can find out all sorts of information which may not be common knowledge. In my case I know there is little they can do right now but, one day, there'll be greater hope for others.'

In that moment, Jenny realised how much she had come to love her aunt – this generous woman who had taken her in and done everything possible to give her a good and happy upbringing. It hadn't always been conventional but it had been good. With this worry upon her, there was no way she was going to burden her aunt further by revealing her pregnancy.

'I'll take a break in my studying to look after you…'

'You'll do no such thing!' The tone of her aunt's voice told her there would be no arguing over this one. 'You must stick at it and get those qualifications. Choose your field wisely and you can write your own ticket around the world. Become your own woman, not answerable to any man – give up your independence because you want to, not because you have to. Do you hear me?'

'Yes, Auntie Clem.' It was a statement her aunt had bestowed upon her many times over the years, a terminal illness wasn't about to stop her delivering it one last time.

'Now, the practical stuff. You are my sole beneficiary, which means everything will come to you – the house, its contents and my savings. Several trust funds have been set up for you – I've never told you about them because I believe people should know how to work for their money – and they mature on your thirtieth birthday. The insurance and compensation from the death of your parents, your sister, and the sale of their house has all been put into trust. I've been to see my solicitor this afternoon and my savings have all been transferred into your name. In keeping with your trust funds, they also become accessible on your thirtieth birthday. If, however, you require money for the upkeep of the house or any emergencies, my solicitors will be able to look into the situation and release money to you if they feel it is merited. Do you have any questions?'

'No, but I don't want your money. I'd rather have you.'

'I'm afraid that's not possible, Jenny, but at least I can die knowing I've looked after you the best that I can.'

It was six weeks after this conversation and Jenny was walking along the high street in town when she saw Oliver on the other side of the road, going into one of the shops. It was October and everyone was back at university for the winter term. Despite keeping an eye out for him, because she wanted to know why he'd behaved so badly, this was the first time she had seen him. Auntie Clem had moved into a hospice yesterday and Jenny was in no mood for taking any crap. This was probably the best day to confront him. She ran across the road, dodging the cars and buses, and waited for him to come out.

'Good morning, Oliver! Long time, no see! How are you?'

She saw his startled look when he heard her voice but he quickly covered it over and plastered on his brilliant smile. The smile she'd once thought so sexy now looked false. Oh, how she had been duped.

'Jenny, how lovely to see you. You're looking really well.'

There was no missing the insincerity in his voice and the look of impatience on his face, so she quickly dumped the speech she'd practised so many times in preparation

The comforting smell of the toast and coffee made her stomach rumble and she realised just how hungry she was. The clock on the wall showed that it was after four o'clock – she'd been walking for over five hours and had no idea where she was.

'Erm, this might sound a bit strange but… Where am I?'

The woman did a slight double take. 'I'm sorry?'

Jenny felt the need to explain. 'It's been a rough day, I've had some bad news and… well… I kind of got lost in my thoughts and my sore feet are suggesting I've walked some distance. I started off in the centre of town but I don't know where I am now.'

The woman smiled. 'I see. Well, love, you've ended up in Abingdon.'

'Oh!' She thought for a moment as she tried to figure out where that was. Her eyes widened. 'Ohhhhh… I've walked quite a way.'

'I would say so. I'm Gina, by the way,' the woman said, sticking her hand across the table.

'Jenny.' Her own hand was firmly squeezed within Gina's grasp.

'Pleased to meet you, Jenny. Now you finish eating and drinking that while I get this place cleaned and closed up.' Gina locked the café door, turned the sign to "Closed" and made her way back into the kitchen.

Jenny could hear the slight strain of a radio coming from that direction as she ate. Gina was right, the warm food was making her feel better physically but it was doing nothing for the turmoil in her mind. What on earth was she going to do now? She couldn't tell her aunt – she was far too ill to be burdened with this. She didn't have any close friends she could confide in. She'd lost touch with Dottie a long time ago for the distance between them had made it too difficult to stay in touch and, after all

199

she'd been through, she'd found it difficult to get close to anyone else. People always talked about their parents and families and it had made her sad. By the time she'd learned to cope with her loss, it was too late. She'd been pegged by her schoolmates as the "solitary weirdo" and no one gave her the time of day. She became more and more introvert as the years passed and, by the time she got to university, she'd become quite the little mouse. The job in the restaurant had been good for her as it had forced her to communicate with people but it didn't help her to make friends. A few people had tried to befriend her but it turned out they'd only been using her in the hope of getting cheap meals at her place of work. They'd found out the hard way – as had Oliver in the end – that she might be a mouse but she was no pushover. She knew how to stand up for herself although that wasn't going to do her much good now.

'Are you all done? I'll take these away and get them washed up.'

'I am, thank you. How much do I owe you? I'll get out of your way so you can go home.'

'No charge, love. Let's call it "medicinal" shall we? You were fair in need of it.'

'No, I insist, I have to pay.'

Gina leant forward and stayed Jenny's hand as she began to rummage in her bag for her purse. 'It's on the house, love. Leave it be.'

Gina's kindness was too much for her. Suddenly, and without any warning, she burst into noisy floods of tears.

'Oh my goodness! Jenny, what's wrong? Oh, love, there… there…'

Jenny felt Gina's arms go around her and hold her tightly as she cried onto her shoulder. She couldn't remember when she'd last been comforted like this and the thought made her cry even harder. Despite all her aunt realising what the girls had done, caused Jenny to seize up in fright and she inadvertently stamped on the accelerator. This threw the car out into the oncoming traffic and the car coming up the road towards them didn't have time to swerve. The next thing they knew, it had crashed straight into the Metro, pushing it over onto the wrong side of the road. A second car coming the other way did manage to swerve and avoid them although it clipped the bonnet and sent the car into a spin. Jenny felt her head thump against the window of her door and then everything went hazy. She heard the girls screaming but it was really faint. As she slipped into darkness, she heard Gina shout, 'RUN!'

'Hello, can you hear me? Hello... Waken up...' Jenny grimaced as she felt a series of slaps on her cheeks. She moaned and the voice spoke again. 'That's it, wakey, wakey!' Her head was aching and she tried to move her hand to rub it but she couldn't. She slowly prised her eyes open and looked down to find her right hand handcuffed to the steering wheel of the car.

'Wha—' she said, groggily.

'Where are your mates? Where's the rest of your gang?' The nasally, gravel-like voice grated through her pain.

'Excuse me, sir, we need to attend to the patient.' A softer voice spoke above her head.

'And I need to question her!' the gravelly tones retorted.

'Well, it's going to have to wait. She's heavily pregnant and needs to be taken to hospital to be checked over so, once again, excuse me!' This time the voice was not so gentle. She was aware of movement beside her and then the dark blue uniform of an ambulance driver came into her line of sight.

'There, there, love. Keep your head still for me while I check you over.'

Jenny tried to do as she was asked but must have blacked out again for the next thing she knew, she was on a hospital trolley and the lights on the ceiling were flashing above her head as she was wheeled along a corridor.

The next two weeks passed in a confusing blur. She spent one night in the hospital for observation before being released into police custody. She vaguely remembered being questioned over and over on the whereabouts of Gina and her cronies. No matter how many times Jenny repeated she didn't know where Gina lived, for she'd never been to her house or flat, no one believed her and they would ask the same questions again a few hours later. She kept telling the police she'd had no idea the women were planning to rob the bank and the first she'd known of it was a few seconds before the car crashed. Unfortunately, the discovery of three sawn-off shotguns in her car was seriously undermining her case.

She was assigned a Legal Aid solicitor who turned out to be a small weaselly man with a scruffy moustache crawling around under a rather large nose, a mullet hairstyle left over from the previous decade, and frayed edges on all his collars, cuffs and hems. His name was David Kerr and he advised her to plead guilty to the charge of aiding and abetting. When she stated she wasn't guilty of anything, he said that with her being so heavily pregnant, she'd be let off lightly and most likely wouldn't do any more than six months. If she pleaded "Not Guilty" it would go to trial, take several months to go through and she could end up doing more time if she was still found guilty.

In the end, Jenny gave in, pleaded guilty as advised

from behind and a sharp prick on her arm. 'I DIDN'T GET TO SAY GOODBYE!' she screamed in the officer's face. 'I DIDN'T GET TO SAY GOODBYE.' She slumped to the ground and, as the blackness rushed through her, she whispered, 'I didn't get to say goodbye...'

Chapter Twenty-Seven

Back in the Future

Jeff pulled Jenny into his arms and out of her memories as her painful sobs reverberated through him. He gently rubbed her back and waited until she had cried herself out. 'Oh, Jenny, Jenny, you poor thing.'

'I don't suppose you have a tissue to hand, do you?' she eventually asked.

'Here, use this.' He handed her a handkerchief from his pocket. 'I'll make us a pot of tea.'

'I'll just use your bathroom, if that's alright.'

'Of course, you know where to find it.'

When she returned to the table, Jeff saw she'd tried to tidy herself up and had put on a spot of make-up to take the redness out of her face. She was unable, however, to conceal the redness of her eyes or the raw pain she was feeling.

In a matter of fact voice, he asked, 'What happened next?' as he sat back down beside her.

Jenny took a few sips of tea before she replied. 'I was

kept sedated for a few days because I became hysterical every time the drugs wore off. Finally, I was moved into the main prison wing where I served my time quietly until I was paroled.'

'What about The Judge and Oliver's mum? What did they say when you told them?'

'At first they didn't believe me. It didn't help that Oliver kept shouting it was all lies. But, when I mentioned the birthmark he has on his inner left thigh, Bernice began to realise I was telling the truth. She gave Oliver a look which said she knew he was the liar. The Judge was spluttering away with indignation until she placed her hand on his arm and said, "Jenny is not only telling the truth but has been badly wronged by this family. It is our duty to sort this out". She then walked over to me, put her arms around me and, while giving me the tightest of hugs, said how sorry she was for all that I'd been through.'

Jeff took Jenny's hand in his. He couldn't get his head around what this quiet, un-presuming, kind-hearted woman had been through. How much inner strength must she possess to have kept going? 'So, did they sort out it? What did they do?'

Jenny tightened her grip on his hands. 'Half and half. The Judge managed to obtain my file with all my case notes and, when he looked into it, he saw I had been very badly let down by the system. The Legal Aid solicitor I'd been assigned was disbarred for malpractice, eighteen months after my conviction. He'd been advising all his clients to plead guilty, regardless of the evidence in their favour, because he didn't want to go to trial. Most of his cases for the previous five years were checked and the clients, where there was insufficient evidence or where it was circumstantial, had their sentences quashed. A few of us, however, were missed because we didn't have any family members to fight for us on the outside. I wasn't informed of his disbarment and knew nothing of it until The Judge told me. He did some further investigation and got my sentence quashed due to a miscarriage of justice. He also managed to get my record wiped from the police records so, despite what Oliver tried to make out, while I have spent time in prison, I don't have a criminal record.'

Jeff wrinkled his forehead in confusion. 'I thought that, once you had a record, you always had one?'

'Prior to about 2006, details on your record could be changed or even removed. After that, it became far more complicated.'

'I see.' He took another drink of tea while Jenny carried on talking.

'Once The Judge had cleared that up, he began looking for Mandy but that wasn't so easy. He called in a few favours, managed to obtain my records from the prison but couldn't progress any further. He just kept coming up against brick walls. Too much time had passed and records weren't fully computerised as they are today, so it was more difficult to trace the family who'd adopted her. Even if we had, reversals were notoriously difficult to get through so there was no guarantee we'd have been lucky anyway. The long and short of it is, The Judge cleared my name but couldn't get back my daughter. He never forgave Oliver for what he'd done and his resentment grew further when they found out, after Oliver's first marriage, that he'd never be able to have any more children because his dose of the mumps had rendered him infertile. The Judge barely spoke to him after that and Bernice tolerates him because he's her son, but she has told me more than once that she'll never fully forgive him for what he did to me and the grandchild he deprived them of.'

'Is that why he hates you so much? Does he blame

you for causing the split in the family?'

Jeff had asked the question before he realised how cruel it sounded. Jenny looked at him and the expression on her face cut right through him. He'd become so engrossed in her story he was forgetting how painful it all was for her. He gently placed his arm around her shoulder again. 'Please, forgive me, that was a rude question. There's no need to answer.'

She leant against him. 'It's okay. You can ask me anything although there's not much left to tell. And, to answer your question, yes, that is pretty much the reason he hates me. He was no longer the apple of his parents' eyes. He'd fallen off his pedestal and landed with an almighty thump.'

'Is there anything you can do to find Mandy now? Times have changed and I know the laws are more flexible than they used to be.'

Jenny blew her nose on his handkerchief again before she replied. 'Not really. Thanks to computers, her records are finally on file and I have attached a request for contact should she ever decide to look into her past. I can't do anything more than that.'

'So you can't look for her yourself?'

'No, it's not allowed. I have to wait and hope that, one day, she'll find me. You know those two seaman's chests which you keep admiring? Well... they're for her. One is full of the gifts I've bought for her over the years. Every Christmas, Easter and birthday, I've placed presents and cards inside one of the chests. The other one holds all my diaries. I began to write a diary the fourth day after she was taken. That's when they stopped the sedation and I was awake enough to think. I want her to know, if she ever does come back into my life, that not one single day has passed when I didn't think about her, talk to her and long to hold her again in my arms. I want her to know she was, and always will be, very much loved.'

When he saw Jenny's eyes fill with tears again, Jeff couldn't help himself – he wrapped his arms around her and held her tightly. He wanted to ease her pain, even though he knew he couldn't. He loved this woman so much and wished with all his soul that he could bring her some comfort.

He heard her speak against his chest but it was muffled. 'I'm sorry, Jenny, I didn't catch that.' He loosened his hold slightly to look down at her.

She looked up at him. 'I said, the only way to describe how it feels is that my life has been lived in black and white from the day I lost her. I've never been truly happy. I've had times when I've been pleased, I've had occasions which were nice and many that were *very* nice but none which made me through and through happy. The nearest I've gotten to how I felt when I held Mandy is this shop. I suppose, in a way, this is my new baby.'

'I know it's not the right thing to say, and this is going to come out wrong, and please know I don't mean it how it sounds but, wouldn't it have helped, even a little bit, to have had another child?'

Jenny gave him a glimmer of a smile. 'You have to have relationships for that to happen.'

Jeff's eyebrows scooted up his forehead. 'Are you saying you haven't… you know… since…?'

'No, I haven't.' She laughed at him then but kindly. 'I didn't trust again for a very long time. What Oliver said and did to me left its mark. When someone calls you fat and ugly in such an intense manner, it really sticks inside you and is almost impossible to forget. It was many years after that – I was well into my thirties – when I eventually went on my first date. He was the son of one of Bernie's friends. I was shy, self-conscious and awkward, he was overbearing and pushy and the evening was a complete disaster. It was also enough for me to know I'd never be able to get close to a man like that again, so I've stayed away from them ever since.'

'Well, you're in my arms now, how does it feel?' Jeff looked down at her. There was silence for a moment before she replied, 'Not too bad, actually. All things considered…'

'Jenny…' He looked her in the eye. 'My timing is probably all to cock here, and I really shouldn't be saying this now, but I feel I must. I love you, Jen, and have loved you for quite some time. Truth be told, it was love at first sight when I met you. These last few months, of being in your life every day, has been total joy for me. Please, give love another chance. You say your life has been black and white up till now, let me be the one to colour it in. Let me try to bring you happiness, please?'

'Oh, Jeff… I don't know…'

'Jen, have you ever noticed that, if you turn a rainbow the wrong way up, it looks like a colourful smile? Let me be your colourful smile, let me be your wrong way up rainbow. I know I could make you happy…'

As he spoke, he watched her beautiful grey eyes become shaded and he felt her pull away from him. Not physically but mentally and emotionally. In front of his eyes, he watched her close down and put her guard back up. He'd pushed too hard, too soon.

'Jeff, I care for you deeply, and I think you're the most honourable man I've ever met, and will probably ever meet, but I'm damaged goods. I cannot love and it would be unfair of me to allude to anything other than that. I treasure our friendship but it can never be anything more.'

'But, Jenny, if you give us a chance… We can take it slowly—'

'NO, Jeff! No! There is no "us" and there will be no

"us"... Ever! Now, I have to go home, the cats need to be fed. You know all there is to know. I hope it won't affect our working relationship and the friendship which I hope we still have.'

'Of course it won't but—'

Jenny stood up and placed a gentle finger against his lips to stop him. 'Say no more, Jeff,' she said, and he heard the break in her voice as she spoke. 'You're a wonderful man and, in another life, I'm sure we could've had something special, but we can never be together in this one. I'm sorry.'

She leant down and softly kissed him on the cheek. When she pulled away, he saw the tears in her eyes before she turned and let herself out of the flat, leaving him sitting alone at the table, wondering what he was going to do now.

he's good-looking?'

'Erm… Well…' She could feel the heat rising in her cheeks as she recalled the odd moments when she'd looked at him moving around the shop and felt a little flutter inside. And she'd never denied to herself that he wasn't rather gorgeous to look at.

'Hah! You *do* fancy him! Look at those cheeks!' Sukie pointed at her with glee.

'Don't! Stop it!' Jenny lowered her head, wishing for the tell-tale redness to subside quickly.

'Jen, don't let this chance slip away. He's a good man and you deserve to have someone good standing by your side.'

'Oh, Sukie, I don't know…'

'Okay, let's look at this another way… How would you feel if Jeff came to you tomorrow, said he couldn't work in the shop anymore and was going back to London? How would you feel if you could no longer see him every day?'

Jenny stopped to think. How would she feel if she no longer saw his wide, happy smile which lit up his face and made his eyes crinkle? If she couldn't hear his footsteps walking around in the room above her every day? Would she really miss the tuneless whistle that floated down the stairs when he was rearranging his displays? Or his shout, every couple of hours, when he asked her if she fancied a cuppa, or his cheeky, schoolboy grin when he sneaked one of Sam's delicious teacakes under the counter for her to eat when the shop was empty?

Sukie's voice broke into her thoughts. 'Well, Jenny, would you miss him?'

'Yes,' she replied simply. 'Yes, I would. Very much…'

'Then tell him. Take a leap of faith. Go for it, girl, you deserve a chance!'

Jenny walked along the path to the Gatehouse. It was dark now and the little solar lights she'd placed in the front garden were twinkling away as she approached. She was mulling over what Sukie had said. Should she take a chance on Jeff? What if it didn't work out and she lost his friendship? Was it worth the risk?

She closed the front door behind her and two dark shadows came running towards her. 'Hello, babies,' she said, bending down to stroke the purring cats winding between her legs. 'I'm sorry I'm a bit late. Let's go and get you guys fed.'

She made her way to the kitchen and put the kettle on to boil while she sorted out the cat food. When it clicked off, she poured the water into her mug and stood, absent-mindedly dunking the teabag. She was thinking about Jeff and her mind didn't seem to want to rest. Now that the idea of him leaving was lodged in there, she couldn't shift it and felt a small twist of fear inside her every time she thought about it.

She suddenly gave a sharp exclamation, threw the teaspoon onto the worktop, turned around and walked out of the house. She marched down the path towards the village, glad of the full moon which lit her way, and almost ran across the village green. The closer she got to the shop, the faster she moved until she was standing in front of it. She looked up to see the open windows of the flat and the sound of The Clash singing, "Should I Stay or Should I Go?" floated down to her. She crossed the road and slipped down the little side alley that brought her to the bottom of the staircase which led up to Jeff's flat.

It was here where she ground to a halt.

Her earlier fears began to slip back into her head, whispering in her ear that she wasn't good enough for him; she wasn't good enough for anyone...

'Oh yes, I bloody well am!' she murmured aloud. 'I am MORE than fucking good enough! For him AND for anyone else!'

With her brave words hanging in the warm, summer air, she ran up the stairs and banged on the door.

The music stopped. A moment later, the door opened and there he was, standing with the light of the flat behind him and the moonlight shining on his face.

'Jenny? What's the—'

Not giving him the chance to say anything further, she reached up, placed her hands on either side of his face, pulled him down towards her and kissed him with every ounce of passion that she possessed.

After a moment, she let go, took both of his hands in hers and said, 'This will not be easy for me. I have many doubts which I need to work on overcoming and there will be days when I'll probably be a total cow because my fears have the upper hand. There will be times when I'll feel I'm drowning in sadness because I miss my baby girl every day but, if you believe you have the patience to ride these things out with me, and can help me to find faith in myself, then I'll give us a go. Can you do that? Can you make that promise to me? Will you bring the colour back into my life?'

Jeff's jaw snapped shut. She saw him swallow. 'Yes,' he whispered. 'I promise. I will be your rainbow.'

She nodded at his words. 'Okay then, let's give "us" a go.'

She turned to walk down the stairs then stopped. She looked back at Jeff. 'I'll see you in the morning. Sleep sweet.'

He smiled at her. 'Sleep sweet, Jenny.'

She walked back across the village green at a more sedate pace, and smiled when The Undertones began to sing about "Teenage Kicks". A tuneless whistle escaped

227

out of the open windows, drifted alongside her and settled inside her head, keeping her company on her short journey home.

Chapter Twenty-Nine

Jenny pushed the small bookcase across the floor. It was Thursday evening, ten days after she'd shared her secret with Jeff and Sukie, and she was altering the floorplan of the shop by moving some of the smaller bookcases around. She was so happy she'd taken Jeff's advice on these because they made her life so much easier. Anytime she wanted to put a fresh display in place, or promote certain books, she simply moved the relevant bookcase into the prime spot in front of the door. It was considerably less work than carting piles of books around, that was for sure!

It was only a week until her first events evening, "A Talk with an Author" and the best-selling crime thriller author, Michaela Balfour, had kindly agreed to be her opening act. Jenny was now arranging a selection of Michaela's books in a prominent display as she began the promotional run-up. She was humming away to herself, placing the books *just so* when she suddenly stopped and stood still. A moment later, Jeff's voice came down the stairs towards her. 'Everything alright down there, Jen?'

'Yes, why?'

'You've stopped singing, I was just checking.'

'It's all good, just concentrating on this display.'

That, however, wasn't entirely true; she'd been unaware she'd been humming and singing to herself and it was when she'd noticed, she'd stopped. She stared out of the shop window, a small pile of books still in her hands, as she thought back over the last ten days.

When she'd gone to bed that Monday night, after she'd been to see Jeff, she had expected to endure a restless night. Instead, she'd gone to sleep as soon as her head hit the pillow and the alarm clock had been ringing a good few minutes before it managed to pierce through the heavy veil of sleep. While she lay stretching, and trying to throw off the groggy miasma that can come from being unexpectedly woken up, she tried to think when she'd last slept right through the night and had required the assistance of the alarm clock to bring her back from the land of nod. Each day since, she had felt so much better in herself. The heavy weight she'd been carrying all these years had been lifted and she actually felt like she had a spring in her step.

She still experienced a sharp, painful, twisting sensation every time she thought about Mandy and wondered where she was, what she was doing and if she was safe, but mostly, she felt relief. She no longer had to hide her true feelings from anyone. Her two closest friends now knew everything and they hadn't judged her, or forsaken her as she had always feared people would do when they found out. Instead, Jeff and Sukie had rallied round her, showing her their kindness and being completely supportive. She'd had dinner with Jeff in the evening a couple of times after work, and he knew exactly what was on her mind when she went quiet. He hadn't said anything on either occasion – he'd simply took hold of her hand, squeezed it gently and placed a soft kiss on her forehead or cheek. He never forced her to talk and just waited until she picked up the conversation again.

Further to her unexpected visit that Monday night, he'd been true to his word and had made no moves of a romantic nature towards her. He was being sweetly old-fashioned and, with the exception of comforting her, only occasionally touched her gently such as when their hands brushed against each other if he passed something to her or gave her a kiss goodnight on the back of her hand. The more he gave her space and kept his emotional distance, the more she found herself wanting to be near him. She didn't know when she would be ready for their relationship to become more intimate, but being close to him was enough for now. He'd promised her there was no rush and she felt quite comfortable with this change in their relationship. Everything else would come along when she was good and ready.

The unexpected ring of the old-fashioned Bakelite phone on the shop counter ripped through the air, bring her back down to earth with a bang as the small bundle of books she'd been holding landed on her foot.

'Eye-ya!' she squealed before hopping over to yank the handset out of the cradle. 'The Cabookeria, how may I help you?'

'Hi, Jenny, it's Percy over at the pub, I was hoping to catch you.'

'Hi, Percy, is everything ok?' She could hear chanting and yelling in the background and was struggling to make out what Percy was saying over the noise.

'You want me to come over, immediately if possible? Okay, give me a few minutes to lock up and I'll be with you.'

Jenny put the phone down. What was this all about,

231

she wondered. She called out to Jeff, told him she was finishing up and mentioned the phone call.

He came down the stairs as she picked up her handbag. 'Would you like me to come with you?'

'Sure, if you want to. Percy didn't say why she wanted me to come over, so I'm not sure what it's all about.'

They quickly switched off the lights, locked up and then hurried over the green to the pub. As they drew near, they could hear the noise from inside and, when they opened the door, it hit them square in the face.

Percy must have been looking out for her; Jenny was barely over the threshold when she ran over and grabbed her arm. 'Come with me!' she yelled.

She pulled Jenny towards the back of the bar. The sound of Beyoncé singing, "Crazy in Love" assaulted her ears and, when she turned the corner, her eyes nearly popped out of her head and her mouth dropped wide open, for there in front of her, dancing on the tables – shimmying and twerking for all they were worth – were Bernice and Sadie.

Chapter Thirty

Amber parked her car in the little car park and walked over to the shop. She'd been lucky because the car park was full but a car was coming out as she arrived and she'd grabbed the space. She noticed the village seemed considerably busier than it had been before. It looked like The Cabookeria had helped to lift the profile of the village, just as everyone had hoped. There was even a small board set up by the telephone box, advertising tours of the church with twice-daily trips up the steeple.

She made her way into the shop and gave a wave to Saffy who was serving a small queue at the till. Jenny was talking to another customer and smiled at her as she walked by. The tearoom, although still busy, was not full and she found herself a table by the window looking out into the courtyard. She had some work to look at while she waited for Saffy to finish. She took a couple of files from her bag and was soon engrossed in them.

'Here, I think you dropped this.'

Amber looked up with a start to see Sam Curtis holding out a tatty, scrunched-up brown envelope. 'Oh, thank you.' She blanched at the sight of it and, hesitating for a moment, put her hand out and took it from Sam.

'Are you okay, Amber? You've gone quite pale.'

'I… I'm fine, thank you.'

'Hmmm, I don't think so. Let me go and get you a coffee, I'll be back in a minute.'

'It's okay, I'm fine…' but Sam had already rushed off.

She returned a few minutes later with two mochas and a plate of macarons which she placed on the table. 'You were lucky, these are the last of them. I remembered how much you like them so I swiped them for you.'

Amber smiled at Sam's kindness. 'Thank you. Yes, they are my favourites although my waistline won't thank you for them.'

'Do you mind if I join you? I need some time out, I haven't stopped all day.'

Amber gestured to the chair opposite. 'Please do.'

'I haven't seen you for a while, is everything okay?' Sam took a sip of her mocha and gave a small sigh of relief. 'Ahhhhh, that's so good.'

Amber smiled as she answered Sam's question. 'Things have been busy at the office the last few months – the hot weather has moved a few projects along quicker than was expected, so we've been able to take on some extra work, and that's kept the old nose to the grindstone. Plus, Saffy likes the feeling of independence that comes with getting the bus home after work, so there's less need for me to come and pick her up. I felt like a run out in the car today so here I am. I'm sure she won't object to being driven home just this once.'

'It's been really busy today, so I'm sure she'll be glad of it.' Sam took another sip of her coffee and looked at the brown envelope still sitting on the table. Nodding at it, she said, 'It won't open on its own, you know.'

Amber let out a sigh and picked it up, turning it this

way and that in her hands. 'I know, it's just that… Well… once I open this, my life will change forever and there'll be no going back.'

'If it's not too rude,' Sam said, 'may I ask what it is?'

Amber looked directly at her. 'My birth certificate.' She saw Sam's look of confusion and explained, 'I found out in January, when going through my parents' papers, that I'm… *was*… adopted. This,' she gave the envelope a small shake, 'is my original birth certificate. In here are the names of my real parents. And I'm really not sure if I want to know who they are or not. As you can see, I've had it for a few months and it's been in and out of that bag more times than you can believe. But, every time, I just can't bring myself to open it.'

'How do you feel about being adopted?'

She thought for a moment. 'I don't know, if I'm being really honest. It changes from day to day. Sometimes I'm angry – angry at them for not telling me. Other days I appreciate how much they loved me, even though I didn't share their DNA. And then there are days where I wonder if they regretted adopting me when their own flesh and blood child came along. But, always in the mix, is the feeling of confusion. Of feeling lost and not knowing who I really am.'

'Were you treated differently when Saffy was born?'

'Not that I can recall. I think, sometimes, you just get a little devil sitting on your shoulder and he likes to pour doubt into your ear.'

'I'm adopted…' Sam picked up her teaspoon to stir up the chocolate which had sunk to the bottom of her mocha glass.

'You are?' Amber was surprised. She'd joined a few on-line groups that dealt with adoption but, to the best of her knowledge, this was the first time she'd been in the company of someone else who was adopted. 'When did you find out? Was it a great shock, or a surprise?'

'I was adopted when I was ten, so I've always known. My brother and sister are adopted too. My mum was adopted, you see, and, knowing how much it had changed her life, she wanted to do the same. My dad wasn't sure to begin with but agreed to try fostering for a time to see how it went. I was fostering with them for three years and then, one day, they asked me if I would like to stay with them forever. My dad had come to love me as if I were his own and, having seen how I'd flourished under the love and care they'd both given me, he understood where Mum was coming from. My brother and sister were younger when they were adopted but my parents chose to let them know as soon as they were old enough to understand. So, we've grown up knowing.'

'Have you ever wanted to find out who your biological parents are? Do you even remember them? After all, you were older...'

Sam shook her head. 'If I'm being honest, no, not really. I know I've always been happy, loved and cared for, so I've got no interest in looking for or finding out more about my real parents. I have some memories of being very unhappy and crying a lot before I was fostered and maybe it's that that stops me from looking into it further.'

'What about your brother and sister? Have they said anything or enquired further?'

'I've never asked them and they've never mentioned it. My parents are quite laid back – they hail from Glastonbury, which moves at its own special pace – and they would never prevent us from finding out if we wanted to. I just think none of us have really felt that bothered about doing so.'

'I see...' Amber twisted the envelope in her hands again.

Michaela herself had arrived half an hour earlier and was currently sipping tea upstairs in Jeff's flat as she unwound from her journey up from Sussex.

Jenny had been most surprised when Michaela had turned up. The only authors she'd met, up till now, had been crusty old professors from the university when they'd released another text book on quantum physics or something equally boring. Therefore, Michaela, in her tight black jeans, figure-hugging T-shirt, black leather jacket and stiletto-heeled boots had been quite a shock. With her long blonde hair swinging loosely behind her and her minimalist make-up, Michaela couldn't have been further from the Barbara Cartland caricature she'd anticipated. She'd also been quite laidback and easy to talk to – Jenny had liked her immediately.

She called Jeff on his mobile. 'Everyone is now seated, so, if Michaela is ready, would you mind escorting her down, please?'

'We're on our way.' Jenny felt the smile cross her face at the sound of Jeff's voice in her ear. A moment later, she saw them standing to the side of the room. She clapped her hands loudly, cleared her throat and announced, 'Ladies and gentlemen, thank you for joining us this evening for the first Cabookeria author event. I hope it will be the first of many. Our author tonight is one the country's best-selling, crime thriller, writers. Several of her books have been adapted for the small screen and Hollywood have recently come a-knocking to put some on the big screen. She is, without doubt, a very special guest and so, without any further ado, please put your hands together and welcome, Michaela Balfour!'

'Jenny Marshall, I think you can safely say that this has all gone down pretty well. Do you have any books left?' Jeff stood beside Jenny as they watched Michaela sign books for the audience who had sat in rapturous silence for almost two hours as she'd read excerpts from some of her books and then explained how she'd come up with the plots, the research involved and how it felt to write in her genre. She'd been funny and witty during the Q & A's and, overall, had ensured the night had been a roaring success.

'Not many. There'll be a large order going through in the morning to replenish my stock,' Jenny replied. 'I'd better go over and see how she's doing.'

She made her way across the room, accepting words of thanks and appreciation from some of the guests who were now preparing to leave. She assured them they would be informed of future events as they were now on her mailing list. Finally, she got to Michaela who was just finishing a conversation with another fan.

'Phew! That was a busy one.' Michaela was rubbing her wrist and flexing her fingers. 'I do love these events but I always forget how painful all those signatures are. I really should have come up with a pen name with fewer letters.'

Jenny smiled at her. 'Thank you so much for tonight. It has been amazing and I can't thank you enough for doing it.'

'Oh, it's no problem. Being a writer means we don't get too many chances to meet the people we slog our souls out for. I'm always pleased to accept the opportunity to get out and meet characters I haven't made up in my head.' She gave Jenny a gentle nudge in the ribs. 'And talking about characters, is that one single, because he's got it all going on, let me tell you.'

Jenny followed her gaze and it came to rest upon Jeff.

'How do you feel about Saffy coming to stay?'

They were in the kitchen an hour later and Jeff was treating Jenny to his special homemade pancakes. He'd just flipped the third one when she asked her question. He flicked a quick look her way. 'Why are you asking me that? This is your home and your guests are none of my business.'

'I know, but you're spending more and more time here. I just wondered if Saffy being around might be uncomfortable for you.'

'It'll feel strange having another person in our space, and I'll need to make sure I put my dressing gown on when I come down in the morning, but I can't see it being a problem in any other way.'

He slid the pancake onto the stack staying warm in the oven and poured more batter into the pan. He had an idea where this conversation might lead and he was ready for it. Jenny had never asked him about his own past and he'd never volunteered the information. The last six weeks had all been about her and ensuring she was comfortable with their new relationship, he hadn't wanted to muscle in and drown her with his own sad facts.

'Jeff, haven't you ever wanted kids? Do you even have kids? Oh my goodness… I've just realised… I've never asked you anything about your personal life. All this time you've let me warble on and I've never once bothered to find out anything personal about you.'

And there it was! It had to happen eventually. Well, it seemed like today was the day. He slipped the last pancake onto the plate, switched everything off and sat down at the table.

As he poured himself a cup of tea, he replied, 'I'm

divorced. And I don't have kids.' The bitter tone of his last few words made Jenny raise her eyebrows.

'I see,' was all she said.

Jeff ran a hand through his hair, wiped it across his eyes and took in a breath. 'I was twenty-four when I met Carol. I'd finished university and hadn't long started my first job in a gallery in Kensington. It wasn't a prestigious gallery such as those you find in Mayfair and Knightsbridge but it was well-known enough. It had a reputation for being a little more on the edge and Carol came to one of our shows. I'd had an unfortunate, short-lived affair a few weeks beforehand and was still reeling from the fall-out from it. She chatted me up, gave me *lots* of attention and wouldn't take no for an answer when she'd make arrangements for us to meet. I tried to decline but, eventually, I gave in to her wishes. Her attentions were a soothing balm to my damaged ego. A year later we were married. We had a small one-bed, ground-floor flat in Vauxhall. It came with a large garden and a shed which Carol turned into her studio.'

'She was a painter?'

He smiled at the surprise on Jenny's face. 'A sculptor.'

'Wow!'

'Wow indeed.'

'Was she good?'

He hesitated before answering. 'She wasn't bad...'

'But?'

'But her creations were... unusual, shall we say...'

'In what way?'

'She had a deep well of personal anger – something I didn't find out until after our wedding – and it came out in her work. It consisted of sharp edges and pointy bits and well... In my opinion, it was all a bit of a mess. She had the talent to create something but not the vision to make a creation. Her colours were all wrong and the end results always looked amateurish. She would ask my opinion but nothing I ever said was right or good enough. After a year of being married, she began dropping hints about me getting her a show in the gallery. I took a few photographs of some pieces and ran them past the gallery owner. I've never repeated his exact words when he looked at them but suffice to say, she was never getting a show in his gallery while he still had breath in his lungs.'

'In other words... over my dead body!'

Jeff laughed. 'You've got it in one. Chuck in a few expletives and you'll have the full gist of the conversation. Anyway, I had to gently break it to her that a show wasn't going to happen but she wouldn't let it go. She kept going on and on about it. One night, in the midst of yet another row on the subject, she said, 'So, what was the fucking point of me marrying you, if you can't get me a show?'

He heard Jenny's sharp intake of breath but carried on talking. 'That was the turning point in the relationship. I began to see how one-sided the marriage was. I was the one doing all the work and all the giving and she was just taking. It all came to a head one day when there was a power cut at work. Some workmen had gone through a cable in the street. The electricity wasn't going to come back on that day so we shut up shop and I went home. I arrived at the flat and found her curled up on the bed, clutching her stomach. My first thought was appendicitis and told her not to worry, I'd call an ambulance. She stopped me and said she didn't need one but she did need some more of the painkillers that were in the kitchen.'

He stared at the table for a few seconds before lifting his head to look Jenny in the eye. 'They were prescription painkillers. She'd had an abortion.'

It still hurt to think of it, even after all this time. He

felt Jenny's hands take his.

'Oh, my goodness! You didn't know?' she whispered.

He shook his head. 'No. There hadn't been any sign. She said she was only a couple of months gone, seven or eight weeks. When I asked why she hadn't discussed it with me, her reply was it was her body and she could do what she liked, no kid was going to stop her from pursuing her career.'

He brushed away the tears gathering in his eyes and felt Jenny move to sit beside him. 'There was no returning from that. I moved out that night and began divorce proceedings the next day. I struggled to cope for a time and my parents began to get quite worried. This was so unlike me – I always had a level head and dealt with things. Gradually, I came out of the funk I'd gone into but I'd lost my job and had nothing to aim for. I decided I needed to get out of the country; I needed to be somewhere away from everything I knew. I contacted a friend from art school who lived in Italy and asked if I could take up his three-year-old offer of a job in the museum his father curated. He said yes and off I went. I stayed there for two years, expanding my knowledge of art along with my linguistic skills. When I eventually returned home, healed and ready to move on, my parents informed me they had been talking about moving out of central London for some time and had made the decision to buy a house in Wimbledon. They gifted their Mayfair home to me and, with a great deal of hard work and effort, it became the gallery I own today. It definitely helped me to move on, although it became my baby and, for several years, it was a substitute for the one I'd lost.'

'Did you ever see Carol again?'

'She had the cheek to turn up one day, about two years after I'd set up the business, and demand I give her a show.'

'Nooooo! What did you do?'

'Let's just say that, on this occasion, diplomacy was not on the agenda. She left the shop knowing exactly what I thought of her work and safe in the knowledge that she would NEVER get a show in my shop, or anywhere else for that matter.'

'Have you seen her since?'

'No. The last I heard, about seven years ago, was that she'd gone to South America. And long may she stay there!'

'Did you meet anyone else after that?'

'No one of importance. There were dates and brief affairs but I found it difficult to trust after that. I was scared of finding myself back in that dark place where I went when I split with Carol. You see, men aren't, or weren't back then, allowed to feel the pain that comes with the loss of a child. We're supposed to be strong and manly. The counselling that's available today was unheard of back then.' He paused and looked at Jenny's hands holding tightly to his. Just like Jenny with her dark secret, this was his and he too, hadn't spoken about it in years. He raised his head and looked out of the window into the garden as he spoke again.

'I *know* the child was gone before I ever had a chance to be a father to it, but it was a chance I wanted. I would have loved to have had children. For it to be taken away in such a cold, calculating manner… it was hard to move on from the pain of that. In fact, the first person who somehow managed to wheedle her way under my armour is now sitting next to me.' He gave Jenny a small smile, and looked into her wide eyes. 'Now that I know your story, I wonder if there was something subliminal that whispered to my soul that you were the right person for me. Maybe our subconscious recognised the other's pain. I don't know. All I do know is that, from the first time I stood beside you, waiting to congratulate Pete and Sukie as we entered the marquee, I felt a kind of peace. Being next to you was soothing. It's really hard to explain but all I knew was that, no matter how long I had to wait, one day we'd be together... because it felt so right!'

He closed his eyes as Jenny gently placed her hand on his cheek and kissed him softly on the lips. He touched his forehead to hers.

'Now you know why I didn't rush to share my past with you. I had to give you time to come to terms with your own traumas, I wasn't about to pile mine on you.'

'Hush, it's fine. I always believe these things come out when the time is right. Thank you for sharing it with me. I'm so sorry you had to go through all that.' Jenny gave him a wistful smile. 'If only you had gone to Oxford University – maybe we'd have met all those years ago and gotten together. Think how different both of our lives could've been.'

'If only, eh...' Jeff drew Jenny into his arms and held her as he reflected on the choices they'd both made and the impact those small moments in time had had on their futures.

He felt Jenny pull away from him. 'Right then, mister, that's enough navel gazing for one day. We've got a visitor arriving in approximately one hour and this place needs dusting and hoovering, so which one are you doing?'

He smiled as he stood up. Jenny's ever-practical nature was exactly what they both needed right now. 'Well, you know how much I like to boogie so I bagsie the vacuuming!'

'Oh, lordy-be!' Jenny rolled her eyes. 'Just promise you won't sing too.'

'Sorry, love, no can do! You know I never make promises I can't keep!' Giving her a small tickle in the side, Jeff jumped up, cleared the table quickly and boogied his way out to the hallway cupboard, while singing very badly, 'I'm in the moo-ood for prancing, feel like prancing, oh, I'm gonna hoover right…'

Chapter Thirty-Three

Amber knocked on the door and wiped her hands nervously on her jeans as she waited for Jenny to answer. She was dreading the next few hours. She saw Jenny through the glass and forced a smile onto her face.

'Amber! It's wonderful to see you.' Jenny's arms came around her in a big hug. She always gave lovely hugs and Amber soaked it up. It was the one thing she missed more than anything – being hugged. Her dad, or adopted dad, had been big on giving hugs. 'Come in, what would you like to drink? Tea? Coffee? Or would you prefer a cold drink? It's a bit warm out there today.'

'Tea would be great, thanks.' She followed Jenny into the kitchen and placed her handbag on the work top. Churchill, Jenny's tabby cat, was lying on the floor, cooling himself on the oak floorboards. She bent down to stroke him and hoped Jenny wouldn't pick up on her agitation – she could be a bit sharp on stuff like that. It was wonderful knowing Jenny cared so much about people but she was also quick to notice when they were out of sorts. And, today, Amber was as out of sorts as it clear the dryness in his mouth. 'A moment...' He picked up his cup and took a deep drink of his tea although what he really wanted was an extra-large malt whisky. 'I'm sorry, forgive me. This is a complete shock. I don't know what to say. I'm guessing it was a shock for you too.'

'Like you wouldn't believe!' she replied, drily.

'How long have you known?' Jenny asked the question he'd been about to ask.

'Just over a week. If it's any consolation, the shock totally knocked me for six!'

'Please, tell me everything. How did you find out? How did it happen? Who was your mother?'

'My mother's name was Kathleen O'Connell.'

Jeff rummaged through his brain... Kathleen...? Kathleen...? Kath? Kathy? Leenie? None of them rang any bells. He looked at Amber, contrition written all over his face. 'Amber, that name means nothing to me. I don't remember any Kathleen, or Kathy, or anything like that.'

'What about Katie?' she asked softly.

His eyes snapped wide open at her words. 'Katie? Oh my God... Katie? You're Katie's daughter. Oh, oh, ooohhhhhhhhhh...' The last utterance came out as a small howl of pain. He felt his face contort and the tears began to slip from his eyes. 'You said she was dead... Katie's dead?'

He saw his tears reflected in Amber's eyes as she witnessed his distress. He got up, walked over to the window and stood looking out over the garden. The room behind him was silent as the two women waited for him to take on board this sad news. Eventually he turned and sat back down, looked at Jenny and said, 'When I told you about Carol earlier, you might recall I said I was on the rebound from a short-lived affair... Well, Katie was that affair and when I say short-lived I really do mean short-lived. We only had two days together.'

'Two days?' It was Jenny's turn to be surprised.

'We met on the Friday night at a party. The usual story, a whole bunch of us ended up in the kitchen. I was in front of the sink and she came in looking for a cloth to wipe her top because someone had spilt a drink down it. Anyway, we got chatting and ended up talking for the rest of the night. We left about two thirty in the morning and went off to find something to eat. We were in Camden, so it wasn't hard to find some little all-night café. We left as dawn was breaking and I asked her back to my flat. I just didn't want to say goodbye to her. We'd clicked and neither of us wanted to leave the other. She came back to the flat, my flatmate had gone off somewhere for the weekend and so, with no one to interrupt us, we simply talked and talked and talked. Obviously there were kisses and cuddles in-between and eventually we fell asleep on the sofa for a while. Well, we had been awake all night!' He gave a wry smile. 'When we awoke a short time later, without any words being spoken, we made our way to my bedroom where we spent the night and most of the next day, making love and making promises. We'd both totally fallen in love. As Sunday evening crept in, she got ready to leave. She needed to go home; she had work the next day. She still lived with her parents and had already said she was going to be in big trouble for staying out all weekend. She wrote down her phone number and I promised to call her. I walked her to the tube station, all the way down to the platform, and blew kisses to her through the window as the train pulled away and disappeared into the tunnel. I stood watching the red tail lights fade away, wishing with all my heart I had gone with her and taken her all the way home. We'd only been apart a few minutes and I already missed her. Katie was sunshine, she was joy, she was happiness in human form. She had a gorgeous big smile, her blonde hair shone as was a pain she didn't have the strength to bear. She said she had two choices – she could kill her mother for the action she had taken, or she could kill herself. The latter was the easiest, and less painful, option.'

Amber looked at Jeff and felt her heart ache at the tears sliding down his face. There was no mistaking the pain he was going through as he listened to her.

'My grandfather hit the roof, or so my aunt tells me. He railed at his wife and yelled that he'd warned her she was being too hard, that they could have brought me up as their own, but she'd refused to listen. The day after the funeral, he had a heart attack. He survived but he never spoke to his wife again. She died of cancer nine years later and, it was in her last few days, that she revealed the news that Jeff *had* phoned, but she'd never told Katie. Katie had died thinking no one cared about her.'

By now both she and Jeff were sobbing as the tragedy of the situation hit them both.

'I would have married her. In a heartbeat! She would not have been shamed into thinking she'd done wrong.'

Amber walked over to Jeff and he pulled her into his arms. As she laid her head against his chest, she realised his hug felt totally right. It was warm and comforting but it was more than that – it was the place where she finally felt she fitted.

Chapter Thirty-Five

Jenny looked on as father and daughter embraced. She carefully loaded the crockery onto the tray and slipped quietly from the room, taking care not to disturb them. She made her way to the kitchen, stood in front of the kitchen sink and let her own tears fall unheeded as she stared unseeingly out of the window.

She didn't begrudge Jeff his good fortune, although it had come at a terrible price, and she was genuinely happy that Amber had found one of her parents, and a damn good one at that. It was a combination of the sadness of Amber's story and her own deep-rooted pain over the loss of her own daughter that was making her cry. Even though she'd known Amber wasn't her child, there had always been a tiny flicker of hope that she might be wrong. The confirmation of Amber's parentage had extinguished that hope and the resulting emptiness within her made her want to fall to the floor and curl into a ball. She couldn't think of any way to let this pain out. The last time she'd hurt this badly had been the day they'd taken Mandy from her.

She didn't know how much time had passed when she felt Jeff's warm hands on her shoulders. He turned her around and pulled her to him.

'There, there, my love…' he murmured in her ear, rubbing her back softly as she sobbed into his chest. 'There, there…'

Eventually, when she was all cried out, Jeff let her go and walked to the sink. He returned with a cold cloth to soothe her swollen eyes. She'd just taken it off him when Amber's voice came from the doorway.

'Hey, you guys, what's taking so long— Oh, Jenny, what's wrong? Why are you crying? Say, you're not worried I'll come between you and Jeff are you?'

Jenny looked up at Jeff. 'You need to tell her,' he said.

'Tell me? Tell me what? What's going on?'

Jeff turned to Amber. 'Amber, do you mind going back into the lounge, please. We'll make a fresh pot of tea and then Jenny can explain.'

Amber looked at them both for a moment before walking back into the front room.

Within minutes, Jenny and Jeff returned and once everyone's cups had been refilled, Jenny told Amber her story. She hesitated when it came to the part about being in prison but realised there was no way of explaining why she'd had to give up her daughter without doing so. When she reached the end, there was silence. Amber said nothing and Jenny waited for her to absorb the details. Eventually she turned to Jenny, her eyes wide in confusion, and said, 'So, did you think I was your daughter? Is that the reason you've been so friendly to me? Were you trying to win me over…?'

'No, Amber, no, absolutely not!' Jenny took Amber's hand and was relieved when the girl didn't pull it away. 'Deep in my heart, I've always known you weren't my daughter. Don't ask me how I knew, I just did. I think it could be attributed to a mother's instinct. That, however, didn't mean there wasn't a tiny little glimmer of hope that you might be. I was not your friend, however, with this in mind. I was your friend, and hopefully still am, because you needed one. You needed someone to help you and give you some support. I'd like to think if my own daughter found herself in a similar situation, or in need of help, that someone would be there for her. I love you and Saffy dearly and your news today doesn't alter that one single bit. I really hope you feel the same.'

Amber looked at her, saying nothing. As she waited for her to speak, Jenny noticed the shape of her eyes were very similar to Jeff's. Funny how she'd never noticed that before.

'It must have been so difficult, losing your baby like that.'

'As difficult as it would have been for your mother to lose you.'

Amber shrugged. 'At least you didn't kill yourself. Your daughter still has a mother even if she doesn't have you right now.'

'Amber, I was on suicide watch for months. I may have been put back out into the main wing of the prison, but everywhere I turned there was a prison guard watching me. And I wouldn't like to say what I would have done, had they not been there. I can't even try to describe the pain of the loss but I do understand why your mother was unable to bear it. Don't think harshly of her, Amber, she loved you so much that death was the more desirable option than trying to live a life without you.'

Tears had welled up again in Amber's eyes as she'd been speaking and Jenny leant forward to embrace her, soothing her in the same way Jeff had soothed her, just a short time before.

Jeff let out a cough and shook the teapot to see if a

refill was required. 'Anyone for more tea?' he asked.

'Oh, blimey, no! I'm all tea'd out! How about a glass of wine? Amber, would you like a glass of wine?'

'Actually, that would be lovely, I could really do with one.' She gave a watery smile.

Jenny patted her arm. 'I think we all could, love. I think we all could.'

'I'll sort that out then.'

Amber looked up at Jeff as he picked up the tea tray and a little smile of mischief ran onto her face. 'When you come back, we'll need to chat about what I'm going to call you... Dad!'

Both women leaned against each other in laughter at the look of horror on Jeff's face as he made a hasty exit from the room.

That night, after Amber had left and they were getting ready for bed, Jenny turned when Jeff said, 'Are you alright, love?'

She smiled at him, 'Yes, I am. I'm fine.'

'You're not just saying that, are you?'

'No, I'm okay. A little bit tender inside, but I'll be alright. I have to be, don't I? What about you? How are you feeling?'

'Numb, if I'm being honest, just trying to take it all in. It'll take time to come to terms with it, I suspect, so for now, I'll take each day as it comes until it sinks in.'

'As surprises go, it was a belter. We definitely didn't see that one coming.'

'No, we didn't. Come on, let's go to sleep. It's been an emotional day.' Jeff patted the bed and she slipped in beside him. He pulled her towards him and held her close until he fell asleep.

Jenny lay in the darkness, listening to his breathing. Her tears fell silently onto her pillow as her heart ached to hold the child she had lost.

Chapter Thirty-Six

Sukie placed the glass of wine in front of Jenny and sat on the patio beside her. 'How do you feel now?'

Pete was upstairs giving the twins their bath and she was relaxing with Jenny in the garden, soaking up the warmth of the early evening sun.

Jenny let out a sigh. 'I don't really know, if I'm being honest. It's been a week since Amber broke the news and I feel as though I've stumbled my way through it. Everything's out of kilter and I'm not sure how to go about getting things back on track.'

'Where's Jeff tonight?'

'He's in London. He's taken Amber down to meet his mum and Charlie.'

'Charlie? But… She's already met him, hasn't she? When the shop was being renovated?'

'Yes, but she hasn't met him as her uncle. Jeff felt it would be better to do a re-introduction, given the circumstances.'

'How's he taking the news himself? That must have been one hell of a shock, on many levels.'

Jenny took a sip of wine before replying. 'I think knowing Amber beforehand helped to reduce the shock. If some complete stranger had turned up on the doorstep... Well, that would have been quite a different story.'

'It has to be said it's one bloody big coincidence though! I mean seriously, what were the chances? It's like something you'd read in one of those trashy novels you sell...' She gave Jenny a nudge in the ribs and they both began laughing.

'You don't think the same thought hasn't crossed my mind?' Jenny sniggered back. 'It is strange though, Sukes. I feel as though the hand of fate decided to stick itself into my life this year and give it a damn good shake up. I'm not complaining because I know I'm happier now than I have been in a long time, despite recent events, but even so...' She gave a small shrug.

'Well, Jen,' Sukie smiled, 'you know my philosophy, things always happen for a reason and usually when you least expect them.'

'I know. I also know I'll be okay and I will bounce back from this. I couldn't be happier for Amber – she's a wonderful girl and she deserves this happiness. She's struggling herself, trying to come to terms with yet another change in her life, but I know she'll be able to deal with it. She's a lot stronger than she realises.'

'What about Saffy, does she know yet?' Sukie liked the spirited teenager and hoped she was able to take this news in her stride.

'She's been away on holiday with her friend from school. She's back tomorrow and is due to come to stay with me on Wednesday. I expect Amber will tell her tomorrow night.'

'How do you think she'll take it?'

A smile crossed Jenny's lips as she answered. 'It's

Saffy, nothing ever seems to faze her so let's hope this doesn't either. She adores Charlie, so to find out he's her uncle – well, sort of – I suspect will make it considerably easier. I think she'll be fine but we'll all keep an eye on her, just to be sure.'

'Well, if there's anything we can do to help, if it's needed, you only have to say.'

'Thanks, Sukie, I'll keep that in mind.'

'Right then, time to change the subject completely.' Sukie topped up their glasses. 'As you know, Essie Walton and I got on rather well when we teamed up to organise the village fete in May. Well, we've been talking and we'd like to do it again for Christmas. We're planning a Christmas Market and Fair and I was hoping you'd like to be involved. We're going to round up the shopkeepers next week and float the idea past them but, if you're already on board with it, that may sway anyone who's not so keen or a bit reluctant. What do you say?' She grinned at Jenny.

'Firstly, I say "wow" and secondly, I say "I'm in". That would be fabulous. Would you do it like the German Christmas Markets you so adore or do you have something else in mind?'

Sukie let out a bark of a laugh as she replied, 'You know me too well, Jenny Marshall. If possible, I would love to replicate the German markets although it all comes down to what the villagers would prefer. The company that provided the fun-fair back in May can supply a number of the little wooden cabins if they're required. I've asked them to reserve them for us although I do need to confirm pretty soon, hence the village meeting being sooner rather than later.'

'What you have in mind for the stalls?'

For the next hour, Sukie bounced her ideas off Jenny and was pleased when her friend began to put forward suggestions of her own. Sukie hoped that being busy with organising the fair might stop Jenny dwelling too much on the reason for her pain. After all, there was nothing that could be done to change the situation, so the best thing, for now, was to find something else to fill her head, even if it couldn't fill her heart.

Jeff and Charlie were sitting in the Chinese restaurant waiting for their takeaway to be prepared.

'Are you alright?' Jeff asked Charlie, because he hadn't said much on the way there. Their mum had sent them out under the pretext of not being in the mood to cook but Jeff suspected she wanted to be alone with Amber and talk to her, woman to woman.

'Yeah, I'm fine. I was just wondering how it must feel to find out you've got a grown-up kid when you're in your mid-forties.'

'It's one hell of a shock, that's for sure. I'm still getting used to the idea. Being friends with Amber before this bombshell has taken the edge off it but even so...'

'And you didn't have *any* idea who she was?'

'None whatsoever!'

Charlie shook his head. 'There must have been something...'

Jeff turned to face his brother. 'Charlie, she's your niece, you met her back in April – did *you* have any inkling?'

'Of course I didn't!'

'Well then! There was no way of knowing. Perhaps if I'd known I had a child out there, somewhere, I might have been more alert to the possibility, but as I didn't...' His voice tailed off.

'Would you have married her mother, if you'd known?'

'In a heartbeat… I would have been thrilled to be her husband. Katie was so amazing. We may have only had forty or so hours together but I felt as though she'd been a part of my life since forever. I can't believe that three lives were ruined because of her mother's bloody-mindedness.'

'Well… I don't mean to be picky here but they weren't all ruined, were they? I mean, yes, Katie's was – that's a given – but you did okay. I know you married Carol on the rebound but you did get the Mayfair house to start up your own gallery as a means of dealing with your divorce and stuff. And Amber, her adopted parents loved her. So much so, they couldn't bring themselves to tell her the truth. Her life has been different from what it might have been but it wasn't exactly ruined, was it?'

Jeff gave his brother a look of disbelief. 'Are you for real?'

'What? It's true.'

'Charlie, how much better would it have been for Amber to have grown up with her REAL parents and possibly have had some REAL brothers and sisters? She could have had that!'

'So, you think you and Katie could have made it work? Do you think a marriage in those circumstances could have survived?'

'Yes, I bloody do!'

'Yeah, right!' Charlie huffed.

'What's that supposed to mean?' Jeff could feel his temper beginning to bubble.

'You? Being in love? You're in your late forties and I've only known you to be with two women – Carol and Jenny. You're not exactly Casanova, are you? How can you possibly say you know what true, lasting love is?'

'Oh, and you do, do you? Mr Love 'Em and Leave 'Em. What do you know about love?'

'I beg your pardon? Have you forgotten what I went through over Elsa?'

Jeff snorted as his mind went back to the short affair his brother had had with Elsa, his manager, last year. They'd only been going out a few months, and it was Elsa's first relationship since becoming a widow several years before, when Charlie had proposed to her on Christmas Day. Elsa had said yes to avoid ruining everyone's Christmas but had broken it off a week later. When he asked her about the timing, she replied it was better to begin the New Year with a clean slate. Charlie had claimed to be broken-hearted but Jeff had his doubts about that.

'Charlie, I know you think you were in love with Elsa, but believe me, you weren't.'

'Yes, I was! How dare you say that?'

Jeff sighed with exasperation. 'No, Charlie, you weren't! You were in love with the idea of being in love. Elsa's rejection bruised your ego, it didn't break your heart.'

'And what makes you so sure about that?'

'Because, when we went for a drink a week later, you were eyeing up every woman in the pub! Something you wouldn't have done if you'd been genuinely pining for a lost love! Furthermore, you've continued to do it every time we've been out since. So don't tell me you know how it feels to be in love because you haven't got a bloody clue!'

He watched Charlie's mouth open to speak and then close again. He hadn't meant to be so brutal but he'd wound him up. Mind you, it needed to be said – he was sick of the "poor me" attitude Charlie had been carrying around for the best part of the year.

'When you think of Elsa now, what do you feel?'

His brother took a few seconds to answer. 'Nothing! I'm not up, down, or anything. Nope, don't feel a thing.'

'Every time I think about Katie, my heart gives a little squeeze. A small twinge that reminds me I still love her. And, even though I now know she's dead, that love is still there. I am, however, fortunate in that I finally know she did love me back and she left me with the greatest gift she could give me – Amber. It'll take time to get used to her being my daughter but I at least have that time, something Katie didn't get.'

'What about Jenny? Do you love her?'

'Yes, I do. It's a different type of love but no less meaningful. Katie was my world back then, Jenny is my world now.'

Charlie nodded that he understood before leaning against the velvet backing of the banquette they were sitting on, and they waited in silence until their order was ready.

Amber looked at the woman sitting across from her on the sofa. She couldn't believe she was related to Brenda Baker. Her dad, adopted dad – oh hell, this was confusing – had been a huge fan and she remembered buying him a DVD box set of her movies one year for his birthday. It had been scary enough meeting the woman who was her paternal grandmother but when her stardom was added to the mix...? Well, Amber found herself almost unable to speak.

'I don't bite, dear.'

She blushed. 'I'm so sorry, Ms Baker, I just don't know... erm... quite what to say.'

'Please, call me Brenda. So, you know who I am? I'm

surprised – I'd have thought I was too old for you young ones today.'

'My dad, err... adopted dad that is, was a huge fan. He had all your movies.'

'Call him your dad, Amber, for that's what he was. He loved you, he raised you and he cared for you. You may not carry his DNA, child, but in every other way you were, and are, his daughter.'

'It's just so confusing. Jeff is my real dad and it feels strange now calling my other dad "dad" – if you know what I mean?'

'Well, unless you're ready to call Jeff, "Dad" – and, even if you are, I don't think he's got his head around that yet – I would suggest you stick with Jeff and keep "dad" for the man who brought you up. I think he's the one who deserves the title.'

'Thank you.' Amber smiled at her gratefully.

'For what, dear?'

'For helping me to sort that out. It's been chewing me up and I didn't know what to do.'

'Well, that's what grandmothers are for.' She raised a hand as Amber was about to speak. 'I'm guessing that probably sounds pretty weird too but it's a fact we both need to deal with. If you wish to call me Grandmother, or Granny, or whatever, I would not be upset – gee, it's a name I've been longing to hear for many years – but I only want you to use it as and when you feel comfortable doing so. Please don't force it, in your own good time.'

'That's very kind of you. And thank you for being so welcoming, I was scared you'd think I was some kind of imposter – a cuckoo in your nest.'

'Come and sit here, Amber.' Brenda patted the cushion next to her on the sofa. Amber walked over and when she sat down, Brenda took her hand.

'Jeff's told me what you've gone through in the last

now felt her life was beginning to even out again. The whole adoption thing had been something out of the left field but she was finally adjusting to it *and* with having a whole new family. She hadn't told Saffy the news yet – she would save it for when they returned from Paris – although she couldn't see Saffy having a problem with it. In fact, if anything, she'd most likely be over the moon because she was extremely fond of Jeff and Jenny.

The office had been quiet as several of her colleagues were out on site and she'd had her head down, concentrating on finishing off the project she was working on before going off for the week. When her phone rang and she was called in to see Mr Hargreaves, the big boss, the last thing she'd expected to hear was that she was being made redundant. She worked for a small firm but it had been perfect for continuing her architectural studies. She had fallen behind in her course work but had been given special dispensation when she'd explained the circumstances to her course lecturer. When Mr Hargreaves, however, had explained that, like most other small firms they needed to tighten their belts and let some people go, her first thought had been on what this meant for her career.

She barely heard the chairman giving her the details of her severance package as her mind began whirling with the news. It had been difficult enough to get the mentoring position in the first place after she'd graduated, so to try and find a new position now, when she was barely halfway through her post-grad course, was going to be near-on impossible. It might be easier if she was prepared to travel overseas but she had Saffy to look after so that wasn't an option.

Shit! Saffy! She looked at her watch. She was picking her up at six pm from Jenny's. She sighed with relief when she saw it was only four o'clock. She had plenty of time, but… well… the sooner she broke the news to folks, the easier she might find it to get her head around it herself. She picked up her bags, left the café and made her way home to pick up the car, all the while wondering why the hits just kept on coming.

Jeff was downstairs with Jenny, chatting, when Amber walked into the shop. One look at her pale face alerted them to something being amiss. Jenny had customers to look after so it fell to Jeff to lead her upstairs to his little showroom which was currently empty of browsers, sit her down and listen to her tale. He was sure his shock was evident on his face even though he tried to keep a neutral expression so as not to put her off.

'Were you the only staff member they let go?' he asked.

'I don't know, to be honest. I was in such a state of shock, I don't recall much once old Hargreaves broke the news. I don't even know if I said goodbye to anyone. All I can remember is hearing the news in his office and then standing outside the building with two plastic bags full of crap! I've got no recollection of anything in between.'

'You don't think you were picked on, do you?' He could already feel his hackles rising at the thought of anyone bullying his little girl. The sudden stab of paternal indignation did not go unnoticed and he knew then that he would fight tooth and nail to protect the young woman in front of him.

'If I'm honest, I probably deserved it due to all the time off I've had since last year. Think about it – my parents disappear, I take time off. My parents are found dead – I take more time off. I have to fly to Vietnam to exasperation. 'You live here too. When was the last time you slept in the flat above the shop? It's been weeks. You do the cooking here, you do your washing here, you mow the lawn and hoover the carpets. You "live" in this house. So yes, this decision involves you.'

'I didn't realise...' Jeff paused for a moment. 'Are you saying we're living together?'

'Err... Yes! You have so many clothes here now, you've got your own wardrobe. Look around this room, that pile of books by the chair you normally sit in are yours, those DVD's by the television are yours and that painting next to the window is yours – the one you found in the car boot sale and thought would look perfect just there.'

Jeff had followed her finger as she'd pointed around the room. He looked back at her now. 'Do you mind that I've muscled my way in? I honestly didn't realise...'

'Jeff, if I'd minded, you'd have known about it. So you may as well do it properly and we can make it official.' She leant over and kissed him, chuckling at the bemused look on his face. She couldn't believe he really hadn't noticed his steady migration from the flat to the Gatehouse.

'Now we've gotten that cleared up, I'll repeat my earlier question – how do you feel about Saffy living here long term?'

She waited for him to think it over. Finally he replied, 'It seems the only workable solution. It's practical and it solves all the problems. Do you think Amber will go for it?'

'I hope she does. She deserves the opportunity to continue her career plus be a carefree young woman again.'

'Then we'll need to cross our fingers that we can persuade her to accept the offer.'

289

Chapter Thirty-Eight

Saffy was once again leaning on the windowsill in her attic bedroom at the Gatehouse. She couldn't believe she was going to be actually *living* with Jeff and Jenny. This was all so amazing. She loved being here in the countryside. She liked being at home in the middle of Oxford too but the air just seemed fresher here and everything was a little more relaxed. She appreciated that, for most teenagers, being stuck in a village in almost the middle of nowhere would be some kind of hell but it worked for her. She adored working in the bookshop, helping out wherever she was needed and, when not there, learning all about the music business from Pete and Jordie. She was seriously considering the possibility of becoming a sound technician – it was so satisfying when they came up with the perfect sound for the track being laid down. This piece of information hadn't yet been imparted to anyone else and she was sure Amber had visions of her becoming a lawyer or something like that, although it had never actually been said out loud.

Thinking about Amber made her wonder how she was

doing. Today was the day she moved to London and she'd be joining Charlie's firm next week. Saffy was so happy Jenny had come up with this plan because she knew Amber needed her own space to do her stuff. Since she'd found out Amber was adopted, she'd been more than a little worried Amber would feel there was no longer a reason to take care of her and might leave her behind. She hadn't really looked into exactly what "left behind" would entail but she'd read enough books to know it wouldn't be anything good.

This dread had increased when, on the trip back from Paris, Amber told her about Jeff being her father – a big surprise – and then about losing her job – a big shock! They'd sat in silence on the train journey from London to Oxford as neither knew what to say. When they'd arrived back home, they'd been delighted to see Jeff and Jenny waiting for them. Jeff arranged for a takeaway to be delivered and then Jenny had put forward her suggestion while they ate. To begin with, Amber had been quite reluctant to accept – she felt Saffy was her responsibility and she'd be shirking in her role if she "palmed her off onto other people". Saffy grinned as she recalled the explosion of denials from Jeff, Jenny and herself when she said that. They eventually got her to admit that working for Charlie would bolster her career immensely and it would be crazy to pass up such a great opportunity, especially when there was a perfect solution to hand which worked for everyone.

Saffy straightened up and closed the window when Jenny's voice came floating up the stairs, calling her for her dinner. Maybe, now that she was going to be here long-term, she could have a word about planting a cherry tree outside her window. As she ran down the stairs, she wondered how Amber was settling in "down south" – she must remember to call her before she went to bed.

Amber stood in the master bedroom of Jeff's flat and looked around. Jeff had been quite insistent she sleep in the bigger bedroom and was currently moving his stuff into the much smaller spare room at the end of the corridor.

'Jeff, are you SURE you're okay with me staying here? It feels like I'm pushing you out of your home.'

Jeff placed the clothing he'd just removed from the wardrobe onto the bed, walked over to her and took her hands in his. 'Amber, I'm barely here anymore, my life is in Oxford now with Jenny. I can't recall the last time I slept in this flat so I could not be more delighted to know that you are here, using it. I'll have peace of mind because I know you're living somewhere safe and that Elsa and Charlie are both very close if you need help with anything.'

'Elsa's asked me to dinner tonight and has even offered to show me some of the sights tomorrow, if I'm interested.'

'Excellent. Elsa only moved down here herself just over a year ago so she can still recall how daunting it is in the beginning. She told me to pass on to you that she's always on hand if you need her and she'd love to hang out with you while you find your feet and adapt.'

'Thank you, Jeff, for everything.'

'Hey, I haven't done anything.'

She looked him in the eye. 'Yes, you have. You've done a lot. You accepted me when I told you I was your daughter; you didn't shy away from the fact. You've worked on making me a part of your family and now you and Charlie are looking out for me again by helping me when my life had all gone to crap. I owe you a big thank you.'

'Amber, you owe me nothing. I'm your father by birth and I hope I can be a father by rights too. I don't want to take the place of the man who brought you up and moulded you into the wonderful young woman that you are, but I do hope I can be a part of your life and continue his work. He would be so proud of you. I know I am.'

She couldn't speak for the lump in her throat but she hoped the hug she gave him conveyed how special his words were to her.

After a moment they pulled apart and Jeff picked his stuff back off the bed. 'Right, this is the last lot and then I'll get going. Get out of your hair, so to speak, so you can settle in. Now, you must make the flat your home. Feel free to rearrange the furniture and if there's anything you don't like, stick it in the spare room or the under-stairs cupboard out of the way.'

When Jeff had left, Amber sat on the sofa, cradling a mug of coffee in her hands, as she tried to get to grips with her new situation. It felt strange to be sitting in this beautiful flat – and it was beautiful, she could see that everything was top quality – knowing she'd be living here for the next three years at least. Maybe longer, depending on what choices Saffy made once she left school. She looked around the lounge and decided that maybe rearranging the furniture might help.

Forty-five minutes later, she flopped down, all hot and sweaty, onto the sofa. She'd read up on Feng Shui a few years ago and had tried to rearrange the room accordingly. She wasn't sure she'd done it perfectly but it certainly felt better. She'd moved around some of the paintings on the walls and swapped one of them for a large mirror hanging in the spare room. It immediately bounced light back into the room and it felt less claustrophobic. Being down in the basement meant all light had to be utilised. She'd located some red tartan throws in the airing cupboard and they now adorned the sofa and one of the large chairs. She'd unpacked one the boxes she'd brought from the house in Oxford and had carefully placed some of the items around the room. Most of the household items had been boxed up and placed in storage in the flat above the shop. Now that Jeff had moved in with Jenny, it was a good solution because it meant their stuff was accessible whenever they wanted anything. The house had been privately rented to one of the large conglomerates in the Oxford area and the plan was to put their overseas staff in there when they came over on international placements. The fact it was fully furnished had been an added bonus. The company had paid the rent a year in advance and it had been split three ways – a third to herself, a third into an account held by Jeff and Jenny to cover expenditure for Saffy and the remainder into a third account to cover any maintenance costs on the house. Everything had slotted into place with such ease, that Amber couldn't help but wonder if her parents were close by looking out for her and helping her along. Now *that* would have been quite awesome!

She looked at her watch and made a bee-line for the shower. Elsa was due to shut up shop in less than an hour and it wouldn't do at all to be sticky and sweaty when she arrived at the front door for their evening together.

Chapter Thirty-Nine

Jenny and Saffy were preparing to go into Oxford to sort out some school items for Saffy in preparation for her return to school in a few days. They had just cleared the kitchen table after lunch when the phone rang.

'I'll get it,' called Saffy. She skipped into the hallway and returned a moment later holding the handset. 'It's for you – a Mr Dalton from that large supermarket just outside town.'

Jenny gave her a puzzled look as she took the phone. 'Hello? Jenny Marshall speaking.'

'Hello, Miss Marshall, my name is Garry Dalton and I'm the manager of Farmer's supermarket out on the ring road.'

Jenny held the phone away from her head as a loud booming voice barged its way into her ear. 'Yes, I know of it,' she said, 'how can I help you?'

'Could you please confirm that you know a Miss Sadie Elsemere and a Mrs Bernice Browning.'

'Yes, I do. I'm sorry but… what is this all about?'

'Miss Marshall, please could I ask you to come to the

shop as a matter of urgency.'

'I'll come now but please, what's wrong? Are they okay?' Jenny began to feel a pinch of fear in her stomach.

'Oh yes, they are both perfectly fine, I can assure you of that.' As he spoke, Jenny could hear giggling in the background.

'Mr Dalton, I'm leaving now. I should be with you in about twenty minutes or so.'

'Thank you.' The line went dead in Jenny's hand. She looked at Saffy.

'I don't know what that was all about but it seems we've got a bit of a detour on our way to town. Are you ready to go now as I need to get there ASAP?'

Saffy confirmed that she was. Jenny picked up her handbag, tossed her mobile and purse inside and they ran out to the car. Within minutes, Brian the Beetle had charged out of the village and was making his way to Oxford as fast as his little wheels could turn.

Jenny threw Brian into the first parking space she found in the supermarket carpark and jumped out.

'Err… Jenny, this is a mother and child spot…'

'Are you a child?' Jenny barked at Saffy as she fumbled about with the key, trying to lock the doors.

'I guess…' came the reply.

'Then we're fine! Come on.' Jenny rushed in through the automatic doors and made her way to the Customer Services desk. There was a small queue waiting to be served but she pushed past them and went straight to the counter.

'My name's Jenny Marshall. I'm here to see Mr Dalton, the manager. He informed me over the phone it was urgent.'

'One moment, please.' The assistant gave a small

apologetic smile to the customers in front of him as he picked up the phone and called through to the manager's office.

'Miss Marshall? He's on his way and will be with you momentarily.'

'Thank you.'

She had barely turned round to speak to Saffy when the loud booming voice from the phone call could be heard approaching.

'Miss Marshall? Mr Dalton. Come with me.'

'Please!'

'Excuse me?' Mr Dalton turned back to look at her.

'Come with me, *please* is the correct way in which to address someone, Mr Dalton. I am not one of your staff and I do not take kindly to being barked at.'

Dalton glared at her with his little piggy eyes which were in serious danger of being lost within the folds of his rather large face. He clearly thought his position, along with his vast, rotund shape, gave him the right to be rude to people. Well she was having none of that. He was all body, bluster and no balls and she didn't have to accept his bad manners.

'*Please...*' he replied, the sarcasm dripping from each letter as he enunciated it.

She nodded and he began walking towards the back of the shop. She caught Saffy's eye and tried not to join in with the giggles the girl was desperately trying to contain.

He led them into an office where she found Sadie and Bernice chatting away to a uniformed security guard.

'Mum, Sadie... What the hell is going on? Are you both okay?'

'Yes, love, we're fine. How are you?' Bernice smiled as she replied.

'Mum,' she hissed, 'I'm not here for a chin-wag. Mr Dalton phoned and asked me to come and I want to know why!'

Before Bernice could reply, the store manager's obnoxious tones filled the room. 'I called you here because these two women have been running amok in my store! They have been causing havoc! Chaos! Pandemonium!'

'Oh, away with yourself, you big bag of bluster. Swallowed a thesaurus, have you?'

'Sadie! Enough!' While Jenny was trying to be stern, she couldn't help but be impressed that Sadie had the same low opinion of the manager she herself had. She turned to face Mr Dalton – not an easy task as the office was small and with six humans in there, one of whom had a girth an elephant would be proud of, it was really rather squashed.

'Mr Dalton, without using four versions of the same word, please could you tell me exactly what has been happening.'

'These women have been caught causing all kinds of damage within the shop.'

'I see. And could you please tell me exactly what they were doing.'

'Well, when they arrived, they made their way to the clothing department and proceeded to remove a number of items from their hangers and replaced them onto hangers with the wrong size on them. So the size ten jumpers ended up on the size twenty hangers. After that, they made their way to the bakery department where they rearranged all the labels on the baskets of bread, causing much confusion between the tiger loaves and the big bloomers.'

Sadie and Bernice let out a snort at this point and, when Jenny looked round at them both, she could see the pair of them were almost crying with laughter. She threw them a fierce look but they took no notice.

'Ermmm… is that it, Mr Dalton?'

'Not quite, Miss Marshall. We finally caught up with them in the Hair and Beauty aisle where they were swapping the dyes around in the DIY hair colouring packages. It was a blessing we caught up with them at this point otherwise some poor woman was going to get the shock of her life when the Ice-Diamond Blonde locks she was expecting actually came out Ultra-Vibrant Red!'

'I see.' Jenny coughed and bit the inside of her cheeks because the giggles and snorting behind her were growing louder and Saffy's high-pitched squeak told her that even she was struggling to maintain control.

'Mr Dalton, while I appreciate the seriousness of the situation, I can't help but feel that pandemonium and chaos may be a little extreme here. These were pranks and nobody was actually hurt.'

'That is not the point, Miss Marshall. I wanted to speak with you before I called the police, in the hope that you might talk some sense into these demented old geriatrics. The senile old buggers shouldn't be allowed out on their own, they're a liability.'

Jenny had been about to respond but when she heard the insults fall out of Garry Dalton's mouth, a flash of ice-cold fury swept through her. She moved to stand in front of him.

'How. Dare. You. Speak. Of. My. Mother. Like. That.' Each word was accompanied with a sharp poke in the chest. 'You want to call the police? Well, be my guest because when I tell them how rude and ageist you have just been to these ladies, I don't think they'll be too concerned about the mischief they've been up to in the face of your discrimination. I'm also quite sure your head office will have something to say when I write to inform them of your unprofessional manner.' She leant across, picked the phone up from the desk and held it out in front of her. 'So, are you going to make the call or shall I?'

'Erm... urm... there's no need to be so hasty, Miss Marshall. I spoke in the heat of the moment... I'm sorry.' The manager's face had turned a deep shade of red and she could see the panic in his shifty eyes.

'I'm not the one you should be apologising to!'

'Ladies, I am very sorry for my outburst.' His panic turned to anger and, just like a sulky child, he muttered insincerely, 'It was rude and I apologise.'

Jenny continued to glare at him for another moment, noting his barely concealed temper growing with each passing second. Eventually she turned away and stepped over to where Sadie and Bernice were sitting.

'Come on you two, let's get out of here.'

Sadie and Bernice gathered up their belongings and they all followed the security guard through the shop to the front door. Once they were outside in the car park, he said, 'I'm very sorry to advise you, ladies, but I'm afraid you are both now barred from the shop. Please don't come back here again.' He turned and walked back inside.

Sadie and Bernice looked at each other before exclaiming, 'YES!' and giving each other a high-five!

Jenny looked at them. 'What on earth is going on here?'

While they were mumbling incoherently and trying to come up with an explanation, Jenny suddenly noticed the clothes they were wearing – leather trousers with padding on the knees, thick-soled boots, leather jackets and, as she watched, two brightly-coloured crash helmets came out of the rucksacks they were carrying.

'What the hell?' She looked from one to the other but Sadie and Bernice refused to meet her eye and neither said a word.

'Right! I need to take Saffy into town. We'll be back

in two hours and then I'm coming round for an explanation. And I will NOT be leaving until I get one! Got it?'

With words which resembled an agreement, Sadie and Bernice walked away, leaving Jenny to make her way back to the car with Saffy in tow. She was just backing out of the parking space when two old-fashioned BSA motorbikes vroomed loudly past, the riders tooting their horns and waving before spinning round the roundabout and speeding off up the hill.

Jenny gripped the steering wheel tightly for a moment before turning to look at Saffy. 'D'ya know, kid, I think I might just be starting to regret pushing those two together!'

Jenny pulled up outside Bernice's house exactly two hours later. The two motorbikes were parked on Sadie's driveway. She knocked on the front door before entering and walked towards the kitchen where she could hear Sadie and Bernie laughing and giggling. They didn't appear to have heard her arrival and she stopped to listen to them chattering.

'Oh my, did you see the colour of his face when Jenny squared up to him? That was hilarious!' Bernie was struggling to talk through her laughter.

'You mean *this* colour…?'

'Oh my goodness, Sadie…! You took a photograph! That is wonderful! Make sure you share it to the group on Facebook later.'

They were both wiping the tears from their eyes when Jenny stepped through the door.

'Right then, ladies! Care to fill me in on what has been

going on around here?'

'No, not really. It's none of your business.'

Jenny sat down beside them at the kitchen table and glared at Sadie sitting opposite. '*Don't* get bolshy with me, Sadie. I've just saved both of your necks from being hauled up in front of the police, and don't think for a moment that that obnoxious lard-ass wouldn't have carried out his threat because he very much would have. So, 'fess up, the pair of you, what was this morning all about?'

Bernice looked at Sadie. 'She makes a fair point. I think we should tell her.'

'Fair enough, but if she tries to stop us, there'll be trouble.'

'Tries to stop you doing what?' Jenny looked between the two of them, trying to fathom out their coded conversation.

'Jenny, since Sadie and I moved here and became neighbours, we've become very good friends and we've shared quite a bit about our lives, past, present and future. We came to realise that there were many things we've never done and that life had kind of passed us by with very little fun or adventure.'

'Yeah, we've been growing old without living our lives,' Sadie grunted.

'But, Sadie, look at all the things you got up to back in the Sixties – you used to tell Sukie and I some quite wild stories.'

'That was over fifty years ago, Jen!'

'And I was the wife of a renowned barrister, who went on to become a renowned judge, so my life was very rigid and structured – letting my hair down was not an option. I had to lead by example.'

'So, we came up with a fuckit list.'

'Sadie, they're called bucket lists.'

'Ours is a fuckit list – as in, "fuck it, we're old, we'll do whatever the hell we please"!'

Jenny tried not to roll her eyes – trust Sadie to put a rebellious twist on it.

'So, what's on this list? Am I permitted to see it? Just so I have an idea of what other scrapes I may need to dig you out of…'

Bernice and Sadie looked at each other again. Bernie shrugged.

Sadie looked back at her. 'You can see but *only* on the condition you don't lecture us or try to change anything on it. It's *our* list, not yours.'

Jenny held her hands up. 'I promise not to make you change anything.'

Bernice got up and walked to the fridge. She took down a piece of paper that was stuck there and placed it in front of Jenny.

FUCKIT LIST

~~Learn to ride a motorbike.~~
~~Attend a Royal garden party.~~
~~Dance on the tables in a pub.~~
Do a skydive.
Do a bungee jump.
~~Get caught speeding.~~
Dance in the fountains in
Trafalgar Square.
~~Get banned from a shop.~~
Do a wing walk.
Abseil down the side of a building.
Smash crockery in a Greek restaurant.
Do 'The Big One' at Blackpool.
Run naked over the village green

on May Day.
Get a date on Grinder.

Jenny read the list twice and then again a third time while she worked on keeping a straight face.

'Ahmm...' she coughed, 'err, this one,' she pointed to the last item on the list, 'you might want to amend.'

'I said no changes,' Sadie growled.

'Sadie, Grindr is a dating site for homosexual people. You might get some new experiences you weren't planning on if you go hooking up with folks from there. I think the site you want is Tinder.'

Sadie and Bernice looked at each other and exploded into laughter.

Jenny looked at them and couldn't help but smile at their joy. She looked at the list again – some of the items on there made her shudder and, deep down, she suspected some may only be there because they looked good. She could not, for the life of her, see either of them doing a bungee jump or a wing walk.

'I'm guessing that today's escapade was with the intention of crossing off this one.' Jenny pointed to "Get banned from a shop" on the list.

'Actually no, that was an unexpected benefit.' Sadie laughed as she and Bernice high-fived again.

'How so?'

'Last week, Archie Wainwright, who lives a few doors along, went to Farmer's for his weekly shopping. He has bad rheumatism and some days he struggles to walk. He always takes his mobility scooter with him in the car in case of emergencies. It's only a little thing, takes up no space at all. Anyway, when he got to the supermarket, there were no disabled spaces free and he had to park quite a bit away from the door. He got on his little scooter and parked it underneath the awning to prevent it getting wet in the rain. Anyway, a certain fat turd we've all come to loathe, came out and bawled at him to move it. He made Archie park it outside in the rain which resulted in Archie getting a wet bottom when he'd finished his shopping. The poor bugger is still recovering from the chill he ended up catching as a result. From what Archie said, he was as rude to him as he was to us today. Archie's son, Gerald, went to see Dalton but apparently he's a bit of a wet blanket and Dalton blew him out too. That's when we decided to take matters into our own hands. We filmed his outburst this afternoon and it's already been posted onto the internet. He'll be lucky to still have his job by this time tomorrow!' Sadie sat back with a very satisfied grin on her face.

'Sadie! You can't do that...' Jenny's first thought was one of pity for Mr Dalton.

'We can and we did!' Sadie folded her arms across her chest in defiance.

'Jenny, you have to admit, he did deserve it.' Bernice gave her a small smile. 'A number of the residents here have had problems with him; Archie was only the latest on a long list. We tried complaining to the head office but they think that, because we're older, we're stupid and don't know what we're talking about. Well, we'll get the last laugh because there'll be uproar over this. The internet won't let him get away with it, that's for sure. Garry Dalton is about to be history.'

Jenny shook her head and stood up. 'You two are incorrigible, you really are!'

'We'll take that as a compliment, thank you.' Bernice smiled up at her.

'And you're not going to stop us from working on our list?'

'No, Sadie, I'm not. You're both grown women, you

can do what you please. You know your own minds, who am I to dictate what you can and cannot do? I'm not your keeper. Enjoy yourselves, just be careful and maybe try not to get into too much bother. I have noticed that being caught speeding has been crossed off but I think the less I know, the less I'm likely to worry. Now, I must go. I'll see you both at the weekend – please stay out of trouble until then if you can.' She gave them both a kiss on the cheek.

When she was back in the car, Jenny sat for a few minutes contemplating what she'd just witnessed. She became aware of the admiration growing inside her. Here were two older women who were determined not to turn into the voiceless pensioners that society seemed to think the older generation should become. Instead, they were rebelling against the restrictions being forced upon them and were showing the world that age would not stop them from living their lives to the fullest. She turned on the ignition and realised that, as she reversed onto the road, she was immensely proud of the stand they were taking. She looked at Bernice's front door again and nodded, saying aloud before she drove off, 'You go, girls! You both bloody well go!'

Chapter Forty

Jenny looked both ways up and down the road before stepping out and turning around to admire her handiwork. It was only a few days till Halloween and she'd been dressing the shop windows accordingly. She couldn't believe how quickly time had passed. It didn't feel like five minutes since Saffy had returned to school and now, here she was, breaking up for half-term. They had settled into a nice routine at the Gatehouse and there were days when Jenny struggled to think what her life had been like this time last year. She'd gone from being a stereotypical spinster, with her two cats and safe librarian job, to a lover, a partner, a business owner and a mother. Well, of sorts... Although, one might wonder who she was mother to as Saffy was far more sensible and grown up than either Sadie or Bernice seemed to be. They were still working through their list and last week they'd given her a few more grey hairs by going to the O2 Arena in London where they'd crossed bungee jumping and abseiling off the list. Jenny, Jeff and Saffy had gone along to watch and they'd all been bursting with pride (and relief) when both ladies had put their feet back on solid ground with their certificates in hand. They'd also struck "The Big One" at Blackpool off their list after they'd organised a trip up there with some of the other residents from the village. Poor Archie Wainwright, his rheumatism had been the least of his worries that day! Bernice and Sadie, however, had caught the roller-coaster bug and had set their sights on doing the Kingda-Ka in New Jersey, USA. Jenny had watched it in action on the internet and that had been enough for her. The pair of them were welcome to it!

Jenny tilted her head to the side as she looked at the window display – did it need something more? She'd stocked up on paranormal romances and spooky thrillers and these were now displayed in the windows along with all sorts of bits and pieces of a ghostly and spooky nature.

When she'd asked around about how the village celebrated All Hallows Eve, she'd been advised the children of the village went out guising each year. This was a Scottish tradition introduced by a Scottish family many years before and it was one which everyone fully approved of. It was very simple – the children dressed up, went around the village knocking on doors and would perform a small party piece, such as sing a song or tell a joke, for which they would receive a reward of some treats. Jenny thought it sounded far more civilised than the Trick or Treat mind-set which had invaded the UK. The philosophy of "give me a treat or I'll play a trick on you" wasn't one she bought into.

With the knowledge of this alternative Halloween tradition, she'd come up with the suggestion of a small party for adults and children in the café and courtyard. There would be bobbing for apples and pin the wart on the witch's nose, along with some of the other more usual party games like musical chairs and pass the parcel.

Everyone had been enthusiastic and now the shop and tearoom were gradually being decorated, ready for the big night. She was also planning to hold a few story-telling sessions on the days running up to the end of the month.

It had been a complete surprise when some of the local mums had mentioned her lack of a children's corner in the bookshop. With all the electronic gadgetry at their disposal these days, Jenny didn't think kids would be all that interested in reading books anymore. The mums, however, had been quick to advise her otherwise on this one, saying they were trying to encourage their children towards proper books again. Never one to dissuade anyone away from a book, Jenny had commandeered the storage cupboard under the stairs and had turned it into a den with children's books filling the shelves, murals on the ceiling and squidgy chairs and beanbags to relax in. She'd even had a hammock installed and it was filled with toys which were all book related. Twice a week, after school, Saffy held a "Storytime" half hour where she read aloud to her young audiences. One session was aimed at the tiny ones and the other was for the older children. Both were going down a treat and everyone, parents and children, loved them.

'Alright there, Jen?'

She looked round and saw Percy from the pub standing on the pavement by the green. She went over to say hello.

'Your window looks fabulous, Jen. If you ever decide to give up the books, you could be an interior decorator. That Lawrence Lollyellen-Brown chap wouldn't know what had hit him – you'd wipe the floor with him.'

Jenny laughed at the compliment. 'Thank you, Percy although I don't think I could ever turn my back on my books. It would be fair to say that Lawrence Llewellyn-Bowen won't be losing any sleep over my possible venture into his territory.'

'Ah well, just a thought for you to hold onto, should you ever change your mind.'

'Are you all set for your Halloween party?' Jenny changed the subject.

'Getting there. I've just been shopping for some cobwebs and luminous skeletons. I can't believe I spend all year cleaning the damn things away and now, here I am, buying some to actually put up around the place!'

'I'm taking a guess here, Percy, that you're referring to the cobwebs and not the skeletons.'

Percy burst out laughing. 'Haha, that would be good, eh? Come on in, the webs are fake but the bones are real...'

Just then, the phone began to ring in the shop. 'Time to get back to work, Percy, I'll catch up with you soon.'

'Sure will, Jen. See you.'

She could hear Percy still chuckling as she walked back into the shop.

She quickly grabbed the phone before it went to voicemail. 'Good afternoon, The Cabookeria. How may I help you?'

'Hi Jenny, its Bernie.'

'Hey, Bernie, how are you? I'll be round to see you shortly – are you needing something brought in?'

'Jenny, I'm not at home, I'm at the hospital—'

'You're what? Are you okay? What's wrong?'

'Jenny... It's Sadie... We think she's had a stroke.'

Jenny rushed through the doors of the hospital, looking around wildly for the directions board. She glanced down at the hastily scribbled note in her hand and back up at the board, scanning it until she found the ward she was looking for.

She quickly sent a text to Jeff who was parking the car.

Level 6. See you up there
xx

One of the lifts pinged its arrival on the ground floor. She dashed in as soon as the doors opened and pushed the button for the sixth floor. It felt like an age before the doors closed and the button was prodded again several more times. Jenny's heart was thudding and she shifted from foot to foot, anxious to get to her friend.

The lift finally made it to the sixth floor and she was out of the doors the second they began to open. She hot-footed it to the ward and rang the bell to be admitted. After an eternity, a nurse arrived to let her in. She dashed to the desk only to find herself waiting again until the nurse there finished her phone call. By now, Jenny thought she was about to burst a blood vessel herself!

'Good evening, how may I help you?'

'I'm here for Sadie Elsemere.'

The nurse looked at her ward sheet. 'May I take your name, please?'

'Jenny Marshall.'

'I'm sorry, Ms Marshall, but I'm afraid it's close family only.'

'She doesn't have any family. I'm her official next-of-kin.'

'Oh, I see. One moment please…' The nurse turned away and went to speak with the ward sister sitting in her office.

A moment later she was back. 'Please, come with me.'

Jenny followed her and was led to a private side room. When she stepped in, Bernice came rushing over. 'Oh good, you're here. Where's Jeff? Didn't he come with you?' she asked, looking out into the corridor to see if he was there.

'He'll be here shortly, Bernie, he's just parking the car.'

'I see.'

Jenny looked around her. 'So, where is she? Where's Sadie?'

'They've taken her for an MRI scan.'

'Do they know for certain it's a stroke? What happened?'

'She fell. I heard her through the wall and rushed round right away. She was on the floor at the foot of the stairs. I recognised the signs when I was checking her over. I may not have been a nurse for long, before I married The Judge, and it may have been many years ago, but there are some things one never forgets. I worked on the stroke ward for a time – I knew exactly what I was looking at.'

'Well, thank goodness you did and that you were there. I know speed is essential if there's to be any chance of recovery.'

'Well, I've been a bit naughty and pulled a few strings…' Bernice blushed as she spoke.

'Why? What have you done?' Jenny gave her a sidelong look while wondering if she would ever get used to the new side of Bernie she'd been seeing this year. Sometimes she missed the slightly uptight, upright, woman she used to be.

'There weren't many perks to being the wife of a renowned local judge but one of the few was that we mixed in some exalted circles when it came to local dignitaries. Meaning, I've made the acquaintance of a few eminent doctors and specialists. A long-time friend is the neurology and stroke specialist here. I made a phone call and he's agreed to take Sadie as a patient.'

Just then, the room door opened and the porters

wheeled Sadie back in. She was carefully transferred back into her bed and the nurse came to tuck her in and make some notes on her chart.

'How is she? What did you find?'

Bernice got her questions out a fraction of a second before Jenny.

'Doctor Sampson will be along shortly and he'll answer your questions.' The nurse smiled as she put the chart back on the end of the bed and left the room.

'I told you both you were too old to go bungee jumping! This is what happens when you do stuff like that!'

'Oh, nonsense! If this was in any way related, it would have happened at the time.'

'How can you be sure? It was very irresponsible of you both. As least, after this, you won't be going ahead with the parachute jump.'

'Don't be so sure about that,' Bernie muttered under her breath.

'What did you say?' Jenny glared at her mum, knowing exactly what she'd said. How could she still go ahead with her dare-devil antics after this?

'Nothing, dear...' Bernice patted her hand before going to stand beside Sadie. She gently lifted a strand of hair off her face.

Jenny stood on the other side of the bed and looked down at her friend. She looked so tiny and frail lying in the large hospital bed. Jenny realised that Sadie's fiery personality made her appear so much bigger than she really was.

There was a knock on the door and a tall distinguished looking man walked in. Bernice made her way around the bed to him. 'Oh, Alistair, thank you so much for agreeing to take Sadie into your care. I know how busy you are, so I really appreciate this.'

313

'For you, Bernice, it's no problem.'

Jenny narrowed her eyes when she saw the doctor give Bernie a soft, sweet smile.

'So, what can you tell us?' Jenny asked. 'Was it a stroke and, if so, how serious is it?'

'This is Jenny, my daughter and Sadie's next-of-kin.' Bernie quickly made the introductions.

'Nice to meet you, Jenny.' Doctor Sampson held out a hand and quickly gave hers a firm shake. He opened his mouth to speak when there was a quiet knock on the door. Jenny opened it and Jeff walked in.

'Blimey, finding a parking space wasn't easy. Sorry it took so long. How is she?'

'We're just about to find out.' Jenny took his hand and looked back at Alistair. 'You were about to say...'

'I can confirm that Sadie has had a stroke. The upside, however, is it was not a severe one. She had a clot on the brain but it was small and we've administered a drug to break it down. We're keeping her sedated overnight to allow the medication time to work. When the clot has dispersed, we'll bring her round and run some tests to assess how she is.'

'How much damage is there likely to be?'

Alistair looked directly at Jenny. 'I don't know. We really can't say at this time. The speed at which your mum got her here will most certainly work in her favour. We'll know more in a day or two.'

'Thank you.' Jenny took some comfort from the soft squeeze Jeff gave her hand.

'Now, I suggest you all go home, there's nothing more to be done tonight. We'll take Sadie down for another scan late tomorrow morning so, if you come back after midday, we should have some news for you then.'

When they left the room, and said their goodbyes, Jenny couldn't help noticing that Alistair Sampson held

Bernie's hand just a little bit too long when they shook hands. She also clocked the faint flush on Bernie's cheeks. How interesting, she thought, I think I need to watch this space – it looks like there could be some developments afoot.

Chapter Forty-One

Barely seventy-two hours later, Sadie was sitting up in bed and arguing with the doctor that she wanted to go home. They'd all been very relieved to find the damage from the stroke had been minimal. There was some weakness on her left side and she'd probably need a walking stick – certainly in the immediate future. *That* little nugget of information hadn't gone down well at all. Her speech was also slightly impaired but not enough to disguise the curses she rained down upon Alistair Sampson when he imparted the information. To say her language was fruity was an understatement. Jeff was on visitor duty that day and Alistair took him to one side after Sadie's tirade. 'Jeff, I need to ask... Would you say the verbal abuse and tone we've just experienced with Sadie could be considered normal?'

Jeff thought for a moment before replying. 'If I'm being honest, Alistair, I'd say it was quite abnormal. She only told you to fuck off twice. Under normal circumstances, you'd have been told to do that at least half a dozen times!'

Alistair's eye's widened at Jeff's words and it was all Jeff could do to keep a straight face. He suspected Alistair had led a bit of a sheltered life.

'I see.'

'Our Sadie is not your normal sweet old lady, and she wouldn't thank you for calling her one. She's independent, feisty, and exceedingly strong-willed. She doesn't give in to anyone or anything.'

'Well, that might not be to her detriment. She'll need a hefty dose of determination to get over this.'

'Alistair, I suspect she'll be running rings around us all again – quite literally – before too long.'

'Jeff, I sincerely hope she is!'

Alistair set off down the corridor and Jeff went back into Sadie's room. She glared at him as he sat down at the side of the bed. 'I'm not using a bloody walking stick!' she slurred. 'I'm not in my dotage yet. I'm quite capable of standing on the two legs I have!'

'It'll only be for a short time, Sadie.' Jeff knew Sadie preferred straight talking so he spoke bluntly. 'It's just until you get your strength back. Like it or not, this is the result of an illness which could have been so much worse. You've been so lucky, but let's not tempt fate, eh? Just follow the doctor's orders on this.'

'Humph!' She lay back on the pillows and stared up at the ceiling. A few minutes of silence passed and then Sadie turned her head to look at him. 'I don't mind dying from this as long as it's quick. A massive stroke or a fatal heart attack is what I've agreed to. I don't want any long, slow, lingering death.'

'What you've agreed to? I don't understand…'

'I've had a firm word with that Death one and I've told him straight – take me fast and quick. Here one minute, gone the next! I don't want to be a burden on anyone and lying around waiting for the end would drive

317

me up the bloody wall.'

Jeff smothered a grin as he replied with a straight face, 'And what has Death said about this? Has he agreed?'

'Well, the miserable bugger hasn't gotten back to me on it so I'm taking his silence as a yes.'

'Then I hope he's too busy to take you for a while, Sadie, because you'll be missed by many when you do go.' He placed his hand gently upon the small, wrinkled one lying on top of the bedclothes and gave it a soft squeeze.

Sadie allowed it to rest there for a few seconds before pulling hers away. 'Oh, don't be so soft! Stop getting all maudlin and dewy-eyed over me. I'm still here now and I'm going nowhere until I see that Jenny one married. So when are you going to sort that out?'

'Eh? What? Married? What are you talking about?'

'Don't look so shocked, young man! I've seen the way you look at her. I'm not blind.'

Jeff coughed as he got his head around the twist this conversation had taken. 'Shouldn't you be resting, Sadie? We can discuss this another time. You should try and go to sleep.'

'I've had plenty of sleep. I'm only lying here because that white-coated commandant won't let me get up. I'm not a bloody invalid, you know. So, c'mon, answer the question... When are you going to marry Jenny?'

'Well, erm... I don't know if Jenny wants to get married. She's rather independent and she's never given any indication of it being something she wants.'

'Have you seen all the blooming romance novels she reads? Of course she wants to get married.'

'Sadie, have you seen all the crime thrillers she reads? By your reckoning, she's also a raging serial killer!'

'Who says she isn't?' Sadie gave him a sly look followed by a little wink.

'Good point, but I like to think I would know about that particular hobby...' He laughed and hoped the conversation would move on.

'So, when are you going to ask her?'

'I'm not. It's too soon – we've barely been together a few months.'

'How long have you loved her? And don't try to fob me off; I was watching you on the opening day of the shop. You had it bad even then!'

'Since the first time I met her, at Sukie's wedding,' he sighed.

'So why haven't you popped the question – you're not getting any younger, you know!'

'Thanks for that, Sadie. Make me feel better, why don't you!'

'Well, you young ones take far too long over the important stuff and not long enough over the stupid stuff. Just get on with it!'

'Sadie, you've never been married so you're not best placed to be nagging me into doing it.'

'You're right, Jeff, I haven't ever been married but that doesn't mean I didn't want to be.'

Jeff leant forward in the chair. 'Seriously? Tell me more, please.'

'Nothing much to tell, lad. In my lifetime, I have loved three men enough to want to marry them. The first was when I was still a teenager – he died in a factory accident. The second didn't love me enough to want to marry me and the third...' She paused for a few seconds. 'The third was called Walter. He was lovely – good-looking, kind, generous... And married! We worked for the same company and we were paired up for a special project. We hit it off from the start. We shared the same sense of humour, liked the same books and radio shows. He was always keen to try new things – be it food, music or the latest fads. He could solve a Rubik's Cube in less than four minutes.'

Jeff noticed a little lop-sided smile on her face as she talked, her mind clearly walking down memory lane.

'He'd been married for five years when we met. It didn't take long to work out it wasn't a happy one. He never said anything – he was too much of a gentleman and, besides, that's too much of a cliché for me to fall for – but it was the little things that gave it away. He earned a good wage yet his shirt collars were often worn. He would just have bread and butter sandwiches for lunch – no meat or cheese in them. I found out from a colleague that his wife demanded he hand over all his wages every Friday night and she looked after the money. I saw her a few times, at work do's, and she didn't stint when it came to spending that money on herself. Top designer clothing, and Mayfair haircuts. One day, I bit the bullet and asked him outright why he'd married her. It turned out she'd claimed to be pregnant and they'd married quickly to avoid any scandal only for him to find out afterwards that she'd lied. Anyway, we began seeing each other outside of work – dates and things – until finally Walter decided to leave her. We were quietly engaged and he began making arrangements, such as finding a flat for us to move into together and sorting out new bank accounts for us and for her. The week before he was due to move out of the marital home, she dropped the bombshell – she was pregnant!'

'No!' Jeff couldn't keep his exclamation to himself.

'Yes! And it was the real deal this time. She was three months gone and had the hospital letter to prove it.' Sadie turned to look at him again. 'Walter was a good man, an honourable man. He'd never been comfortable with our affair which was why he intended to do the decent thing and leave his wife. It also meant he wouldn't leave her when there was a baby on the way.'

'So what happened? Did you carry on with the affair?'

'No, we didn't. We broke up and I left the company. Walter offered to hand in his notice but, he had a baby coming, he needed his job. So, I gave up mine instead, left London, and moved to Oxford to begin a new life for myself, far away from the painful memories which followed me everywhere, and far away from the risk of ever bumping into him.'

'Was that the last you saw of him?' Jeff was intrigued. He'd never given much thought to Sadie's past or her younger days. Like too many people, when he met folks older than him, he just took them at face value and how they lived their lives today. He felt a bit guilty that it had taken Sadie's illness for him to get to know her better.

'No, I saw him once more, about sixteen years later. I rarely visited London after that but there was one occasion when I had to visit for a business trip near Charing Cross. I arrived early so decided to kill some time in the National Gallery by Trafalgar Square. In true Hollywood fashion, he came out of the revolving door as I walked in. After a few seconds of staring at each other, he asked me to join him for a coffee. He informed me that staying with his wife was the biggest regret of his life. They'd had a boy and she'd made him hers. He had no time for his father and had become his mother's son in every way. Eighteen months after we'd split, he'd tried to find me but with no success. He'd stayed because he had no one to leave her for. In that moment, I saw his true colours. He *was* a nice, kind man – as I said before – but he was also a weak man. He didn't understand, or didn't have the courage, to leave the relationship for his own wellbeing. He needed a reason and didn't think that *he* was a good enough one.'

'Did he ask to see you again?'

The lop-sided smile appeared on Sadie's face once more. 'Yes, he did, but I declined. I'd changed since then, moved on, and he was no longer the man for me. Had we gotten together, all those years before, we would have grown together. As it was, we'd grown apart and our paths were never going to cross again.'

'So what did you do?'

He watched the smile fade and saw sadness slip into her eyes. 'I thanked him for the coffee, kissed him softly on the cheek and declined his request. I told him our time had passed and he had to move on. I also told him he deserved a happy life but he'd never find it if he stayed where he was. If he wanted change then he had to be the change. I'm not sure he really got what I was saying to him. I turned away, walked out of the café and didn't look back.'

'Has there been anyone else since then?'

'No one that really mattered. I've dated a few men, and had two proposals, but I didn't love them enough to walk down the aisle with them.'

'Do you regret those choices now?'

Sadie didn't answer immediately and Jeff began to wonder if he'd overstepped the mark. Just as he was about to apologise for being rude, she answered.

'No, I don't. I've had a good life, made good friends along the way and am still making good friends now. I've known you less than a year and yet, here you are, sitting by my hospital bed keeping me company. There's no guarantee that family would do that. I know people who've done all the marriage and kids thing and they're far lonelier than I've ever been. No, Jeff, I don't regret anything and I wouldn't change anything.'

'Yet, here you are, insisting I propose to Jenny!'

'Jeff Rowland! Haven't you listened to *anything* I've just said? Don't be a Walter! Don't wait for life to come to you, you have to go to it. You're saying you don't know if Jenny wants marriage, but what about what you want? Do you want to marry Jenny?'

'Yes, I do. I'd marry her tomorrow, given the chance.'

'Then ask her and get on with it. Don't waste another minute second-guessing what Jenny wants. This is also about what you want. Marriage is not just for women so, if you really love her, then go and damn well get her! You've got a pair of balls, haven't you? Try bloody using them!'

This was too much for Jeff and he burst out laughing. It was a few minutes before he was able to speak again and, even then, he was struggling.

'Oh, Sadie, you crack me up, you really do. Okay, I'll ask her.'

'When?'

'Soon, I promise.'

'You'd damn well better. And, when she says yes – because she will, trust me on that one – tell her that you and I are organising the wedding. All she needs to do is turn up.'

'We're WHAT?' The last vestiges of laughter drained out of Jeff's body. 'You want *us* to organise the wedding?'

'Hell, yeah! Have you seen that program on the telly where the groom does all the stuff and the bride just turns up? It's hilarious. I love it! We won't be as mental as them – some of the things they come up with are bonkers – but we can give that lovely woman a very special day. She's looked after me, and looked out for me, for all these years. I want to give her something back. It'll be my way of saying thank you. After all, she never accepts my thanks any other time, so it's the only chance I'm ever going to get!'

'Right... I see...'

'Ach, don't panic, lad! We'll put on a grand show. Now bugger off. I'm tired and the Hitler with the stethoscope won't let me out of here if I'm not at least eighty percent on the up so I need to sleep. Come back when you've done the deed and we can begin planning. Bring some of those wedding magazines too – we'll need them for ideas.'

'Sadie, you'll be home by the time I propose—'

'I'd better not be! You get this done ASAP, Jeff. Remember, no hanging around.'

'Okay, Sadie. You win. Now sleep, I'll be back soon.' He stood up, leant over the bed and kissed Sadie on her soft papery cheek. She was asleep by the time he left the room.

Chapter Forty-Two

Jeff made his way back to the car at a pace that would have seen a one-legged donkey overtake him. The discussion with Sadie was rocketing around his head and he was trying to figure out how he'd just been manipulated into agreeing to propose to his girlfriend of barely a few months. He needed some time to think before returning home, so when he drove out of the car park, instead of turning towards the A40 and home, he instead made his way towards the city centre. Jenny would pick up on his frazzled state of mind in an instant. And frazzled it definitely was, for he hadn't left the house that morning thinking, '*I must pick up an engagement ring and propose to my girlfriend tonight!*'

He reached the town centre, parked up, and made his way towards the shops. He wasn't thinking about where he was heading, he just let his feet do the walking. After about twenty minutes of mindless meandering, he found himself in a small cobbled lane. A little smirk ran over his lips when he realised where he was. Of course! Where else should he be but here? He walked on a few feet more until he came to the door of a little antique shop. It was owned by an old family friend who made an excellent cup of coffee and, right now, that was exactly what he needed.

He rang the bell and, as he waited for Hershel to answer, he found himself feeling relieved. Hershel had been a close friend of his father's and Jeff had turned to him more than once over the years when he'd needed advice on certain paintings which had come onto the market. Many masterpieces had been stolen by the Nazis during the war and, if Jeff wasn't happy with the provenance being provided, he would speak with Hershel who had a greater knowledge of these things. They'd never discussed personal matters but, as he no longer had a father he could talk with, Jeff supposed it was only natural for Hershel to be the one he'd turn to at this time.

'Jeffrey, it's wonderful to see you! Come in, come in.' Hershel ushered him into the little shop, which was crammed from ceiling to floor with antiques of all shapes and sizes. He'd once owned a much larger establishment in Belgravia in London but, when his wife died of breast-cancer in her mid-forties, he sold up and moved to Oxford to be closer to his brother and two sisters. Jeff was convinced that all the stock from the larger shop had been brought to Oxford because there wasn't an inch of space to spare.

Hershel led him to the back office and sat him down. 'Can I tempt you with a cup of my finest Turkish brew?' he asked, holding up his old, battered, coffee percolator.

'Always, Hershel, always!'

'So, my boy, what brings you to my door today? It's wonderful to see you, although I sense you have trouble in your eyes. Is it your beautiful mother? Is she keeping well?'

'Hershel, she is very well indeed and, if she knew I was here, she would be sending you her love in return.'

'So, what's bothering you?'

'Why would anything be bothering me?'

'Because you always phone ahead when there's a problem with any artwork. So, for you to turn up unexpectedly… well, this tells me you are bothered about something else. So, I am going to make you some nice coffee and then you are going to tell me *all* about it.'

Forty-five minutes and two cups of delicious coffee later, Jeff had spilled his heart out to Hershel. He told him everything – how he felt the first time he'd met Jenny, how he'd carried a torch for a woman he barely knew for almost four years, how they now worked and lived together and finally the conversation he'd had with Sadie. When he was finished, he sat back in his chair, feeling drained from all his talking but also relieved to have shared his feelings with someone else – someone who knew him, and had known him for a very long time. Someone who he could trust to give him good, solid, advice.

He looked at his old friend who was sitting with his eyes closed and his chin resting on the pyramid he'd made with his fingers. Suddenly his eyes sprung open and Jeff felt himself being pinned underneath their gaze.

'Why oh why, do you young people today make everything so difficult and complicated? You take a problem with a simple solution and twist it around until it becomes a tangled mess. Oy vey, Jeffrey, it is so simple. Tell me, yes or no, do you love this woman? This Jenny?'

'Yes, I do.'

'Jeffrey, do you love her with all your heart and soul and would you do anything for her?'

'Yes, I do, and yes, I would.'

'See, my friend, you didn't even hesitate.' Jeff sat

quietly, knowing Hershel had more to say. 'Jeffrey, we both know that life can be short and we should never waste a moment of it. Not a day goes by when I do not wish I'd had extra minutes with my Rebekah. The days I stayed late at the shop when I could have been at home with her, enjoying her wonderful company and basking in her glorious love, are my biggest regrets. If I had known how little time we were going to have, I would've stretched every day out to its fullest. I would've made every second feel like a year and every minute feel like a century. I'm sure you've felt the same over the loss of your father. So, don't waste this opportunity. Ask this woman to be your wife and cherish every moment. Don't waste your energy letting your head argue with your heart. Your heart knows what is true.'

'But what if she says no?'

'Then you respect that, give it some time, and then ask her again. A faint heart never won fair maiden. You only walk away when she tells you she does not love you. Until that happens, you hang on in there.'

Jeff nodded as he listened to the wise words Hershel was speaking. He was right! Neither he, nor Jenny, were getting any younger and, while they weren't exactly old and decrepit, it hadn't passed him by that Jenny was about the same age as Rebekah when she'd died.

'In that case, I think I need to buy an engagement ring, it seems I have a proposal to make!'

'Come with me, Jeffrey, let's see what I have in my safe...'

It didn't take him any time at all to select what, he hoped, was the perfect ring. Hershel had placed a tray of a dozen rings in front of him and one had immediately stood out. It was a round cut, half-carat emerald set in eighteen-carat gold with four gleaming quarter-carat diamonds – two on either side – set into the shoulders. It reminded him of Jenny on the day they first met when she looked so beautiful in her emerald green dress. He loved it and he just knew Jenny would too.

Hershel walked with him to the door and gave him a warm embrace of encouragement. 'You'll be okay, my boy, trust your heart. Your father would be so proud of you.'

'Thank you, Hershel, for the coffee and the advice. You must promise me you'll come to the wedding, if she says yes.'

'Of course she will say yes – she might be too good to let go but so are you, my boy, so are you.'
With a last hug and a handshake, Jeff made his way back down the lane, anxious now to get home and ask the most important question he'd ever asked in his life.

Chapter Forty-Three

Jeff parked his car by the gate and stepped out, picking up the bouquet of roses from the passenger seat as he did so. He retrieved the two bottles of champagne from the boot and made his way to the Gatehouse. Pete and Sukie had installed a number of antique styled lampposts since Jenny had moved in and these made it much easier to find his way in the dark. With his hands so full, he'd have struggled to carry a torch. He sincerely hoped the champagne wasn't too bold a move but they could either drink it in celebration or he could drown his sorrows in it. Either way, it would be consumed tonight.

On the drive home, he'd mulled over the myriad ways he could make his proposal. He could book a flash restaurant and ask them to bake the ring in a dessert... Or, he could wait until Bonfire Night – which was drawing near – and do it with fireworks exploding behind him... He'd even considered the possibility of hiring a small airplane to pull a banner behind it or write his words in smoke up in the sky... But all of them felt forced and affected. Did true love really need such grand gestures or did it work best when it was kept simple and pure? Jeff had always been one for keeping things simple but this wasn't just his proposal – it was also Jenny's. He wanted it to be perfect for her too. Had she always dreamed of a proposal straight out of a Hollywood movie? Did she read of proposals which had been planned right down to the last, minute, detail in her romantic books and wish for one of those? The biggest problem was, now the idea was in his head, and the ring was in his pocket, he didn't want to wait a single second longer than was necessary to ask her the question.

He arrived at the cottage and found it in darkness with the exception of the lamp in the lounge, which was on a timer. He made his way into the kitchen where the clock on the wall informed him it was just after five o'clock. He had approximately half-an-hour until Jenny and Saffy came home from the shop. Sukie was helping out with covering the shop rota so everyone could take a turn of sitting with Sadie.

He put a bottle of champagne in the freezer to chill quickly and the other in the fridge while also taking out the pre-prepared casserole they were having for dinner which he placed on the table while the oven warmed up. The bouquet was decanted into a vase and cat food was decanted into bowls in an attempt to keep Winston and Churchill away from the flowers. Once there was nothing left for him to do, Jeff paced back and forth between the kitchen and the lounge window, looking out for Jenny and Saffy coming home. Finally, after what felt like an eternity but was, in reality, only fifteen minutes, he heard Saffy's laughter floating on the air.

He met them at the front door and helped Jenny with her coat while breathing a small sigh of relief when Saffy ran upstairs saying she wanted to send Amber a quick email before dinner. Jenny made her way through to the kitchen and he followed behind.

'Oh, Jeff, what beautiful flowers, they're gorgeous.'

'Roses are okay, aren't they? With the cats, I mean. I know lilies are banned but I was sure you'd said these were safe if they ate them.'

'Yes, roses are absolutely fine. Thank you.' She turned and gave him a kiss on the cheek. Jeff pulled her into his arms. 'The flowers might be beautiful but they fade to nothing when compared to you.' He held her tight and kissed her deeply. 'I love you, Jenny. More than I could ever possibly put into words.'

He smiled as she blushed at the compliment.

'Oh, will you shush! You've made me go red...' she giggled.

Jeff took her by the hand and led her to one of the kitchen chairs where he sat her down. He pulled out the one next to it, sat in front of her and took her hand in his.

'Jenny... I love you. I have loved you from the first moment I set eyes on you. All the days since you've became a part of my life, have been the best days I've ever known. Tom Cruise said in that film of his, "You complete me" – well, Jenny, I totally get that because *you* complete *me*! I really, really, hope you feel the same about me because I want to be your whole world just as you are mine. I want to spend every last moment I have on this earth being the reason you smile every day because you are the reason for mine. I want to be the colour in your life, your upside-down rainbow. If you will let me, I want to walk beside you, sharing the good, and the bad, that life throws our way. Jenny, what I'm trying to say is...'

He slid off the chair and onto the floor, knelt on one knee and took the ring from his pocket. He opened the box, held it up in front of her, and taking in a deep breath, said, 'Jenny Marshall, will you do me the great honour...

of allowing me to be your husband? May I marry you?'

Jenny looked at Jeff kneeling in front of her. She could taste the shock of his proposal in her mouth. Of all the things she might have expected when she got home from work tonight, this didn't even come close to being on the list.

'I... I... I really don't know what to say.' Her mouth opened and closed as she tried to work out how she felt. A proposal seemed so sudden – they'd only been a couple for a few months – and yet... Somehow... it also felt so right.

'I'm not in any rush for an answer, my darling, but my knees aren't growing any younger and this wooden floor is a bit cold and hard.'

'YES! Yes, yes, yes! You may marry me!' She loved his choice of words. It was so "Jeff" to make his proposal all about her.

He stood up, slipped the ring onto her finger, pulled her to her feet and smothered her within his embrace. 'Thank you,' he whispered in her ear. 'Thank you.'

From the corner of her eye, she saw Saffy loitering just outside the kitchen door. 'Saffy, I know you heard all that, so you may as well come in.'

'OMG! OMG! OMG! Jeff that was SOOOOO awesome! You totally rocked that proposal.' She turned to Jenny and gave her a big hug. 'Congratulations, Jenny. You guys are the best and you so deserve to be happy together! Jeff, come here and have a big hug too!'

Jenny looked into Jeff's shining eyes as he looked at her over Saffy's shoulder. *I love you*, he mouthed.

I love you too, she mouthed back, smiling.

And she did. With all her heart. She never thought she'd find someone so perfect for her, who knew all of her past and yet still loved her. She'd always been so scared to let anyone into her inner sanctum because the fear of losing them, the way she'd lost Mandy, was too much for her to bear. And yet Jeff had somehow slowly eased his way in, gaining both her love and her trust. His proposal had come out of the blue but her heart was making it clear that accepting it was one of the bravest, and rightest, things to do.

'Darn it, we haven't got anything bubbly to celebrate with. A cup of tea is all well and good but sometimes—'

'Stop right there, my darling wife-to-be, flowers and a ring were not the only thing I brought home this evening.' Jeff walked to the freezer and pulled out the perfectly chilled bottle of champagne.

'Oh wow! Do I get to have some too?' Saffy eyes sparkled at the thought of being allowed a glass of wine.

'You may have a buck's fizz, young lady, and it'll be heavy on the orange juice.'

'Awwww! Can't it be fifty-fifty? Pleeeeeeeeeeeeease?'

Jenny rolled her eyes at Saffy's pleading. 'You might not like it – have you had it before?'

'Yes, I was allowed a glass at my parents' fiftieth birthday party.'

The mention of Saffy's parents gave Jenny a sudden reality check. For the briefest of moments, she felt as though time was standing still, and it hit her just how lucky she actually was. Yes, she'd lost – through no fault of her own – the daughter who she loved beyond everything, but life had tried to make that up to her in so many ways since and she hadn't really taken on board how blessed she was. Saffy had lost both her parents in a terrible tragedy, but she still grabbed life by the throat each day and wrung every bit of joy out of it that she possibly could. Jenny realised she would do well to take more than a few leaves out of Saffy's book.

'Okay,' she relented. 'As it's a super-special occasion, you can have sixty-forty bubbles to OJ.'

Saffy grabbed her in another tight hug. 'Jenny, I know Jeff loves you, but I love you too.'

Jenny was glad of the glass of wine Jeff handed to her just then because the lump in her throat made speaking impossible.

'Oh, can I make the toast?' Saffy didn't give them a chance to say no. She held up her glass and said in her clear, sweet, voice, 'To Jenny and Jeff – As you both walk on this new path together, may you never have stones in your shoes and may all your days be blessed with sunlight and happiness.'

'Amen to that,' said Jeff and he chinked his glass against Saffy's and Jenny's.

'Amen indeed,' whispered Jenny, taking a large sip as she worked on preventing the tears from falling. 'Amen indeed.'

Chapter Forty-Four

'So, now we need to sort out a date. Can I be a bridesmaid?' Saffy's excitement was contagious as they sat down at the table to eat dinner.

'Well, we don't have to rush it and I do believe the correct etiquette on bridesmaids is that you wait to be asked.' Jenny was smiling again as she handed round the bread. Her sentimental moment had passed and she now felt all light-headed and giddy. She was going to be married. She never thought she'd see the day.

'We don't want to wait too long, Jen, I want to be your husband as soon as possible. I'd marry you tomorrow if I could.'

'I think that might be a bit soon, Jeff. These things take a bit of organising and, right now, I'm kind of busy with the Christmas Fayre. I know Sukie's an understanding person but I suspect she'd have something to say if I dropped her in it with less than two months to go.'

'Well, funny you should say that because Sadie already has a suggestion—'

'Sadie? What has Sadie got to do with anything? Did *she* put you up to this? Is that why you proposed – because Sadie told you to?' Jenny heard her voice growing higher and louder and she took a deep breath to bring it back under control. Had Jeff just proposed because an old lady had given him an order to do so?

'No, she didn't "tell" me to propose, she merely opened my eyes and made me see how much I love you. She told me her story—'

'She told you about Walter?'

'Yes, she did and how he regretted not taking the chance to grab happiness when he had it in the palm of his hand. Then, when I spoke with Hershel—'

'Hershel? Who the bloody hell is Hershel?' Jenny felt herself becoming more and more flustered with every word Jeff was uttering. Why *had* he asked her to marry him? She needed to know. 'Jeff, just start from the beginning and tell me everything.'

So Jeff did. When he'd finished, he was astonished to see both Saffy and Jenny sitting there with tears in their eyes. 'What now?' he asked.

'Rebekah,' said Saffy.

'That's so sad and Hershel's words about not wasting a single moment…' Jenny looked at him as she wiped her tears away. 'He's right. We shouldn't waste any time, we don't know what each day is going to bring. Look at Sadie, look at poor Rebekah… Okay, you can do it! You and Sadie can arrange this wedding. Just promise me one thing…'

'Sure, what is it?' Jeff smiled.

'Don't let her come up with anything too wild. I know how much she loves that reality show and I DO NOT want anything like that. Capiche?'

'Capiche! I'll make sure it doesn't get too wild.'

'Can I help, please?' Saffy leaned into Jenny and

mock-whispered behind her hand, 'If you let me in on the arrangements, I can make sure they don't do anything mental such as having you parachuting out of a plane...'

Jenny recalled Sadie and Bernie's bucket list. 'Good point, Saffy. Jeff, I agree on the condition that Saffy is allowed to be a part of it. Strangely, I feel I can trust a fifteen year-old girl more than I can a seventy-eight year old woman!'

'Excellent!' Saffy fist-punched the air. 'Jenny, I promise to keep these guys in line and I'll make sure your wedding is everything you deserve and more. That Sadie one won't get the better of me, I can promise you that!'

They all laughed but Jenny knew she'd made a valid point. She wouldn't put it past Sadie to go for something totally bizarre and Jeff wouldn't have the heart to refuse her. At least with Saffy on board, she stood a good chance of having a wedding that was not too outlandish and, hopefully, even romantic.

Chapter Forty-Five

'For goodness' sake, girl! Will you stop fussing! I am quite capable of walking into my own home by myself!'

Sadie shrugged Jenny's hand off her arm and stomped up the pathway, her walking stick making little staccato noises as it hit the paving stones with some vigour. Sadie wasn't happy with the fact she needed to use it and treated it as if it were an alien growth in her hand which she couldn't shake off. It was thumped down hard with every other step and Jenny despaired of it lasting any length of time.

It was three days since Sadie had helped Jeff to come to his senses – as she so delicately put it – and she'd been champing at the bit to come home and get immersed in the wedding arrangements. Jenny was holding a carrier bag full of the wedding magazines Sadie had instructed Jeff to bring to the hospital and she could see post-it notes sticking out of several pages. That was all she could see, however, for Sadie had given her extremely strict instructions to, "keep her beak out"! Saffy and Jeff were already becoming secretive and she'd walked in on them a few times around the house, with their heads together, whispering quietly.

They walked into Sadie's house, Bernice bringing up the rear with Sadie's holdall in her hand, and headed straight for the lounge.

'I'll just put the kettle on and make us a brew,' said Sadie.

'No, you won't, Sadie, *I'll* put the kettle on, you'll take a seat and rest.' Jenny placed the wedding bag at the side of Sadie's favourite chair.

'Don't boss me around in my own home, girlie! I'm quite capable of making a pot of tea!' The old lady's sniping tone was too much and Jenny snapped back. 'For God's sake, Sadie, will you JUST SIT DOWN! You've only been out of hospital five minutes, for crying out loud!'

Both Bernice and Sadie gave her a startled look.

'I'm sorry. Sadie, forgive me for being rude. I'm just tired. We had the Halloween bash at the shop last night and I didn't sleep so well afterwards. Please, just let me make the tea this time.'

Sadie muttered a few choice words under her breath but didn't argue any further. She made her way to her chair as Jenny headed towards the kitchen.

She was filling the kettle under the tap when Bernice came up behind her. 'Are you okay, poppet? It's not like you to be snappy.'

'I know, Bernie, I'm sorry. I just don't think Sadie realises how much we care for her and want her to be safe.'

'And maybe you don't realise how scary it is for her to be losing some of her independence.' Bernice turned Jenny around to face her. 'Jen, you know how she's always been proud of being able to look after herself and, in her words, not being a burden on anyone. This stroke, albeit a small one, has really frightened her. She's trying to prove she's still the same person she was before it happened. You know what a determined little sod she can be, she'll go out fighting all the way. Try to cut her some slack, eh?'

'You're right… again! I don't want her to come to any harm and I'm being over-protective. I get it.' Jenny gave her mum a small smile.

'I think you and I both know what she'd say to being wrapped in cotton-wool.' Bernie's grin made Jenny feel better.

'I think the words "shove it" and "sun don't shine" might make up most of the sentence…'

'Oi, you two! If you've quite finished talking about me, is there any chance of getting that cuppa today? My throat's drier than a camel's flip-flop!'

'Just coming, Sadie.' Jenny poured the water into the teapot and had just placed it on a tray when her mobile started ringing. She fished it out of her pocket. 'Bernie, do you want to take that through to her majesty while I answer this? Thanks.'

She turned away from the door to answer her phone. 'Hello, Jenny Marshall speaking.'

'Hello, Jenny, its Adrian Crookson here, how are you?'

'Hi, Adrian, I'm well, thank you. How are you?' She exchanged the usual pleasantries but one thought was buzzing around her head – why was the family solicitor phoning her? As fast as the thought came into her head, she felt a stirring of excitement. Maybe he had news on her daughter. There were two addresses logged on Mandy's file – the Gatehouse and also that of the solicitors. Maybe there had been contact…

'Jenny, I'll get straight to the point. Oliver has demanded a meeting. I've been trying to fend him off for a few months but he won't give up. He's making noises regarding his father's will. I'm not sure exactly what he's expecting but are you able to come in to the office tomorrow afternoon?'

Jenny let out a sigh. She hadn't heard anything further from Oliver since he'd stormed out of the shop in the summer. She'd hoped he'd spoken in temper and had since calmed down and come to his senses – it would seem he hadn't.

'Sure, Adrian, I can come in. Would two o'clock suit?'

'That would be perfect. I also need to speak to Bernice and ask her to join us. I'll phone her now.'

'No need, Adrian, she's here with me. Let me just get her for you…'

She called Bernice and, telling her who was phoning, passed the mobile across and made her way into the lounge to sit with Sadie.

A few seconds later, Bernice walked back in and returned her mobile phone. 'I wonder what that little shit wants now!' she said.

'Bernice! You can't say that about your son…' Jenny had heard Bernie call Oliver a few things over the years, ever since she'd found out about her lost granddaughter but she'd never spoken with such venom before.

'I can and I will! He's getting worse as he gets older and I've had enough of it. He's a selfish, self-centred, arrogant man and I am appalled that I managed to create such a creature. They say hindsight is a wonderful thing and it's very true. I know it's my fault for indulging him but that doesn't mean to say I have to like him now.'

'I wonder what he wants…' Jenny mused aloud.

'Well, we only have twenty-four hours till we find out.'

'YOU WANT TO DO *WHAT*?' Bernice yelled at her son while Jenny looked on dumbfounded. Like their mother, she couldn't believe what she'd heard. Oliver had just informed them of his intention to contest his father's will *and* he wanted a Power of Attorney drawn up to give him full control of Bernice's finances as he didn't believe she was competent enough to take care of them herself.

Adrian Crookson, the solicitor, stepped in before Bernice had the chance to really lose her temper.

'Oliver, the first question I need to ask you, is why are you making these requests?'

'Well, regarding the will, I don't think *she*,' he glared at Jenny, 'was entitled to any share of it and, regarding the POA, *she* has clearly wrapped my mother around her little finger and is sponging cash from her. My mother needs me to put a stop to it. Ever since we've been told some fairy story about a child who, surprise, surprise, can't be found, my mother has bent over backwards to give her everything *she* wants. Well, that needs to stop.'

'I see. Thank you for explaining that, Oliver.'

Jenny watched as the solicitor took his time before responding further and suspected he was doing it on purpose in an attempt to maintain peace within the room. When he began speaking again, she noticed he was using a rather slow and ponderous voice which in no way resembled his normal day-to-day tone.

'Oliver, have you taken any legal advice before coming along today?'

'No, I don't need to – I know what my rights are.'

'Well, I am very glad to hear that because you won't need to request a refund for their services.'

Jenny drew in a deep breath and held it to stop herself from giggling. In those few words, Adrian Crookson had intimated that Oliver didn't have a leg to stand on with either of his requests. She sat back to watch the show, relaxing now she knew Oliver couldn't cause trouble, no matter how much he wanted to. She took Bernice's hand and gave it a gentle squeeze. When Bernice looked at her, she gave her a small wink and hoped she understood what she was trying to convey. The slight lift at the corners of her mouth told Jenny she'd got it. Bernice's shoulders dropped and, like Jenny, she relaxed back into her chair.

'I'm not exactly sure what you mean by that.' Oliver had turned his glare onto the solicitor.

'Then please, allow me to explain. I'll try to keep it simple. Firstly, you cannot contest the will for two reasons. Number one – you can only contest within the first six months after probate has been granted. As your father died over eighteen months ago, and probate was granted within six months of his death, you are almost a year too late. Secondly, *had* time been on your side, you still could not have contested it because you were not financially dependent upon your father. Furthermore, your father left you a reasonable bequest and it is highly unlikely a court would award you a greater sum, especially as the main beneficiary was your mother.'

'I don't want more money, I want *her* to give back what she got as she's not entitled to it.'

'Oliver, Jenny is entitled to whatever your father chose to give to her. She is regarded as a "child of the family" and your father made sure all legalities in this matter were covered.'

'I'm still going to contest it!'

Jenny couldn't believe she was watching a grown man actually pouting because he wasn't getting his own way. She so wished she could bring out her camera. She'd love to have a photograph to show Jeff later.

'Oliver, you can't. It's too late. So forget it!'

'I also want Power of Attorney for my mother.'

Adrian looked to Bernice. 'Bernice, are you agreeable

to Oliver holding a POA for you?'

'Over my dead body! He will NEVER have a Power of Attorney for me.' She turned to her son. 'However, thank you for bringing the matter up, Oliver. Having one would be the responsible thing to do so I'll be making arrangements for *Jenny* to hold it for me. I will never let you have control of my finances or be in charge of my welfare.'

'But, Mother, don't you see, *she* is syphoning your money from you. You clearly don't see it now but it won't be long before you have nothing left.'

Jenny had had enough of listening to Oliver's whining. She moved in her chair in order to look directly at him. 'Oliver, what on earth makes you think I am taking money from Bernice?'

'Well, how else could you afford to be the owner of that shop? That's one big building and shops in little country villages in the middle of the Cotswolds do not come cheap. The last I heard, librarians don't earn bucks big enough to afford a place like that.' The sly smile on his face suggested that he thought he'd caught her out. Well, she'd had enough of his crap – it was time to kick his shit to the kerb. She looked at the solicitor. 'Adrian, tell him!'

The solicitor gasped. 'What? You want to inform him of…' His voice trailed away. Jenny knew why he was surprised, she'd always maintained her personal information was none of Oliver's business – and it wasn't – but she now realised there was no reason for it all to be a big secret. What difference did it make if he knew or not? If it got him off her back, then it would be worth it.

'Yes, Adrian, tell him everything.'

'Very well!' The solicitor shuffled through some folders on his desk and pulled one towards him. Upon opening it, he glanced at the top page then looked directly at Oliver. 'Oliver, at Jenny's request, I am at liberty to inform you that Jenny has never taken a penny from your mother or your father. The bequest left to her by your father has been placed in trust for her daughter.'

'But... what about the cost of the shop? It said in the newspaper she was one of the proprietors.'

'That is correct, Jenny does own half of the premises.' Adrian paused to look at her again. She nodded at him to continue.

'Oliver, Jenny was the sole heir when her parents and aunt died. Various trust funds and insurances, along with real estate and interest, contributed to make Jenny rather wealthy. At this time, Jenny has funds totalling over four million pounds.'

This time, Jenny showed no restraint. The look on Oliver's face was priceless and she made sure she got a photograph of that one!

Chapter Forty-Six

Saffy looked around her bedroom and gave a little nod of satisfaction. Her friend, Brioney, was having her first sleepover tonight and Saffy wanted it to be perfect. Jenny and Jeff had tried to replicate Anne Shirley's bedroom, from her favourite book, and hadn't done too badly. With Sukie and Pete's permission, they had sanded the floorboards in the attic room and varnished them. In the middle was a round, braided mat which one of Jeff's craft suppliers had made for her – it didn't specify a colour in the book so she'd chosen a red one. The walls had been painted white and the dormer windows had white muslin curtains across them. Jenny had pointed out that, with the carpet up and the old-fashioned wooden windows, which were not double-glazed, it might be cold in the winter so they'd agreed some heavy red, velvet curtains wouldn't be too much of a deviation from the room at Green Gables. Jeff, in his travels around house-clearance shops and car-boot sales, had even managed to find a small three-cornered, three-legged table. There had been some discussion over the "prim yellow chair" which Jenny believed would probably be small, straight-backed and wooden – not unlike an old-fashioned, rustic, kitchen chair. Once again, Jeff had sourced something that fitted the bill and it had been painted a lovely bright sunshine yellow and her old, battered, teddy bear now sat upon it. The only concession that had been made, in this replication, was the bed. In the book, Anne had a wooden bed frame but Saffy had always hankered after a white, cast-iron frame and this is what she now had. There had been no description of Anne's bedclothes so Jenny had suggested that, given the era in which the book was written, there was every chance a patchwork quilt may have been on it so they'd gone for plain white cotton bed linen with a proper patchwork quilt over the top. There was a small walk-in cupboard in the corner which should have been a wardrobe area but, so as not to interfere with the olde-worlde décor of the room, Jeff had asked Robbie to create a built-in desk and work area where she could sit to do her homework and studying but could then hide away her modern-day computer items when the cupboard door was closed.

Saffy walked over to the mantelpiece above the small fireplace – something which hadn't been in Anne's bedroom but there was a limit as to how identical it was possible to be – and slightly moved the vase of holly and mistletoe she had placed there. Ideally, it would have been a vase filled with cherry-blossom but, as it was now the middle of December, that wasn't possible so she'd decided to be more festive instead. She felt sure Anne Shirley would have approved.

With a final sigh of happiness, she spun around and left the room, scooping up Winston as he tried to sneak in to sleep on her bed. 'Oh, no you don't, you little ginger monster, my room is currently spotless and I want it to stay that way until Brioney arrives.' She nuzzled the cat under her chin as she walked down the stairs and into the kitchen where Jenny and Jeff were getting ready to leave. They were both dressed in Dickensian costumes because today was the day of the Christmas Fayre. A Victorian theme had been the popular choice between the shopkeepers, as they felt it was in keeping with the Victorian theme of the May Day Fete and Jeff was resplendent in his high-collared shirt, cravat, waistcoat and long frock coat. He had a top hat and cane sitting on the table which would complete the outfit perfectly. Jenny had taken some time to decide on her style of outfit as the era had been quite varied when it came to women's fashion. In the end, she'd opted for an outfit from the late 1800's which consisted of a long midnight-blue skirt with a bustle at the back, a matching midnight-blue jacket with glorious puffed sleeves and which cinched in at the waist with a small white belt. A white blouse was visible underneath and the whole ensemble was finished off with a high-collared white cape, edged with midnight-blue piping. She'd pinned her hair up and a small blue hat with a white feather perched daintily on top. Together, they looked stunning and Saffy pulled her phone from her pocket.

'You guys look amaze-balls! Let me take a piccie before you go.'

When she'd finished uploading the shot onto Instagram, she made her way to the toaster.

'What time is Brioney arriving?' asked Jenny, as she pulled on her gloves.

'Around eleven.'

'Then we'll see you later.' Jenny came over to give her a hug and a kiss, her long skirt making a swishing noise on the floor as she walked. Jeff dropped a light kiss on top of her head as he said, 'Remember what I told you, only put a small amount of your money in your purse, keep the rest secure in the inside, zippy pocket of your jacket. It's going to be rather busy, and these kinds of events always attract the less-honest in society.'

'Got it, guv!' She gave Jeff a mocking salute and a big smile. She was planning to do some Christmas shopping today and she'd worked a lot of hours in the shop to earn her spends – she certainly had no intention of losing it to some light-fingered thief.

She called out her goodbyes as she buttered her toast and then sent a short text to Brioney asking her to get there as soon as possible – she couldn't wait to show her everything.

Jenny smiled as she placed two books in a bag and handed it to the couple in front of her. When they'd moved on, she quickly leant down and pulled another copy of "A Christmas Carol" and "The Snowman" from the stockpile hidden by her feet. As she placed them along the front of the counter, she looked out at the spectacle in front of her. She was delighted to see all the little Christmas cabins had a healthy number of customers hovering around them. Hilda, from the haberdashery shop, gave her a quick wave. She was doing a roaring trade in Christmas ribbons and tableware. Her daughter, also called Hilda, had come up from London for a few days and was helping out in the shop. Jenny had to assume it was as busy at the other end, beside the pub, because she was unable to see that far thanks to the funfair which filled the centre of the green. The village pond had been covered over and the neighbourhood ducks were safely tucked away in the barn of one of the local farmers. The perimeter of the green, and the pavements on both sides, had cabins lined up side by side, all selling everything from Christmas jumpers, to cakes, biscuits, decorations, floral winter bouquets and much, much more. The overhead Christmas lights had been switched on by Pete in mid-November and they twinkled away in the frosty air. Carols were being played quietly through a discretely-placed tannoy system. When they'd advised the tour companies of the intention to hold a Christmas Fayre, they'd been told to expect large crowds and the companies hadn't lied – the place was rammed. It may have only been going for a few hours but Jenny already sensed it was a roaring success. She caught the eye of Sukie, who was running a snow globe stall nearby and gave her a thumbs-up. She received a quick one back before the crowds moved again and her view was blocked. She picked up her phone to text Amber to ensure everything was okay in the shop as it was all hands on deck today. Charlie was covering the shop for Jeff, who had his own crafts and candles cabin going on, Robbie was running the bakery stall for Sam, and Amber had taken Jenny's place in the bookshop. She'd just hit "send" when Bernice and Sadie appeared in front of her. Standing behind them, with his usual sulky face, was Oliver, his hands full of bags.

'Hi, Jenny, how's it all going? Have you been busy? Everything looks fantastic.'

'Oh, Bernie, I've barely stopped. Any concerns I had over whether a Christmas book cabin would work have been completely dispelled – the books are simply flying off the shelves. The children's books have been the biggest hits but the ladies romance novels aren't far behind them.'

'Is this one any good?' Sadie was holding up a Trisha Ashley novel. Her other hand was lying on Bernice's arm – her replacement for the much-loathed walking stick.

'Oh, yes! That's one of my favourites, Sadie. I read it every year.'

'And it's not too lovey-dovey? You know I can't be doing with all that schmaltzy shit!'

'I can assure you, Sadie, it's not like that. I think you'll enjoy it.'

'Okay, I'll give it a try then.'

Bernice had been flicking through some of the children's books on offer. She held up a particularly beautiful edition of "Twas the Night Before Christmas". 'Jenny, this book is gorgeous. Look at these stunning illustrations... If only I had a grandchild to buy it for!' She gave Oliver a fierce look as she spoke. Jenny raised an eyebrow at Bernie's tone – it was quite unlike her to be bitchy, even to Oliver.

The recipient of her disdain gave a small cough. 'I'll just... erm... go and put these purchases in the car. I'll be back shortly.' He threw Jenny a wide smile before scurrying off.

'What was *that* all about?' Jenny looked at Bernie as she put the book back on the stall.

'Oh, he's being his usual pain-in-the-ass self! Since he found out about your financial status last month, he's been going on and on at me to put in a good word to you on his research. Apparently one of his investor contracts ends in January and he's trying to find a replacement. I'm afraid he's set his sights on you, Jenny.'

Jenny couldn't help laughing. 'I do not believe that bloke! Well, that explains the smile. After everything he's done to me, how can he honestly think I'd have any kind of involvement with him? I swear his ego is bigger than his IQ and that's saying something! Well he can take a long walk off a short pier, Bernie, he'll get nothing from me.'

'That's what I told him but he refuses to listen, so be

prepared for a charm offensive, Jenny.'

'Thanks for the heads-up, at least I'll be prepared for it.'

Bernice gave her a smile before turning to Sadie and saying, 'Shall we make our way over to Percy's and try out her mince pies and mulled wine?'

'About bloody time – that mulled wine is the only reason you managed to talk me into coming to this shindig.'

'Oh, Sadie, you don't mean that surely.' Jenny passed over Sadie's bag with her purchase inside along with a couple of other books she'd slipped in which she thought might be to the older lady's taste. 'I thought you loved Christmas – we've always had good times together.'

'When you've seen as many as I have, Jen, they eventually lose their sheen. The only thing I enjoy is the convenient excuse to eat mince pies and get pissed! If we ate and drank at any other time of the year, the way we do at Christmas, we'd be told we were raging alcoholics with eating disorders! It's all a sham!'

'Right then, on that cheery note, we'll be off. See you later, Jenny. I hope you have a great day.'

Jenny waved them off and smiled cheerfully at the family who'd taken their space but inside she was seething at the news Bernie had imparted. How *dare* Oliver think he could soft-soap her into giving him any of her money – he really was a piece of work! Well, let him try, she'd have great fun telling him where to go!

Chapter Forty-Seven

Jenny put the last few bits and pieces in her overnight bag and zipped it closed. She looked around her bedroom, checking she had everything. It was the night before her wedding and she was staying at the manor with Sukie and Pete. She was feeling both excited and nervous but had yet to decide if she was excited and nervous about being married or what the big day may bring since she'd had no hand whatsoever in the organising of it. She hadn't even seen her wedding dress. She'd been instructed to present herself to Hilda, in her haberdashery shop, to be measured up and go through a list of materials to weed out any she disliked. When the time came to try on her wedding dress, she'd been blindfolded, and had been helped in and out of several dresses and items to ensure she remained in the dark. It seemed as though Jeff, Saffy and Sadie had thought of everything.

Sukie had planned a small get-together for tonight which included Sadie, Saffy, Bernice, Sam, Amber and Elsa. Her hen night had been arranged by Sukie and had taken place the first weekend in December. Everyone had been whisked over to Salzburg on one of Pete's private flights and they'd had a great old time going round the Christmas markets, visiting some of the locations from the Sound of Music film and indulging themselves with apple strudel and mugs of hot chocolate on the roof-top terrace of the hotel where Sukie and Pete had first met. There had been much laughter when she'd told them the story of how they'd come to be friends. Tweety-pie…! Even now, it made her smile.

Saffy stuck her head around the door. 'Are you ready to go? Jeff's going to be here in a few minutes and you're not allowed to see him. It's bad luck!'

'You do know that's an old wives' tale and has absolutely no truth in it, don't you?'

'Yup, it probably is but,' Saffy smiled at her, 'I ain't taking no chances so move yourself, lady! We need to get out of here now!'

'So bossy for one so young!' Jenny murmured, as she picked up her holdall.

Saffy led the way down the stairs and out the door, barely giving Jenny time to pause which, she concurred, was probably a good thing. When they arrived at Sukie's front door a few minutes later, they walked in to laughter and loud singing. It seemed like the other girls had arrived and were already murdering the Christmas songs being played.

'Come on in,' Sukie greeted them enthusiastically at the door. 'Let me show you to your rooms before you join the merry throng.' She led them upstairs and showed Saffy where she was sleeping that night and then took Jenny to her bedroom. It turned out be one of the larger rooms in the manor. 'You're going to need plenty of space tomorrow for getting ready, hon,' was Sukie's reply when she commented she'd need a map to get from the fabulous four-poster bed to the en-suite bathroom.

'Talking about tomorrow, how much do you know about it?' Jenny asked her.

'Enough, but I can't tell you anything. I'm sworn to secrecy!' She tapped the side of her nose with a finger.

'Oh, go on! Tell me something... I promise I won't tell Jeff...'

'Jenny, I'm not scared of Jeff, I can handle him. Sadie, on the other hand... Uh-uh! I'm not crossing her!'

'Hmph!' Jenny let out a sound of exasperation. 'This was all her bloody idea!'

'I'm sure it's all going to be just fine and you'll have a wonderful day.'

'We'll see...'

Sukie walked over and took hold of her hands. 'How *are* you feeling, Jen? Are you okay?'

Jenny thought for a moment before replying. 'Yes, I think I am. I'm not at all concerned about whether I'm doing the right thing or not because I know I am. I never thought I'd hear myself saying this about anyone but I love Jeff to the moon and back. He's everything I could want and more. After everything that has happened in my life, the only thing worrying me is the thought of losing it all. I mean, let's be honest here, there's form in that department.'

'You can't think like that, Jenny, you'll drive yourself daft.'

'I know, and I do my best not to, but sometimes... Well, the thought has a way of popping up every now and again and it's not always so easy to push it away.'

'Well, tomorrow is the start of a whole new life and I just know you'll never need to worry about being alone again – Jeff will always be by your side.'

'I know he will,' she smiled. 'Also, I can assure you that, with not having had *any* involvement whatsoever in this wedding, I've got no worries over anything going wrong because I won't actually know what should *be* right or wrong. I suppose some would say that's a good thing. I'm just going to take the day as it comes and whatever will be, will be!'

'That's the spirit! Now, c'mon, let's get down those stairs and have a few glasses of bubbly stuff. It's your last night as a single woman – we need to see you out in style.'

'Okay, you can open your eyes now!'

Jenny waited for a moment longer before she dared to look. She'd told herself the dress would be the early alert on how the rest of the day was likely to pan out. She took a deep breath, counted to three and…

'WOW!'

She looked at the vision reflected in the mirror. This couldn't really be her… could it? The woman staring back at her was *stunning*. Her dark auburn hair had been curled and then piled up loosely around her head, giving it volume and depth. A few little tendrils hung down and these had been curled to soften the line of her face. A golden tiara, with pearls woven through it, sat snugly at the front of the hairdo.

Her make-up was subtle yet effective, making her grey eyes large and doe-like, her cheekbones sharp and pronounced, and shapely lips that even she wanted to kiss. Margie, from the hair and beauty salon in the village, had done a wonderful job. Jenny turned to her to say thank you but found her eyes swimming with tears.

'Don't you bloody dare cry,' said Margie, springing over with a tissue in her hand to dab away the moisture before it ran down her face.

Jenny smiled at her administrations before turning

back to the mirror. She ran her hands gently down the front of her pale gold wedding dress. It had a soft satin bodice which began at the top of her breasts and dipped down into a gentle V-shape below her waist and was embroidered with emerald swirls enhanced with small flashing diamantes and tiny seed-like pearls. The top of the dress, from her collar-bone to the top of the bodice, was delicate lace with a mandarin collar and a sweetheart neckline. The sleeves were also lace and finished in a point across the back of her hands; small diamantes graced the tips. The skirt of the dress was flat and smooth down her front, flaring out on the sides and had soft pleats at the back which led into a small train. There was also a small line of emerald embroidery around the bottom. She turned to get a better look at the back and let out another small gasp of surprise when the front of the dress parted to reveal an inset panel of emerald satin. The design most definitely had its inspirational foot in the medieval period and she loved it. The gold colouring suited her perfectly and enhanced the radiant glow of her face.

'Well, do you like it?' asked Sukie. She was her matron of honour and Saffy was her only bridesmaid and they both looked equally as stunning in the dark gold sheaths they were wearing. The matching bolero jackets were also delightful.

'I'm speechless... It's absolutely gorgeous. I love it.' She gently turned from side to side to get a better look and smiled every time her actions caused the emerald panel in her skirt to wink through the gold.

'It's not quite finished, there's one more item.' Natali from the ladies' dress shop stepped forward with a large suit bag draped across her arms. Jenny hadn't even noticed her presence in the room until then. She took a look around her and saw Hilda standing behind Natali, a small sewing basket in her hand. Next to her stood Sadie and Bernice, both dressed in emerald dresses which matched Sukie's and Saffy's in design.

Everyone in the bedroom exclaimed loudly when Natali unzipped the suit bag and brought out a velvet coat in the same shade of gold as her wedding dress. She held it up and Jenny slipped her arms into the emerald satin-lined bell sleeves. It had a stiffened collar which was high at the back and sloped down towards her chin. The front had a number of pearl buttons which stopped at the point of the V on her bodice after which, the coat was cut away to reveal the golden skirt of the dress beneath it. As the weather outside was cold and frosty – perfect Christmas weather, in fact – the addition of the coat was most welcome.

Jenny took another look at her wedding outfit. It was absolutely perfect and she was filled with confidence that the day would be too. She had nothing to worry about.

Sukie came over and touched her gently on the elbow – it was time to go.

The ladies made their way down the stairs and, at the bottom, Sukie handed out the small bouquets which were lined up waiting. Sadie and Bernice each had a posy of red roses with long trailing gold ribbons that matched the dresses of Sukie and Saffy. Sukie and Saffy had the same posies but theirs sported long trailing emerald ribbons which matched the dresses Sadie and Bernice were wearing. Jenny's bouquet was a more elaborate affair of red roses and dark green holly with trailing ribbons in both green and gold.

When she looked at everyone standing together in the hallway, with their flowers in their hands, Jenny knew Jeff had taken control of this arrangement. His eye for colour and detail was evident in the precise way everything had been put together.

The photographer, who'd been discretely taking photographs throughout the morning, lined them up for a few more shots. When she was done, she nodded to Sukie who turned and said, 'Okay, Jenny, this is it, time to be on our way. Are you ready?' She stood by the door, preparing to open it.

'As ready as I'll ever be,' replied Jenny.

Sukie slowly swung the door open to reveal the two horse-drawn carriages waiting on the driveway.

Jenny's eyes turned to saucers when she saw them – this she had not expected. She looked at Sukie who smiled widely back at her.

'I believe the expression is, "Your carriage awaits, m'lady!"'

Chapter Forty-Eight

'I now proclaim you husband and wife. You may kiss the bride.'

The church bells began to peal as Jeff took Jenny in his arms to kiss her. Her eyes were shining and he couldn't recall her ever looking this happy. For the first time since he'd met her, the shadow that always hung around her was missing. This made him smile even more because he wanted this day to be one in which all her troubles were forgotten. He guessed there would be a moment of reflection at some point, where she would dwell on those who could not be with them on this special day, but he hoped she'd be able to put the pain to one side and enjoy all the festivities they'd arranged.

They took their time strolling back up the aisle, greeting friends and smiling for the photographs being taken all around them. The church looked stunning, bedecked as it was in shades of green, gold, and red. This had been part of the arrangement he'd made with Jeremy, the vicar, who normally declined to perform weddings on Christmas Eve as he had to get the church ready for

Midnight Mass. When Jeff had informed him he could use their wedding flowers and shared the secret of the colour scheme, he'd relented and agreed to do it. Jeff had been ecstatic for he knew this was one thing Jenny really wanted. As modern as she was, she still had her toes steeped in some traditions and a church wedding was one of them.

They made their way outside and waited for the photographer to take all the group shots. Jeff had always abhorred the way the guests were made to wait ages after the church ceremony while the obligatory five hundred photographs of the bride and groom and family were taken before the rest of the invited guests were able to participate. Now it was his wedding and he'd made sure the group shots came first so the guests could make their way to the reception location and take some time to refresh themselves before he and Jenny arrived.

'How are you doing? Are you okay?' He slipped his arm around Jenny's waist and pulled her against him.

She transferred her bouquet to her other hand and placed the free one upon his and squeezed it. 'I'm doing wonderfully, my love, how about you?'

'It's the happiest day of my life.'

'How much longer are these photographs going to take, it's bloomin' freezing?' Jenny gave a small shiver.

The photographer, overhearing her, called back, 'Only a couple more. The light is fading fast now...'

She was true to her word and, ten minutes later, Jeff was helping Jenny back into the horse-drawn carriage. The hood had been partially raised making it cosy inside. Red velvet throws lay on the seat, waiting to be draped over their hands and legs.

'So, how is your wedding day shaping up? Have you liked it so far?'

'Liked it? Jeff, I have LOVED it. Everything has been

stunning.'

'Is it what you would have chosen?' He tried not to sound too nervous – as the day had drawn closer, he'd really begun to question the wisdom of allowing Sadie to talk him into making all the arrangements.

'Jeff, I don't have your artistic eye. I don't think I could have put together anything as near as good.'

'And you were okay with both Sadie and Bernice walking you down the aisle?'

When the bridal march had begun, and he'd turned to see her walking towards him, with Sadie and Bernice on either side, their dark green outfits making her golden creation shine even brighter, he'd had to wipe away a tear. He hadn't known it was possible for her to be any more beautiful.

'That was perfect. Thank you. I know it meant as much to them as it did to me.' She placed a soft kiss on his cheek.

He put his hand gently on the side of her face and directed her lips towards his.

They were so lost in their kiss, they didn't feel the carriage stop and only realised they'd arrived at the reception when Sukie's voice called out in laughter, 'Oi you two, get a room!'

Jenny pulled away and looked round. 'Good grief! That has got to be the biggest marquee I have ever seen!'

The marquee had been placed on the village green, and green and gold fairy lights twinkled along the covered pathway leading from the road to the entrance.

Jeff helped her down, placed her hand in the crook of his arm and, together, they walked into the marquee while their friends lined up outside, throwing confetti over them.

'Don't worry,' he whispered in her ear, 'I made sure it was one hundred percent biodegradable.'

She let out a laugh as, yet again, he'd known exactly what she'd been thinking. They stepped through the canvas entrance and Jenny drew in a sharp breath as they walked through a darkened corridor lit only with ice-white twinkling fairy lights. Suddenly, the sides lit up and, projected onto the walls, was a snowy forest scene. As if that wasn't surprise enough, snow began to gently fall down upon them.

'Oh, Jeff, this is just... Amazing! I really don't know what to say...' She looked all about her as her throat choked with emotion. It was beyond her wildest imagination.

They walked the short distance to where there were two sets of double doors. Above one was a sign saying "BAR". There was nothing above the other.

Jeff stood her in front of the anonymous doors, 'Close your eyes.'

Jenny did as he asked. She heard him knocking on the doors and felt the air around her move as they were opened. With his hand gently touching the small of her back, he guided her forward a few steps. 'You can open your eyes now...'

When she did, Jenny was incapable of making a sound. The vision in front of her was so exquisite it rendered her immobile for several seconds. Her eyes grew larger as she tried to take in all that she was seeing.

'Is this okay? You've gone so quiet...'

She looked at Jeff and saw the worry on his face – he'd misinterpreted her silence and thought she was disappointed. He couldn't have been further from the truth.

'It's... It's... It's breath-taking! I just don't know where to start to describe how I feel. There aren't...

There aren't enough words…'

The interior of the marquee had been transformed into a winter wonderland. A vast array of white and blue fairy lights twinkled above her head and around the walls. The ground beneath her feet was covered with a white snow blanket and narrow brick-effect paths wound their way around the room and through the tables. The centrepieces on the tables were swinging, shepherd-crook lanterns, lit with flickering candles inside, and the floral displays were made up of white and red roses woven through frosted holly garlands. Instrumental Christmas music played softly in the background.

Jenny turned to Jeff. 'I think letting you, Sadie and Saffy organise this wedding, was the best thing I could have done. *Never*, in a million years, could I have come up with something like this. It's beyond my ability to put into words how wonderful I think this is. Thank you, thank you so much.'

Jeff gave her a smile. 'You might want to add Sukie to your list of organisers. She managed to pull some strings in certain quarters that we could never have done. Apparently being married to a rather famous rock-star comes with a few perks…'

Jenny giggled at this. 'So it would seem.'

'Come, my dearest wife, allow me to lead you to your seat and let the festivities begin.' As they walked towards the top table, their guests began entering the room behind them and, judging by the gasps and wows hanging in the air, she wasn't alone in being blown away by its splendour.

Two hours later, when the tables had been cleared and glasses were being filled in preparation for the speeches, Jenny spotted a guest she hadn't expected to see on her special day. She leant over to Jeff. 'Darling, why did you invite Oliver?'

'I didn't.'

'Oh! I'm sure I just saw him. I must have been wrong. It's dark and it was one of the tables at the back. It's probably just someone who looks a bit like him.'

'Then he has my sympathies...'

'Jeff, you're naughty... although, I quite agree!' They shared a quiet laugh and then sat up straight when Bernice stood and tinkled a spoon against her champagne flute.

'Ladies and gentlemen,' she began, 'thank you for joining us today...'

Jenny slipped her hand into Jeff's as she listened to Bernice singing her praises and telling Jeff how lucky he was to be marrying such a wonderful woman. Her eyes, however, were discretely scanning the room. She was sure it was Oliver she had seen. If it was, why was he here? Surely he wasn't so petty as to try and spoil her wedding day? A little voice in her head answered the question, *You know he is!* She pushed the thought away. She was not going to entertain thoughts of him on this special day.

She tuned back into the speeches, giggling as Charlie – who was naturally Jeff's best man – shared a few stories she hadn't been aware of about her new husband. Charlie's naturally ebullient personality soon had everyone crying with laughter and she forgot her concerns as she joined them.

Once all the speeches and toasts were over, Charlie announced there would be a fifteen-minute break and then the happy couple would be taking to the floor for their first dance as husband and wife. Jenny looked around her – there was no dance floor that she could see. She was about to ask Jeff if the tables were being moved when she saw four of the waiting staff move across to one of the side walls, push aside the silk curtains and open a partitioning wall to reveal a dance floor on the other side. In keeping with the winter theme, there were snowmen and snow-covered trees around the perimeter and yet more twinkling lights above it. A small stage was situated at the end furthest from where they were sitting and she could see a DJ on one side, messing about with his headphones and decks.

Just then, Charlie came over. 'Right, you guys, you're on, as they say!'

Jeff stood and held out his hand. 'My darling wife, would you care to join me for a dance?'

With a smile a mile wide, she placed her hand in his. 'It would be my pleasure.'

As they made their way through, the DJ announced, 'If I could please ask all the guests to make their way to the side of the dance floor, the bride and groom are about to have their first dance.'

Jeff took her in his arms and waited for the music to begin. She looked up at him and asked, 'So, what is "our" song? We've never discussed this.'

'Wait a moment and you'll see.'

He'd barely finished speaking when the soft tones of Simon Healy's voice filled the air around them, singing the opening line to "Forever with You".

The Acid Kows had been described as Britain's Bon Jovi and Jenny thought they were wonderful, along with most of the world if the media hype was to be believed.

'Oh, Jeff, I LOVE this song!'

'I know you do, my darling, it's the only song you ever really sing along to. When I hear you singing, it fills me with happiness and so it has become my song too. Therefore, it is now *our* song.'

Jenny buried her face in his shoulder as she tried to

stop the tears in her eyes from spilling. She knew Jeff wasn't perfect but, by golly, he wasn't far off.

Jeff guided her around the floor and she let herself become immersed in the beautiful rock ballad. It was just reaching to her favourite bit, where Simon sings softly as the music builds up to the powerful, goose-bump inducing, finishing crescendo...

BANG!

BANG!

BANG!

'WHAT THE HE—'

She opened her eyes to find glittering stars falling down around her and, when she looked at the stage, the curtain which had been hanging there had fallen to reveal The Acid Kows on the stage singing right at her and Jeff in front of them!

This was just too much and the jaw she'd managed to keep closed through all of the day's surprises hit the floor! She looked at Jeff and then back to the band on the stage. Simon gave her a wink and a smile as he brought the song to a close.

She looked at Jeff again and mouthed, 'Sukie?' at him. He nodded and pulled her close as the band moved effortlessly into their next song.

Along with the rest of their guests, they stood and swayed, danced and clapped through the short five-song set the band performed. As they finished with their massive break-through hit, "Patiently Waiting", Jenny turned to Jeff and said, '*This* should have been our song because you certainly used a lot of patience waiting for me.'

Jeff took her into his arms and said, 'You were worth every second of it, my love,' before kissing her deeply once again.

When the band had taken their bows and thanked everyone for the rapturous applause, Jenny excused herself and made her way to the toilets. Her wonderful wedding organisers had thought of everything and this included a private bathroom purely for the use of the bride and groom. She slipped through the curtain behind the top table and was making her way along the small corridor when a body stepped out of the shadows and grabbed her by the wrist.

'Hello, my dear *sister*,' said a slightly drunken voice.

'Oliver! What the hell are you playing at?' She pulled her hand away and rubbed her wrist to soothe it after being gripped so tightly.

'I had to come and wish you well on your wedding day, didn't I? That's what brothers do, is it not?'

'Except you're not my brother, and have never had any inclination to behave as one, so I'll ask you again, what the hell are you doing here?'

'Oh, Jenny… Don't be so fierce, not after I bought you such an expensive coffee machine as a wedding gift.'

'If you had been officially invited, you'd have known we asked for donations to be made to charity instead of gifts, but not to worry – I'll organise a charity raffle and that can be first prize.'

'Why are you always such a bitch?' Oliver stuck his face up close to hers as he spoke.

'Me? A bitch? I think you're confusing me with someone else, Oliver, because, if I'd been a bitch, I might have had the street-smarts to avoid a scumbag like you. Anyway, you don't need to answer my question, I know what's brought you crawling out from under your rock – you want me to invest in your research.'

'Bernice never could keep her mouth shut, interfering old bitch!'

Jenny was appalled at the contempt in his voice. 'Oliver! That is your mother, show her some respect.'

'Look, I haven't got all day to listen to you. You owe me and now you're going to pay. Bernice has made you her power of attorney – I needed that authority, I needed her money.'

'But you...' Jenny stopped as his words sunk in and she realised what he'd been planning. Or rather, had planned! Thankfully, Bernice knew what he was capable of. 'You were going to rob Bernice behind her back, using the POA to access her funds.'

'Not rob, as such, just take what will eventually be mine anyway.'

'You know, you really ARE a nasty little shit, aren't you?'

Her words must have hit a sore spot because the next thing she knew, Oliver was pushing her up against the wall with his hands around her throat.

'I NEED that money. You're a rich bitch now, you won't miss it. I've got debts and no investment. The only other option I have is to move to the States but the role on offer is a step down the ladder, not up. It won't help me.'

'And neither will I!' In the blink of an eye, Jenny reached down, grabbed him between his legs and squeezed hard. Oliver's hands fell from her neck and he stood stock-still.

Keeping hold of his short-and-curlies, Jenny stuck *her* face forward into his. 'I might be rich but let me tell you something – I would give away every last penny if it would bring my family back. No sum of money can replace them or give me back the life I lost when they died. That's why I never touched it, that's why the investments grew – because I didn't want it! It was tainted. You see, Oliver, I would have given *anything* to have my family around me, all you want to do is throw yours away. You're a spoilt, ungrateful, bastard, and you don't deserve any of what you've got. Well, I *suggest* you take that job in America, because you're getting nothing from me. Not now and not ever.' She tightened her grasp a little more and Oliver let out a squeak of pain. 'Do I make myself clear?' she asked him through gritted teeth.

'But I—'

'I said, DO I MAKE MYSELF CLEAR?' She squeezed even tighter.

'YES! YES, I GET IT!'

'Good! Now get out of my sight, you snivelling little shit before I make you even more dickless than you already are!' She allowed her hand to make a sharp twisting movement before letting go. Oliver fell to his knees with his hands over his crotch.

She looked down on him and simply said, 'Despicable' before turning on her heel and walking away.

When she got to the bathroom, and had ensured the door was securely locked, she sat down trembling on the chair. Good grief, what had gotten into her? She poured a glass of water and sipped it slowly, waiting for the adrenaline rush to pass. Eventually her legs stopped shaking and she was ready to make her way back to the party. She checked her dress in the full-length mirror and looked closer to ensure there was no bruising on her neck after Oliver's assault. She glanced at her face to check her make-up was still intact but stopped when she looked at her eyes. Staring out of the mirror was a strong, capable woman in total control of herself. Jenny had never noticed her before, she'd always thought of herself as the victim in her life – and she had been – but that victim had grown up to become a woman who had finally learned the worth of herself. She lifted her chin, unlocked the door and, checking the corridor outside was clear, made her way back to her wedding reception.

When she arrived at his side, Jeff put his arm around her waist and held her close against him. 'Is everything okay, my love?'

She accepted a glass of champagne from a passing waiter, and before she took a sip, she replied, 'Everything is absolutely perfect, darling, absolutely perfect.'

'Come with me a moment.' Jeff guided her over to the side of the dance floor. He put his hand in his jacket pocket and pulled out a velvet box.

'My wedding gift to you,' he said, as he placed the box in her hands.

'But, Jeff, you've done all this,' Jenny made a small sweeping gesture with her hand, 'I don't need anything else.'

'Yes, you do. Open it.'

Jenny lifted the lid and, this time, she couldn't stop the tears from falling. She looked up at Jeff and whispered, 'Thank you.'

Jeff took the box from her, lifted out the enamel rainbow bangle and placed it on her wrist.

'For you, my love, so that every day may be lived in colour.'

And So It Ends...

Amber Fisher looked around the room as she reflected on how much her life had changed. One year ago today, her life as she'd known it had completely fallen apart. After everything she'd gone through with her parents' death, the knowledge that she was adopted had been too much and she'd felt as though life had picked her up and smashed her against a brick wall. Through the strangest quirk of fate, she'd been put back together by the kindness of a stranger – a stranger who was now her step-mum and who she loved completely. She may have lost one family when her adopted parents had died but here, in this room today, was the new family she'd gained. They would never replace the people who had adopted her and raised her with so much love and care but she didn't want them to. They were a new family and she was enjoying the thrill of getting to know them along with discovering the little foibles that came with their shared DNA. Her father, Jeff, was a kind man with a gentle heart and a generous soul. Her uncle, Charlie, was a relaxed, happy-go-lucky man with a slightly roguish tint in his nature, and her grandmother, Brenda, was funny, caring and full of mischief. Amber could see her in both of her sons. She wished she'd met her grandfather, Arthur, he sounded like a good man and both of his sons spoke of him with love.

She heard Saffy laughing and looked around to see her younger sister chatting with the two older ladies who'd helped Charlie and Jeff to find the hidden wonders in the shop. She knew their irreverence, especially Doris's, would appeal to Saffy. Finding out that Saffy wasn't her sister by blood had been a hard blow but she'd realised blood wasn't needed when it came to family and love. She would always love Saffy and look out for her, no matter what. Amber heard a noise and looked over to see Jenny struggling through the door with a large platter of sandwiches in her hands. She rushed over to her. 'Here, Jenny, let me take those for you.'

'Thank you, sweetie, that's much appreciated.'

Amber grinned at Jenny's term of endearment when she handed over the heavy plate and, as she made her way to the table, she smiled to herself when she felt a bubble of joy float up inside her. This was going to be a great New Year.

Jenny was checking if the sausage rolls were ready to come out of the oven when the doorbell rang. She knew it would be Sam because she was the last to arrive.

The last week had been a quiet one with just her and Jeff at the house. The shop had been closed, Saffy had been in London with Amber, and Sam had gone home to Glastonbury. Jenny had really enjoyed the quiet bliss of not getting up on an alarm clock and relaxing with long walks, reading books and watching films – all in the circle of Jeff's arms. They'd both agreed a little soiree with all their family and close friends, to celebrate both the New Year and the changes in all their lives, would be fun.

And it had to be said, when she stopped to think about it, her life had changed beyond recognition in the last twelve months. All it had taken was one small incident, when her car wouldn't start, to put in motion a chain of events which had brought her to this point. Last January, she'd been a librarian who was single, with two cats, a clapped-out Beetle and a past which was weighing her down and sucking the joy from her. Meeting Jeff had changed all that. He'd taken her dream and helped her to make it a reality. He'd taken her past and helped her to realise she could live again and the pain of what she'd gone through should not be holding her back. He'd helped her to let it go. As a result, she was now a happily married, successful businesswoman, although she still had the two cats and the clapped-out Beetle. Well, there's a limit to how much one should change all at once.

There was only one thing left which would have made her year better but she'd finally come to terms with the knowledge she may never see her daughter again. It had been hard to deal with that one but it had been necessary if she wanted to make a better life for herself. Amber and Saffy could never fill the void of losing Mandy but they both went a long way towards easing some of the pain.

She heard the doorbell ring again. Clearly no one else was going to answer it so she slammed the oven door closed with her foot, put the hot tray on top of the cooker and made her way down the hallway. She could see two figures through the stained glass. That's strange, she thought, she was sure Sam had said Robbie was going back to Ireland for the festive period.

She opened the door and was immediately drowned in a massive embrace from Sam. 'Happy New Year, Jenny, wishing you all the best for it.' A noisy kiss was planted on her cheek.

Sam carried on talking as Jenny stood back to let her in. 'I hope you don't mind, Jen, but I've brought my little sister along. She and her boyfriend have just split up so I thought a change of scenery might help her through.'

'Of course I don't mind, Sam. The more the merrier.'

She turned as Sam's sister pulled off her woolly hat and released a waist-length waterfall of brilliant Russian-gold coloured hair. When she turned around, Jenny found herself looking into a pair of sparkling cornflower blue eyes.

'Jenny, this is my rather poshly named sister, Amanda Clementine—'

'Oh, Samantha Jane Curtis, will you just shut your lips!' Pulling a face at Sam, she moved towards Jenny and stuck out her hand. 'Hi Jenny, I *am* Amanda Clementine but most people just call me Mandy…'

The End

Dedication

This book is dedicated to the memory of Jeff Rowland
who passed away in November 2018. Although I had
known of Jeff's battle with his health for many years,
he'd always managed to beat the odds and so many hoped
he would do so again. As it was, it turned out that there
were only so many battles he could win.

The first draft of 'An Incidental Lovestyle' was only a
few days away from completion when I heard the news of
his passing and finishing those last few chapters was
difficult because I knew he wouldn't be here to read the
end result.

When I first asked Jeff, three years ago, if he would
mind me using his name for the art dealer in my debut
novel, he was delighted. We had a chat about how he
would like me to portray his alter-ego and, when he
expressed his great admiration for the actor Clint
Eastwood, it seemed only fitting to create *my* Jeff in his
likeness. As the Lovestyle series developed over the
course of time, Jeff's character grew into being more than
just a 'bit player'. When I informed I had developed a

storyline which would see him in the role of the leading man, he was beyond thrilled and couldn't wait to read how I had portrayed him. I can tell you that, while he may not have looked like his Hollywood idol, the waistcoats, funky footwear, malt whiskey and love of punk rock are all 'pure Jeff'.

It saddens me deeply to know he will never see the finished product but I hope that his literary persona brings some joy to all of those who knew and loved him as well as to those who are only just learning of him. His stunning art work will ensure he is remembered for a very long time. I hope this book helps to give a small taste of the wonderful human being he was.

A Rock 'n' Roll Lovestyle

Not everyone wants to be famous...

Sukie McClaren is a thirty-something singleton. She's a cat lover, a Sound of Music Fanatic, and a happily independent, woman with a razor sharp tongue. She enjoys her anonymity so when she is sent to Salzburg on a business trip, all she is hoping for is some time to see the locations in her favourite film. Befriending the worlds number one rock star is the last thing on her mind.

Pete Wallace is a cynical, reclusive rock-star and the world's Number One, male solo artist. After a three year hiatus, he's preparing to go back on the road again. A week in Salzburg, schmoozing with the music press, is one of his worst nightmares. Making new friends is the last thing on his mind.

When Pete and Sukie meet, sparks fly, but despite Sukie's reservations over his fame, their friendship flourishes. However, when life throws up a cold, calculating Italian, intent on seeking vengeance, Sukie has to make tough decisions.

Could their new friendship die, before it has a chance to bloom?

An Artisan Lovestyle

When falling in love is the only way to stay alive...

Elsa Clairmont was widowed barely five years after marrying her childhood sweetheart. She has struggled to come to terms with the loss and, six years later, has almost ceased to live herself. She does just enough to get by.

Danny Delaney is the ultimate 'Mr Nice Guy'. He's kind, caring and sweet. A talented artist in his teens, his abusive mother ruined his career in art and he turned his back on his exceptional gift. Now, he does just enough to get by.

On New Year's Eve, both Danny and Elsa are involved in unrelated accidents which leads to them having to make some serious lifestyle changes and face up to the consequences of their actions. They need to *begin* living if they want to *keep* living. Will they succeed in altering the paths of their lives? Will they find love before it's too late?

An uplifting tale of second chances and appreciating every opportunity life gives you.

Printed in Great Britain
by Amazon

75306915R00224